Black Ink Publications Presents
Dolla and Dyme: Jackin' For Love
A Novel By
Sa'id Salaam

I0619743

Email: saidmsalaam@gmail.com

Facebook: Free Sa'id Salaam and Black Ink Publications

Cover: Michael Horne

"Is that him?" Dolla asked, squinting through the dimly lit club. The ice on the target's neck illuminated him, putting him on his radar from all the way across the room. The dancer in front of him looked in the direction he was looking while still popping her caramel ass cheeks in his face.

"He shole look like the one," his equally ambitious partner Dyme said, licking her lips at the tasty lick in front of them. A good lick has a taste, and it's sweet. After wearing a three-thousand-dollar designer outfit and another ten around his neck, they were going to need a shot of insulin after this one. "It sure looks like him."

The mark must have wanted to get robbed when he pulled out a wad of cash and made it rain on the two dancers dancing in front of him. It was mainly ones and fives, but he still wouldn't have been doing it if he wasn't caked the fuck up. He could be charged as an accessory to his own robbery for flossing so hard. His Instagram post could be used against him in a court of law or holding court in the street.

"Yeah that's him, daddy," she purred like she does when her kitty is stroked. He wasn't supposed to be touching it since the club had a no touching policy but it was his pussy, so he would touch it when and where he wanted. "See, if I bust a nut on your hand you gone swear I did you wrong."

"You do and I'm gonna bend you over this table and give you the business. All of it!" he warned and lolled his head back in laughter.

His bright smile contrasted brilliantly against his dark skin and turned heads. The same heads quickly turned back away since Dyme was quick to beat a bitch up over her man. He felt the same way and stopped fondling her when some locals watched him play in her pussy from a few tables over. He used the liquid she leaked to smooth the thick waves on his head since it worked better than Murrays.

"I'm down," she dared and would have done it if he wanted. Dolla was the first man to treat her right, so she was down for whatever he

1

wanted. What he wanted now was to relieve all the cities clowns of their money.

Dyme was what's known as a fine muthafucka. She stood five foot six inches and had an athletic body, as in an ass as round as a basketball and firm breast the size a regulation soft balls. What set her apart from most of the highly made up strippers was she was naturally pretty. As pretty as she was, she was as rough as a dirt road. Her round face needed little embellishments to turn heads. A little lip-gloss on the thick lips beat all the beat faces in the club. She further drove the value of her vagina up by not tricking with the ballers. Now they chunked bands at her to get her home and fuck. She accepted a few times but they were the ones who got fucked. Fucked out of their money, drugs and jewels that is. Not one lived to tell about it.

Chapter One

"Yo! Yo! That's her B! That's the bitch I was telling you about!" Yayo shouted and pointed when he spotted the same girl from a week ago. Her round, brown ass was jumping and jiggling under a short pair of shorts now just like it did last week. Except last week he was with one of his baby mamas and couldn't pull up. Now he was with his partner Que, so he pulled up and hopped out.

"Silly nigga," Que said and shook his head. His boss just hopped out an eighty thousand dollar car to talk to some hood rat eating a twenty five cent bag of chips. "Bitch bad though!"

"Ayo, ma! Hole up, shorty!" he said and grabbed her hand. She twirled around and shot him a look that cut like a blade. It didn't draw blood but did get him to let go. "My bad, ma. I'm just tryna meet you."

"Well, you have, so..." she said and twisted her sexy ass away. Dyme had a naturally nasty walk just from the proportion of hips to ass, but she did turn it up a little since she was certain he was watching. He was right along with every other male on the block. Old to young, all looked at as she passed by. Even a baby boy spit out his pacifier and gave her a gummy smile.

"Swing and a miss for strike three!" Que teased when he returned empty handed. It was actually a good thing since they had business. Yayo was one of those clowns who thinks with their dick. He would have blown off their drug deal in a heartbeat if he had bagged the girl.

"Yo, bet a hunnid I bag that bitch!" Yayo dared. Que twisted his face up to show what he thought of betting a hundred dollars on some pussy.

"Or, we could go make a hunnid off this deal. How 'bout that?" Que asked.

"Yeah, I guess," he sighed like he'd rather fuck the chick instead of sell a couple of bricks.

3

"Girl, what Yayo ass talm'bout?" Dyme's cousin April asked when she made it back to the group of girls she hung out with. They called themselves G.M.G for Get Money Girls, but B.A.B was closer to the truth because these were some broke ass broads.

"Same as all the rest of these Brooklyn niggas talking 'bout some sss!" Dyme shot back. She'd been tricked out some pussy a couple of times and wasn't falling for it again.

"Word. I know that's right. Fuck these niggas," they all said even though Yayo had been inside everyone of them. Including April on some late night, last second back seat action when he caught her coming home from a party.

"Word," Dyme agreed and opened her bag of chips. She regretted it instantly when every hand extended for a chip. They shared it just like shared blunts and dick.

*****

Yayo didn't give up easily. In fact, he downright stalked the block for weeks on end trying to get the girl. She finally gave him her number and they began to talk and text and 'like' and 'share'. Persistence pays off in any pursuit, especially the pursuit of pussy and Yayo got that pussy.

Weeks of movies, food, weed, cash, and even some much needed outfits did the trick and they ended up inside a swank hotel. Her friends fucked in motels, back seats and even staircases, but Yayo took her to his main house. He set out the champagne, exotic weed and even a new phone inside a new purse. In return, she set out some good, clean, wet, tight pussy. It wasn't tricking since he swore they were in a relationship now.

"Don't play me," Dyme pouted when Yayo settled on top of her. Her body was ready, but her mind needed a little reassuring.

"Never that. You, my, lady," he assured her with soft kisses as commas. He reached down and rolled on a condom like she insisted. "We are now an us."

"Okay," Dyme said as she gave in and gave it up. She let out a hiss and winced from the pressure when he entered her. She got her breathing together and settled in to enjoy her new man.

"Mmm," Yayo grunted and screwed up his face. She did too, wondering what was wrong since he just got inside of her. Two strokes later, he was moaning and groaning like he was about to cum. "I'm about to cum!"

"Huh?" she asked because that just didn't make any damn sense. He wined and dined her for months and only fucked her for a few seconds. He couldn't even be called a minute man since you have to stay in the pussy for a whole minute. April always said that if a dude bust that quick it's only because a chick got that good-good, wet-wet. It's to be expected, but they will last longer the second go 'round. Could be true but there would be no second.

"Mmm, shit! That was good. I gotta go," Yayo announced and stood. Dyme was already confused by the micro sex but when he pulled out and got up, he wasn't wearing the rubber.

"The fuck, yo?" Dyme demanded when she reached down and felt the slimy semen he deposited in her vagina.

"My bad," Yayo shrugged and got dressed. It was no big deal to him since he always pulled the trick condom act on young chicks. Meanwhile, Dyme was still in shock, trying to figure out what just happened. His "my bad" echoed in her head the whole way back to the hood. She was in her shower still shaking her head at his "my bad".

Yayo was always throwing her a hundred here or a hundred there but the hundred he gave her when he dropped her off at her Aunt Lynn's house seemed tainted. It felt dirty and she would have thrown it away if she didn't need it so damn much. The only thing she could do was cry, so she cried. Cried herself a river in the shower while washing his seeds out of her.

*****

It took a week of unanswered calls and texts before Dyme accepted that she'd been played. It just didn't make sense if he was one of them fuck 'em and duck'em dudes as long as he could beat the pussy up a little bit. He spent all that time, energy, money and good game to fuck for a few seconds.

It took a month to figure out that she was pregnant from the brief encounter. She was the only chick she knew had knocked her up without a calendar and phone records to match up dicks. No question, Yayo impregnated her which made her calls and texts even more urgent. She saw the nigga everyday when he was stalking her but didn't see a trace of him now.

To add insult to injury to her pregnancy, he didn't pay the bill on the phone he gave her so she couldn't even call or text anyone. Now she never saw him at all. Until today that is.

"Hmph! There go that sexy ass Dolla!" April said with gusto when she spotted the hood's most elusive pretty thug. Just a sighting of the dude made every coochie on the stoop throb. Even Chattie and it sent up a puff of funk in the air.

"He a'ight," Dyme was said when she saw Yayo pulled up to go into the bodega ahead of Dolla. She hopped up and made a beeline over to the corner store, almost getting hit by a gypsy cab when she blindly crossed the street.

"Fuck she got going on?" one of the B.A.Bs asked since she didn't even have a quarter for a quarter water.

"I'on know?" April asked but kept a keen eye out to find out. Especially since Dolla was heading to the same store. She wanted to run over and ask if she wanted her to roll his blunt, light it for him and then suck his dick while he smoked it.

Dyme didn't even notice Dolla as she rushed past him and into the store. He noticed her and bit his lip as he watched her fat ass wiggle by. Dyme finally had this nigga Yayo and he was gonna have to tell her something about something. She caught him in the cooler picking up wine coolers.

"Awe, man!" Yayo groaned when he saw her coming.

"Awe, man what?" Dyme shouted on verge of hysteria. All she wanted to do was tell him she was pregnant so he could break bread to pay for the termination. No way would she even entertain the thought of being baby mama number eight.

"I ain't got time for you," he said and stormed off. He saw they had an audience so he had to put on a little, even if it was a lie. "Plus, yo pussy stunk! That's why I ain't come back for seconds!"

A lifetime of unspoken disappointments flooded Dyme's mind and pushed all reasoning aside. That bullshit her own mother pulled, putting her out over some nigga. Living with her shady aunt and ratchet cousin. Having to hang out with the brokest broads in the borough and now her pussy stank! No, that wouldn't do at all. She made sure to keep a nice, clean vagina.

"Ain't got time for me?" she growled and pulled her straight razor as she followed him from the store. She couldn't have stopped herself even if she wanted to. She didn't want to though, so she savagely took a swipe that opened his face from earlobe to his chin. "Got time for stitches?"

"Oh shit !" the whole block shouted. That included Que sitting in Yayo's car, the G.M.Gs sitting on their stoop and Dolla who had just arrived.

"Did you cut me?" Yayo asked mainly from everyone else's reaction since the super sharp blade was almost painless. For a moment, followed by the burn and gush of blood that seemed to explode on his shirt.

Mind your business Dolla, Dolla said to himself. He had a little thing for Dyme but didn't like the company she kept, so he kept that thing to himself.

"Bitch, I'll kill yo' ass!" Yayo shouted with his cheek flapping as he spoke. His teeth and tongue could clearly be seen through the cut. He snatched Dyme completely off her feet and into the air by her throat. Que reached for his door handle to go help her because he didn't like seeing women beat up. Neither did Dolla who was closer.

"Shit!" Dolla fussed at himself when he realized he wasn't going to be able to mind his business. He pulled a pistol from his back and rushed over. Que fell back to watched the show.

"Choke me!" Dolla dared and gave him a backhand smack with the gun that made the block go, "Ooooh!"

Yayo let Dyme go and she stumbled away and coughed in search of her breath. Dolla wasn't done yet, so he shoved the gun in Yayo's mouth until he gagged. Que just shook his head at the spectacle and sat tight.

"Do it," Que heard himself say like most sidekicks will do. Every right hand man wants to be the man instead of the man next to the man.

Dolla felt his finger tightening on the trigger until he was a millisecond away from splatting his brains on the "rest in peace" mural on the wall behind him. Something shook Dolla's head "no" and he left the pressure off the trigger. He pulled the gun out of Yayo's mouth and dismissed him with a swift kick in the seat of his expensive jeans. Que shook his head again as Yayo ran and got into the car.

"Ain't nobody need your help!" Dyme snapped on Dolla instead of thanking him. Her pride was hurt about getting put on blast and almost getting choked out.

"Whatever. Keep ya legs closed and shit like this won't happen," Dolla said and continued on his mission.

Chapter Two

"Roll a blunt?" Que reeled in response to Yayo's request as they rode away from the incident. He took another look at his friend's battered face and confirmed, "Nigga, you need a doctor! Some stitches or sutures or staples or something!"

"Is it that bad?" Yayo asked hopefully. All that hope was lost when he pulled the visor down and saw his face in the mirror. He had a classic "buck fifty" that would stay with him for life like a case of herpes. "That bitch cut me!"

"Yup," his partner nodded as he steered towards Kings county hospital. "And that nigga Dolla stuck his tool down your throat."

Both men paused to process those facts. Both recalled the embarrassing sound of him gagging on the barrel of his glock. They both relived the "ooh" of the crowd when Dolla slapped a spark out of him. Yayo was content to be alive but Que knew he had to do something. To do nothing would invite the whole borough to try him. He would be considered soft and soft niggas are bait. Especially ones with bread like Yayo and Que were getting. He was too young to move to Florida and retire so "get back" was the only option.

"Well?" Que asked since he saw the wheels turning in his head. If he punked out, he would pull over and kill him now so he could take his spot. There may not have been any lions and tigers, but the streets of Brooklyn were the jungle.

"I'ma buss that nigga is what," Yayo said unconvincingly. He heard his own whiny tone and tried again. "Nigga gone slap me with the tool! Yo, I'ma knock son block off! That's on Brooklyn!"

"Humph," Que huffed. It always amazed him when people swore by shit that ain't theirs to swear by. He didn't swear much but when he did it was by Allah. In fact, he secretly swore by Allah right then to take Yayo's spot first chance he got. He didn't know who the connect was, so he had to wait. Wait and plot. So, while Yayo was plotting, Que was plotting, but both were being plotted on at the same time.

****

"Been wanting to rob his soft ass anyway," Dolla growled to himself. He never really liked Yayo but a bit of jealousy played a part in it. He was a ladies man himself so he got just as much ass as Yayo but Yayo had that check. Money allowed him access to some chicks out of Dolla 's pay grade. For now anyway, because he was plotting on a come up.

His heart broke when word got out he'd sexed pretty Dyme. Her good girl rep made her wifey material since no one wants a hoe for a housewife. Not that a hoe can't be tamed, it's just a lot of work. Similar to breaking a wild horse and no one has time for all that.

Then hearing Yayo putting on that her pussy stunk just added insult to injury. Dudes can tell from two and a half blocks away chicks who pussy stank and Dyme wasn't one of them.

Dolla peered out his window and saw Dyme and her little crew of girls smoking on the stoop of her brownstone. A half smile turned a corner of his mouth up as he watched her theatrics as she spoke. She waved her hands, flipped her hair and dipped her hip to help make her points. He could only guess she was telling them what happened with Yayo earlier, and he was right. Some of the girls saw and others heard about it but it was still a good story.

"So, I was like 'Sup, now nigga!' He was like 'chill yo'. I ain't got no chill yo. I let that nigga get it!" she said and demonstrated the swipe of the blade that opened his face. "Then son grabbed my neck—"

"Told you not to mess with that fuck 'em and duck 'em ass nigga anyway!" her cousin reminded. She would know since Yayo fuckd her and ducked her too. The other girls nodded since they had experienced the same as well.

"Ooh, then fine ass Dolla came out of nowhere..." Chattie exclaimed and told that part of the story. "Yayo had her in the air and—"

"And what you and Dolla got going on?" April asked, needing to know right away. She'd been throwing pussy at the pretty thug like a white girl tossing a Frisbee in the park.

"I'on even know that nigga!" she shot back. His words from the bodega came back to her. *Keep your legs closed,* replayed in her mind and threatened to make her smile. She knew he had to care to say that to her.

"Girl, that nigga is a beast!" Chattie said and bit her lip like she had firsthand knowledge. She threw herself at him too, but he had spotted her two and a half blocks away. Besides, he didn't really like fucking with girls around the way. They talked too much and that was dangerous in his line of work.

Dolla was a Jack Boy and chicks talked too much. They gave up so many details on dudes they bedded, it made it easy to rob them.

"Bitch, puh-leeeze!" April said dramatically. "If that nigga turned his nose up at me I knooooow he ain't fuck with you!"

"Cuz yo' pussy stink," Monica nodded helpfully. The rest of the crew nodded since it was singing it's salty song right now.

"My um, pH balance be...and um..." she stammered in defense of her funk box.

"Can I finish my story?" Dyme wanted to know. She got no objections and continued. Her girls oohed and aahed as she played it back for them. At the end of her show she took questions from her audience. Everyone wanted to know more about Dolla, except April.

"What you gone do about Yayo? He may be soft but you cut his face, yo. He gotta do something about that!" she spelled out as correctly as an Indian kid in a spelling. R-E-VE-N-G-E, revenge.

That soft smile came back to her face as Dolla 's voice rang once more, *Next time keep your legs closed.*

Nah, she thought. *Next time I'ma spread them for you!*

Chapter Three

"Y'all fast ass girls don't never listen!" Dyme's aunt chimed but no one really listened. Not that she minded since she liked hearing herself talk, even if nobody else did.

"What you talking 'bout now, ma?" April asked since she wasn't listening either.

"Talking about she cut that boy face and he gone see about her. And y'all getting dressed for some party like she ain't give dude another smile on his face.

"Well, I ain't about to let him stop me from doing me!" Dyme shot back foolishly. Mainly because she had a fool for an advisor who gave negligible advice.

"Word! Fuck that nigga! We out here!" April insisted. She knew good and damn well that Yayo had to clap back for getting cut. The world was watching and the wolves were licking their chops. She fucked two dudes already who were scheming on Yayo after he got punked. If something happened to Dyme, she would inherit her clothing. Especially the matching bra and panty sets she just bought.

"We out here!" Dyme repeated even though she knew she shouldn't be. She wouldn't run into Dolla again if she didn't so yeah, "We out here."

The rest of the G.M.Gs piled into the small apartment and blazed up the few dime bags they scrounged up. It usually took two or three of them to chip in on a ten dollar bag of weed. Then, they all had to go buy it together so no one would skim a few buds off the top.

They were all cute girls but their lack of morals and ambition turned them into thots. Their stock value decreased with every dude who ran through them. Dyme was nothing like them but was stuck with them. A reality that forced her to dream of a night in a shiny wave cap to come save her.

13

"What you over there smiling about?" April fussed when she saw that faraway gaze and slight smile on Dyme's face. She didn't like seeing anyone around her too happy. After all, misery loves company and she wanted everyone to be miserable with her.

"Oh, nothing," she sang and tried to wipe the smirk from her face. It was hard because Dolla's words kept playing in her mind, *Keep ya legs closed*.

"Yo, let's hit this spot while we can still get in free!" Chattie said since they couldn't afford to pay the cover. Plus, she had temporarily tamed her pussy and wanted to bag a man before it crunk up again.

Dyme was still pinching off the last hundred she got from Yayo since she literally didn't know where her next buck was coming from. Then she had to hide what she did have so April or her Aunt Lynn wouldn't beg or outright steal. She had to go so far as to separate coins in separate pockets so they couldn't hear the jingle.

"Yeah, we need to get up in that piece!" April said and led the charge out the front door. Everyone fell in step, but everyone wasn't invited. "Un huh, where you think you going?"

"Huh? Oh, I was gonna come with y'all," her mother said. She wanted to wind her backside and turn up too.

"Nah!" April said and pointed back to the house. Lynn pouted and stomped back into the house. All wasn't lost since one of these thirsty dudes would definitely come looking for April to trade weed for pussy. She had a pussy and liked to smoke so...

*****

"It don't even look that bad. I can barely see it," Yayo said as he inspected his face. The doctors did do a great job, but the cut was still there.

Que sucked his teeth and shook his head. He knew Yayo was looking for a reason to let the diss slide. He kept trying to hire a hired gun to gun Dolla down but Que wouldn't hear of it. Yayo got a pistol shoved down his throat and he had to handle that himself.

Then when they saw Dolla a week later, he had to make Yayo jump out the car to shoot him. He had the drop on Dolla but couldn't shoot straight. He hit everyone and everything except Dolla. Then jumped back in the car like he did something.

"Shitting me! That shit is a buck fiddy!" Mitzi laughed and got slapped down.

"Fuck you talking 'bout?" Yayo shouted down to where he knocked her.

"Save some for Dolla, killer," Que said sarcastically. He lost the last shred of respect for him since he was quick to hit a chick but wanted to let getting gagged on a gun slide. "You need a ride, Mitzi?"

"Nah, I'ma stay here," she said, wiping her mouth. She was so used to being abused she would stay and suck dick with a bloody lip.

"Well, stay. I'm about to hit the club. You need to handle your business," he warned him over his shoulders and was gone. The wheels were turning in his head just like the ones on his car. He had to do something, and soon.

Que was a VIP in Brooklyn, so he bypassed the line and walked straight into the club. He heard the chickens clucking as he walked by, but he was too deep in thought to listen.

He posted up with a bottle of expensive bubbles and lit an expensive blunt of fruity weed that cost more per gram than most people make per hour. A group of winding asses on the dance floor caught his attention. One in particular, so he made his way over to shoot his shot.

"Look-it," Lala said when she spotted Que approaching. On cue, the whole crew slipped razor blades from their mouths and got ready. The club didn't allow guns inside, so she carried the blades between their cheeks and gums. They were so good at it, they could eat, speak and give head without even taking them out. Que would get cut to ribbons if he was on some bullshit.

"Sup, ma?" Que greeted with his hands raised and movement in his hips like he just came for a dance.

"Sup with you, daddy?" she shot back inquisitively. She wasn't sure if he was here for beef but his eyes ran over her body like she was a piece of meat. He was cute, had that bag but she didn't fuck friends of dudes she fucked. She was barely fucking as it were but wouldn't be passed around whole crews like her whole crew was.

"Just tryna dance, so you can untwist them lips," he said and disarmed her with a smile. She smiled back since she knew her face was balled up.

"Ya man still whack!" Dyme insisted. "Now he 'sposed to be coming for me?"

"Eh?" he shrugged. Lord knows she would be on RIP t-shirts had she cut his face but she was right, his man was whack.

"I'on even know how you work for a nigga like that," she put out since she heard he asked the same thing in his tone. If he protested, she would fall back. He didn't, so she pressed on. "I know you loyal and wouldn't move on him, but—"

"But what?" he asked so intently, she knew she had him. Dudes were always distracted by her pretty face, fat ass and slim waist, but Dyme was one smart girl.

"But what if it just happened to happen? Then, the man next to the man could slide over—"

"And be the man!" he finished with stars in his eyes. She pressed her body against his and winded and grinde'd until he bust in his pants. They exchanged numbers to put their plan in motion. The deal was sealed, but Dyme still needed one more piece to complete the puzzle.

*****

"Dolla! A-yo, Dolla!" Dyme shouted up and down the block. She didn't know which apartment building or window belonged to him so she just shouted his name. She was lucky enough to find out which block he lived on but that was all. So, she just kept calling his name.

"The fuck?" Dolla fussed when he peeked through the blind and saw the girl. She cupped her hands like a bullhorn and kept on calling. After ten minutes, he accepted she wasn't stopping or leaving, so he grabbed his gat and stepped outside.

"A-yo Dol—" she said but stopped in her tracks when he barged out of a building taking long, angry strides towards her. She felt her pussy twitch in reaction to the pretty thug in a crispy white wife beater. There was nothing she could do to stop the moisture from gathering in her panties.

Dolla didn't even tuck his tool when he came out. Yayo had just bust at him. so he let the gun swing freely as he walked. He doubted she was there to set him up since she was the cause of the beef. He was used to girls stalking him after dicking them down real good but that couldn't be why she was here.

"What the fuck is wrong with you?" Dolla barked outwardly but inwardly thought, *damn this is a bad broad*. Dyme dressed down as much as she could but couldn't hide all that fine.

"Well, actually there's a lot of things wrong me, but I ain't here for all that," she admitted. His fine didn't go unnoticed either but she wasn't here for that either.

"So, what are you here for then?" he asked again and scanned the block once more.

"Same nigga looking for you is looking for me. I may just have a way to find him before he finds us," she suggested.

"Do you know what you getting yourself into? Huh?" Dolla shot down at her. "This ain't no little hood rat game you little hood rats be playing!"

"First of all, I ain't no hood rat! If I was, I wouldn't have did what I did. I got honor and dude dissed me. I'll die about mine!" she said with a fire in her eyes that lit his fuse. He pursed his lips in contemplation as his head began to nod.

"Okay, I'm listening," he said and listened to her plan. She wasn't sure to be proud or pissed when she saw April come out of a building and look directly at them. On one hand, she liked being spotted with the hunk of the hood but then again, her cousin couldn't hold water. She would repeat seeing them together and where far and wide.

"Can we go inside?" she asked so they wouldn't be on front street.

"No," he said so quickly, she had to try to remember what the word meant. They did duck inside the bodega since it wasn't safe to be outside. By the end of her plan, he was all in. They exchanged numbers and glances up and down before they departed. Neither would admit it at that moment, but it was on from that moment.

Chapter Four

"That's where he be taking chicks to bone them," Dyme said, nodding towards a brownstone. She would know since that's where he took her to bone her. Her face scrunched in disgust as she replayed the incident.

Yayo was supposed to be all that but was none of that in the sack. In fact, he was quite whack. He had a nice sized dick but what's the use since he didn't know how to work it. Problem was, he was selfish in the sack. Only concerned with his own pleasure. He stroked the vagina like it wasn't attached to a real person.

He pursued her for months only to fuck her for a few minutes. In fact, he spent more time showing off his stash of money and dope he also kept in the house. He mainly fucked gold diggers so it served as an aphrodisiac. For all his flossing, the only thing he gave up was the dick. She was still hurt when he chumped her off after the deed was done. Chicks will stay with a man with a weak stroke if she digs him.

"I'll wait," Dolla said sarcastically when he saw her drift inside her own head. He was glad to see disgust and not lust on her face since he was sure she was thinking about Yayo.

"Anyway, he strapped though. He had a tool in each room. Plus a closet full of guns," she recalled from her tour. Yayo was definitely getting to the money and had his hand in a little bit of everything.

"All I need is one!" he growled. He was taken in by his father's brother upon the death of his aunt. The Iraqi war veteran was certified crazy but taught Dolla how to fight, shoot and blow shit up. Dolla was deadly with his hands and a fool with a tool.

"Don't talk like that cuz I don't have a change of panties," she laughed but was serious at the same time. Dude had her fucked up and she knew it. It was more than his chocolatey good looks that gave her a wet dream the night after he shoved his hand down Yayo's

19

throat. It was something deep down in him that seeped from his pores. She was in love with him and it scared her to death. Nothing ever worked out in her short life, so she expected the worse. Ironically, that's sometimes when you get the best.

"Word," he laughed but was too dark for her to see him blushing. He planned to bag the pretty girl and keep her. She was young enough to mold but smart enough to shape him, as well. They both had a lot they could learn from each other.

"He talking to this broad named Kimba now. She a'ight, but she got kids," Dyme said and relayed the info she extracted from Que. She remembered she wasn't gossiping with her girls and got back to the point. "Anyway, I heard they was going out to eat. That's when he gone try to bring her here. You know he can't take her to the crib since his sister's always around."

"And that's when I'ma run up in there on him," Dolla decided. "The best time to catch a nigga with his pants down is when his pants are down."

"You say the craziest stuff!" Dyme laughed and lit up his life. He never felt what he was feeling now ever before. He wouldn't know love if it bit him since it had been so long. He hadn't felt any type of emotions except anger since his parents died. He loathed his aunt and was loyal to his uncle. He loved Dyme but couldn't identify it.

"Yeah, my uncle used to say stuff like that all the time. I ain't always get it but it seemed to fit," he recalled fondly. He just passed recently and Dolla was all alone. Until he bagged the chick sitting beside him.

"Only thing, babe..." Dyme said with worry in her voice. "Yayo soft but this nigga Que!"

"Ain't talking about nothing either," Dolla responded sharply. Everyone knew about Que's rep because he was loud and flamboyant. No one knew about Dolla 's because real bad boys moved in silence and violence. That didn't stop a smile from spreading on his face from her calling him babe.

"He tried to holla at me, too," Dyme admitted shyly. She knew it was only because Yayo bragged on her box. Dudes tell other dudes how good the pussy is so they want some, too. Chicks do too but can't understand why their girls fuck behind them.

"Well, holla at him," he said, causing her to snap her head is his direction for explanation. "Go to the movies like Abraham Lincoln."

"Ah yes!" she nodded when she got it. Yayo was about to get robbed and Que wasn't going to be able to do shit about it. They like to ride together so they could die together.

*****

"Whoa, shorty. Save some room for desert!" Yayo told Kimba from across the table. She was smashing her chicken and waffles while he picked over his.

"Mmhm, and what's for dessert?" she dared as if she didn't know. Every chick in the hood knows dick comes with dinner and a movie.

"This dick!" he laughed. She laughed too since he was paying. "Come on, let's bounce."

"Bounce on that dick?" Kimba giggled. He was a known playboy so her goal was to fuck him and suck him so crazy, he'd have to come back for seconds and thirds. Every dude in the hood knows if they wanna keep fucking a chick, it was going to cost. Either way, she was paid to go on this date.

He tossed money on the table for the bill minus the tip and pulled her from the restaurant. She had to open her own door since he opened his own and hopped behind the wheel. She never had a dude open a door or pull out her chair, so she couldn't miss it.

"Go on and warm that motor up," he dared and nodded at her legs.

"Mmhm," she hummed and put her feet on the dash and pulled her panties aside. The little circles she made on her clit made her, "Mmm, sss!"

"Damn, shorty!" he said and mashed the gas to hurry home and smash that ass. He was lucky Brooklyn cops had bigger fish to fry than him speeding through the borough. The car came to a screeching halt in front of his brownstone but it was being taped off by the gas company. "The fuck? Yo, my man. What's going on?"

"Gas leak," the utility worker said from behind the mask covering his mouth and nose. "We have to find the owner to shut it off from the inside."

"This my shit! Come on!" he said and led the way up the stairs.

"You better stay out here," the man told Kimba before handing Yayo a mask of his own.

"A'ight, yo," Kimba said and sucked her teeth. She had waited patiently while he fucked her whole crew. Now it was some bullshit when it was her turn. A smile turned her lip up as she watched the utility worker follow Yayo inside with his tool box. Her work was done so she raised her hand and hailed a gypsy cab.

"It's in here!" Yayo said, pointing to the basement door. He turned around and saw Dolla pull down his mask and pull up his gun. "Son, I thought we was good about shorty?"

"Oh we are," Dolla assured him with a nod. "I'm over that. This is a robbery, homie."

"She told you where I be at," he said, shaking his head at his own stupidity. Que warned him on many occasions to stop bringing chicks to the stash spot.

"Yup, now let's get this bread upstairs," he said. Yayo let out a sigh and led the way up to the second floor. He unlocked a locked door where bundles of cash sat neatly on a table.

"Put them in here," he ordered and opened the empty tool box. He complied and accepted his loss.

"Man, that's almost eighty bands," he moaned when he put the last of it in the box. He wasn't hurt though since he had twice that on the street.

"Now, I'ma need them hammers," Dolla advised. He had buyers for the guns lined up already.

"She told you about that, too?" he whined. He already knew the answer and led the way to where he kept the guns. The box of brand new MP5 machine pistols brought a smile to Dolla 's face.

"I'ma have to keep one of these for myself. Two maybe? Yeah, two," he decided. "Now, I heard something about some work?"

"Nope! Que got everything in the street. Ain't nothing here but a few pounds of green!" he said as if he one upped the jack boy.

"Well, run that!" Dolla growled, ready to slap the smirk off his face.

"Oh, yeah," Yayo agreed when he remembered he was getting robbed. He led Dolla into the bedroom to retrieve the weed. Dolla 's face morphed into a mask of murder when he saw the king size bed in the room. It had a handle on the headboard, and one of those special pillows for back shots. He assumed correctly that this had been the scene of the crime. The place he sexed Dyme and it was about to become a crime scene again.

Yayo gagged even louder this time when Dolla shoved the plastic pistol in his mouth. He chipped a tooth but that was the last of his worries. Dolla grabbed his throat and looked him square in his eyes.

"You dissed my woman!" Dolla demanded.

Yayo tried to shake his head no, but it was too late. A tug on the trigger blew his mind literally, as the wall turned a custom pink from blood and brain matter. He saw the lights in his eyes go out when his soul left his body. There was no turning back now. If you can't turn back, you turn up!

*****

"So, what made you come hang out with me?" Que asked when he and Dyme got seated for dinner. She agreed to dinner and a movie knowing what came with it. It didn't matter what was on the plate because dick was for desert.

"You asked me," she shrugged. "Better question is why you wanna hang out with me? After what I did to your man's face."

"Cuz Yayo told me you left a puddle in his bed. Not a wet spot, a whole fucking puddle!" he admitted.

"True, but he also been running around telling errbody my shit stink!" she said, getting mad about it again now. Not for long before a text from Dolla made her smile. Most chicks would have been grossed out by the gory picture of Yayo with his brains on the wall. Not Dyme, though. She let out a little giggle.

"Nah, I knew that wasn't true. A nigga can tell if a chick pussy stink from a couple blocks away. Son be bugging, yo," he nodded with his own decision to take over his spot. "He on his way out anyway."

"Mmhm," she giggled again since she knew he was already headed to the upper room. He was right behind him and didn't even know it. "Anyway, I did leave a puddle behind. I can't help it. My pussy get so wet I be having to carry extra panties in my purse."

Que felt his dick jump in his jeans when she said that. Then got an instant erection when she pulled a pair of yellow panties from her purse. Que had heard all he needed to hear when he saw the dainty drawers.

"Fuck this food, yo. Let's get out of here!" he said and rushed her from the spot.

"I got a room," she offered coyly.

"Word?" he asked cautiously. He could give a fuck about saving motel fair. He just wanted to hurry up and take a dip in that puddle. He reached over to feel it but it was not to be.

"Chill, B!" she said and knocked his hand away. She pledged her pussy to Dolla and vowed to never let another man touch it. "I got a room over in Red Hook. My cousin rented it, but they at the club."

Que nodded and steered the car towards the Red Hook section. He found the motel and parked outside. Que scanned the area for friends or foes before stepping outside, pulling a 40 cal from under his seat.

"What you need that for? I'ma give you the pussy. You ain't gotta steal it!" she laughed.

"Word," he said and squinted his eyes into evil slits. He was a killer himself and killed quite a few dudes just like this. As soon as Dyme unlocked the door, he rushed in with the gun eye high and cleared the room like in a cop show.

"Clear!" she called out and cracked up when his search of the room came up empty. "Really, bruh? You think I was tryna set you up?"

"Nah, I even do that when I go to my grandma house," he laughed and sat the pistol on the night stand. That was mistake number two. Number one was taking her call in the first place. "Now get them clothes off!"

"You first. Slow, papi, so I can watch," she said and twirled her tongue around her thick lips.

"Oh word? You want the Chippendale shit, huh?" he said and grinded his hips.

"Un huh," Dyme said and bit her lip so she wouldn't laugh. He made a big show of unbuckling his belt and letting his expensive jeans fall to the floor. He had a decent size lump of dick in his boxer briefs, but it was about to go to waste.

"You like that?" he asked and she nodded and bit her lip a little harder. Que reached down and slowly pulled his shirt over his head. When he did, he came face to face with his own gun. It looked totally different from this side. The huge barrel looked like the Holland tunnel but Jersey wasn't on the other side. "Chill, ma. That shit is loaded!"

"I know," she smiled and pulled her phone. "Come on, babe."

Que knew what was up and wasn't going out without a fight. He was pretty sure that wasn't April she just called, so he had to make his move before whoever it was arrived. She eased over to the door to open it and he sprang into action.

"Bitch!" he barked and lunged towards her. Lunging requires legs and a quick shot to his knee nearly took one of his off. The gun barked and sparked and down he went. "Yeeooow!"

"I bet," Dyme giggled at his howled and turned the knob to let Dolla in.

"You okay? I heard a woman scream," he laughed as he entered the room. He grimaced at the mess the 40 cal made of dude's knee. "Son, you sounded like an opera singer."

"Fuck you, fuck her," he said defiantly. He lived like a man and would not die like a bitch. "Could at least let me fuck her first!"

"I'll take care of that," Dolla said and raised his gun to Que's face.

"Wait!" Dyme shouted just before he bust him. Dolla twisted his face up, wondering why she wanted to spare him.

"The fuck?" he asked.

"Let me?" she asked with a wicked grin.

"You sure?" he asked cautiously. He knew once a person opens that door, they can't close it. Murder is habit forming like smoking weed or masturbation. She nodded, he shrugged and stepped aside.

"Not with my own shit, yo!" Que protested when she raised his own gun to his face.

"Beggars can't be choosers," she reminded him and sent a speeding bullet into his face that sent him speeding into the afterlife. She cocked her head and studied the mess she made. Dolla realized he just created a monster. Not that he cared because she was his monster.

"Come on, ma. We gotta bounce!" he urged and pulled her out of the room. They tucked their guns and rushed to his car.

"Yo, I'm mad horny!" Dyme said. It was time to take their relationship to the next level.

Chapter Five

"Well, this is it," Dolla said almost nervously when he pulled to a stop in front of the Park Hill motor lodge. He knew there would be heat after both Yayo and Que got their shit twisted. Fingers would certainly point his way since he dissed him. Yayo had a mean team, so he stepped off the scene for a moment. Things would die down once Yayo's old crew finished their power struggle and a new leader emerged. Dolla and Dyme would rob him too on their quest for a million dollars.

"Yup," Dyme said just as nervously. They both knew tonight would be the first night of the rest of their lives.

"You hungry?" he asked despite them just eating an hour ago.

"Nah," she said and followed him into the room that would be their home for a while. She hid the money and weed in her Aunt Lynn's house. She found a hole in the closet wall that April would never find.

Small talk was over once they entered the room and sat on the edge of the bed. The first kiss was a memorable peck after locking eyes. The others were lost in a blur of furious sex.

Dyme practically ripped Dolla's clothes as they made out. Then her own without breaking the lip lock. His sweet tongue only came out of her mouth long enough to pull her shirt over her head. Next, they found themselves face to face on the bed.

"I'm going to love you so good. That's my word!" Dyme vowed when they locked eyes once more at the moment of truth.

"And I'm going to love you even better," Dolla declared as he lubed the head of his dick in the slippery froth between her legs. She relaxed and gave herself up to him completely.

Dolla was well hung but it didn't hurt when he entered her. She was far too turned on and slippery wet to register any pain. She was going to be sore later but only felt pleasure at the moment. A moment that literally lasted for hours as they explored each other in search of what the other liked.

"I'm about to cum," Dolla announced like he was confused as to what he was supposed to do about it.

"Cum then," Dyme purred and clamped her already snug walls around his dick. He grunted and spasmed in the throws of a good nut. Holding back only intensified the sensation and damn neared killed him. He could have sworn his heart stopped for a second as he filled her with his seeds.

Neither recalled going to sleep but they awoke huddled together in a ball the next morning. His morning erection didn't go to waste because Dyme mounted it and rode off in search of her own orgasm. She found it and rode him to one of his own. They cuddled again and caught their breath.

"Mmm," Dolla moaned as he felt her contractions convulsing on his dick. They milked him dry and made him wonder, "Are you on the pill? Or a shot or implants?"

"No, no and no," she giggled and wiggled. He didn't go soft, so she kept right on rocking and rolling on the dick. His tone was funny but the question was valid. Especially with all the kids he just sent speeding up inside of her.

She'd only been with KC twice and Yayo once. KC went raw but she survived and Yayo strapped up or so she thought until she knew.

"Well let me show you the Dyme special," he offered and patted her ass to get her up. That was easier said than done since she found her rhythm. He was helpless when she began to coat his shaft with that thick cream only the best pussy can produce.

"I'm cu—" she began then began to cum. She didn't get to finish his statement but he got the point when she busted another nut. He could feel a river of juice run down his balls and between his legs.

She went limp, making it easy to roll her off and roll her over. He positioned her face down on her belly and used a pillow under her hips to tilt her ass forward. Her fat vagina popped out like a jack in box and he slid into her box. He lifted up on his hands and toes as if about to some push ups but pushed in.

"Oh, wow!" was all Dyme could say in reply to the long solid strokes. She said something else when she came once more, but it was in a language neither of them spoke. Good sex will have people speaking on tongues and reaching for shit that ain't there.

Dolla could relate as the sensation began to tingle from his toes to the back of his knees. He made the mistake of looking down at himself sliding in and out and it was over. It quickly shot up his legs and exploded out the tip of his dick, but not before he snatched out her soaking wet snatch.

"Ugh! Shit! Whew!" he shouted and shivered as his dick spit and quivered, send globs of unwanted children onto her back. He collapsed on top of her and struggled to catch his breath.

"Okay, daddy. I'll go to the clinic in the morning," she relented. Having him pull out felt like kicking a man out of his home when he needs you the most.

She would love to have his kids one day, just not this day nine months from now. Not in this place either.

"Okay, baby," he said. He wanted her to have his kids as well but now wasn't the time and New York wasn't the place. Anywhere was better than here to raise a family.

"We should move. Let's move to Atlanta!" she shouted and rolled out from under him.

"Word?" Dolla asked and thought of his own pros and cons. First, it wasn't Brooklyn, and the score was four to one in favor of the Atl.

"Hell yeah! It don't snow. It's mad money down there. Cost of living is way cheaper," she said, pushing the score to twenty to one.

"We still got sixty bands that Yayo donated to us," he said since they ran through twenty is the week since the robbery. He let her stash the cash since he didn't want to keep it in the room he rented in the rooming house or in the motel room they shacked up in.

"Yeah, I stashed it real good in my auntie's house," Dyme said. She was now happy Dolla put the breaks on their shopping or she would have spent in all. She spent five grand on a chain and wanted to spend five more on matching earrings and bracelet but Dolla talked her out of it.

He spent his ten on a used Lexus and new Timberlands. He'd been broke and homeless before and vowed to never be again. No matter who had to get robbed.

"Well, go get it tomorrow, after... the clinic, and we out," he said and rubbed her booty. She smiled wickedly and set off round three.

"Let's bounce. Let's get up out of here!" Dolla decided seemingly suddenly.

"From the room or..." she asked hopefully that she had sold him on her idea of moving down to Atlanta. It was the land of milk and honey compared to the bricks and bullshit of Brooklyn.

"From New York," he said. It wasn't quite as spontaneous as it seemed since he had been weighing it all day. He had no family left and friends were more trouble than they were worth. Dyme was all he had and he wanted a fresh start with her.

"Thank you! Thank you! Thank you!" she cheered and planted more kisses all over his face. That led to round two for the day and it was still morning. Once they wrapped up and showered, Dyme set off to collect her clothes and his money. He had to make a few moves of his own and they agreed to meet up later. When they did meet up it was more of the same.

*****

"We need to hit that clinic now if it's not too late," Dyme moaned after Dolla filled her full of early morning cum.

"For real, though," he agreed since pulling out is much easier said than done. It's unnatural to get to that point then, abandon what got you there. He pulled his deflating dick from her and got up.

Dyme joined him in the shower and ended up with even more cum in her. Neither had any self-control when it came to the other. They were soul mates and only death could separate them, unless they died together.

Once they fucked and finally washed, they got out the shower and got dressed.

"Let me help you," Dyme fussed and fixed his collar like he was her son. She hoped to have his son, then sons and a couple of daughters. Ten if it were up to her. She didn't want her children growing up lonely like she did as an only child. So they could protect each other so scumbags like her mother's boyfriend James. He got tired of sneaking and eating her out. Now he wanted to fuck her. She confided in KC but he got mad and cut her off.

She ran away to her Aunt Lynn and cousin, April . Life was crowded and chaotic but no grown man was sneaking in her room trying to fuck her either, so it balanced out. Her biggest problem was ratchet ass April wearing her clothes and going through her belongings.

"Thanks, babe," he said once she fixed his collar. They looked around the motel room to make sure they didn't leave anything since they would not be coming back. They rode over to the clinic to put her on something before he knocked her up.

"Um, excuse me?" Dyme fussed at some young chick staring at Dolla like he was a rap star. He did have that look and that aura about him. He was larger than life and she would just have to learn to live with the attention it brought. "Ain't you here to get rid of them crabs?"

"Chill, Dyme," he said, holding her arm as the girl rolled her eyes and stole another quick glance. He was used to the attention but humble enough to still not understand it. Chicks dug him everywhere he went.

"Let me catch you looking at him when I come out!" she dared when her name was called. She went to the back and got a six-month subscription for Dolla to cum in her. Once that was done, it was off to Aunt Lynn's house.

"You just missed your cousin," Lynn said when Dyme walked in the house.

"Missed her where?" Dyme wondered since April never worked and it was too early for the club. It was too late in the afternoon for a booty call since dudes would drop her off first thing in the morning.

"Girl, she done picked up and moved to Atlanta! I believe she done met some nigga on Facebook," Lynn said, since she had met one herself. In fact she had just put some pussy pics in his inbox before Dyme arrived.

"Say word! I..." Dyme began until a sinking feeling came over her. Her heart sank and she knew what she knew before she got upstairs to check. "Oh no!"

Chapter Six

"Yo, I can't believe this—" Dyme began but stopped short of lying to herself. Why wouldn't she believe that April would steal from her when she'd been stealing from her since she arrived? First the change out her pockets, to socks and panties. Now she just snaked her for everything she had and what she didn't have, including Dolla's dough from robbing Yayo. A man died for that and she just walks off with it for free.

"What's wrong, chile?" Dyme's Aunt Lynn asked in response to the scream Dyme let out when she found her closet and stash spot empty. Even she knew something was up when her daughter suddenly bounced with more stuff than she owned.

"April jacked me. She took everything I own, yo. She ain't leave me nothing. Not even my dirty clothes!" she whined. "And my man's money. Tens of thousands of dollars!"

"That girl ain't shit!" Lynn slipped. She usually stuck up for her sorry child no matter what. She was now as mad as Dyme hearing how much money she ran off with and didn't leave her any money. "I heard her telling someone she was moving to Atlanta."

"Wow. She even stole my plans. Now how I'm supposed to tell Dolla?" Dyme moaned. She failed him and all their money was gone.

"Suck his dick first. Then give it to him straight," she suggested. It was actually a good idea but deceptive, so she decided to give it to him straight. Still she had to make up for it, so she searched her mind for a quick lick. She saw a name and number on a piece of paper April had left behind. She saw why she left it behind once she read the name.

"Shit ," she fussed when she read the name Goose's name and number. He had plenty of money but was known to be a sexual sadist. Chicks threw the pussy at him because he was rich but he still took it anyway because he was rapist.

Knowing she had to make up the loss, she picked up the paper and made the call.

"Who?" Goose asked and frowned up when he answered the unknown number.

"Dyme, April cousin," she repeated. "From Marcy. You don't remember me? Wow!"

"Oh yeah! Young pretty bitch, with that fat ass!" he recalled. He had checked her out as much as he checked out April when he rolled up on her. She looked young and didn't have a reputation so he didn't pursue her.

April went out with him once and wasn't the same when she returned the next morning. She had a few hundred dollars in her knock off purse but was in shock for a couple of days.

"That's not exactly how I would describe myself but, yeah. So what's up, you tryna hang out or nah?" she cut through to the chase.

"If you fucking. You fucking?" he wanted to know. And if nothing else, he should be given credit for transparency. He wasn't with the movies, or dinner and didn't even have a subscription to Netflix. He was trying to put his dick in some pussy, end of story.

"I mean, we can go. I'm saying I, I," she stammered.

"Nah, yo. If we fucking, say we fucking. If not, get off my phone. There's plenty of pussy in Brooklyn, so don't waste my time."

"Okay, we fucking. Dang!" Dyme fussed. It was crass even for a chick from the projects. They made the plans and she got off his phone. She stayed on hers and called her man.

"Sup, ma. I'm headed your way now," Dolla said when he took her call.

"K," she said and decided to wait until they were face to face to tell him. In the end, she took her aunt's advice and gave him some head before breaking the bad news to him.

"I'm about to—" Dolla warned when he reached the point of no return. It was enough warning for Dyme to get him out of her mouth and finish him off by hand.

She smiled in amazement when the baby batter exploded from his dick and landed some of everywhere. She stroked his thick shaft until he was spent, then went to get a soapy wash cloth from the motel bathroom to wash him off.

"Okay, now what's up wit' you?" Dolla asked knowingly. The upside to having a soul mate is them knowing you like a book. The downside is them knowing you like a book. He knew something was eating her before she ate the dick.

"Man, April done hit the stash. You trusted me to keep your money and she found it Stole err cent. Even my dirty clothes. I ain't got shit except what I got on!" she whined.

"Damn, yo!" Dolla shouted and shook his head. He felt as bad for Dyme as he did about the money. He knew the streets were talking about Yayo getting hit up and people knew they had beef. "How we supposed to move to the A now?"

"I got us another lick. Dude named Goose from Bed-Stuy."

"Goose the killer? The nigga who be raping chicks for money? You bugging, yo," Dolla insisted.

"I'll do it myself. Just give me the banger," Dyme offered.

"Oh you a killer now, huh?" he laughed and was actually a little turned on. "Got one little body under yo' belt and now you ready to go murk something, huh?"

"Yup!" she insisted and stuck her chin up.

"Okay. We gone see what you talking 'bout, but uh..." he said and reached between her legs. She gladly gave him what Goose was never getting and would die trying.

*****

"Yoooo! This some HGTV type shit right here!" Dyme sang as Goose led her into his waterfront loft in downtown Brooklyn.

"Thanks. Nothing like that small time cat Dolla, huh?" he asked and laughed at her shock. "Oh, a nigga did his homework. I'on just stick my shit in anybody.

But you'll fuck a nobody, Dyme thought to herself. Dolla told her sometimes it's best not to say nothing and just listen so that's what she did.

Goose lit a blunt of some fruity flavored weed and introduced her to the good life.

"Dom P, while you was drinking wine coolers," he said as he retrieved a bottle from the ten thousand dollar fridge.

"Mmhm," she said with her lips pressed tightly so nothing else would come out. Especially that good weed he had. She hoped there was a stash of it somewhere so she could take it, too. If not, she would clip the blunt so she could save some for her man. The conversation started off weird then got worse.

"Most people like to do things the easy way. Me, I like things the hard way. Feel me?" Goose asked and handed Dyme a glass of champagne.

"Not really," she said and took a sip. "What exactly does that mean?"

"It means I'm gonna take that pussy. I want you to try to stop me. I mean like really fight me. I'ma hit you off real good, but I like what I like," he explained.

"Yo, that's the craziest shit I ever heard in my life. Straight up, and I'm not with it," she said and took a final pull on the blunt.

"That's what the fuck I'm talking about!" Goose cheered. He assumed she was getting into character and it turned him on. He had her on tape saying we fucking, so it was whatever with him at this point.

"I'm out, yo," she said and went for the front door. She really did want to get away from the sicko but knew Dolla was on the other side of the door. A switch hit inside of Goose's twisted mind and he snapped.

"Drink my bubbly and smoke my weed and you talking 'bout you out!" he shouted and attacked. He ran up and tried to get her down so he could rape her right there on the spot.

"Get off me, nigga !" she shouted and fought for her life. Dyme had been fighting her whole life but fighting not to be raped gave her energy and strength she didn't know she had.

"That's what the fuck I'm talking about!" Goose cheered when she split his lip and scratched his face. He was rock hard and ready to fuck. Dyme put up a better fight than most and actually made it to the door. She managed to unlock it before Goose snatched her away and threw her down. He had her right where he wanted her and went for his pants. He was so focused on getting his dick out, he didn't hear death rush through his front door.

"Sick ass nigga !" Dolla growled as he wrapped his muscular arm around his neck. Goose was so used to fighting chicks he was no match for a man. He could only pull at the meaty arm cutting his wind off. A body needs oxygen to fight and he quickly ran out of both.

Dolla felt him go limp but kept on squeezing. He squeezed until he passed out, then kept on until he passed away. He dropped him next to Dyme and went to check on her.

"You a'ight, yo?" he asked even though she was clearly shook up.

"That nigga is crazy!" she shouted and scooted away from his corpse.

"Go wait in the car!" he demanded and pushed her to the door. Once she was out he pulled his gun and pumped a couple rounds in-to Goose's head for Dyme, then got to searching for valuables.

"Jackpot!" Dolla cheered and pumped his fist. He was glad Dyme was in the car so she didn't see the little happy dance he did. The safe was closed but not locked, so a simple turn of the latch gave up its goods as quickly as Chattie on a first date.

"Man," he said and twisted his lips at the content inside. There were a few hundred thousand dollars' worth of bonds which were worthless to him. They came with tracking numbers and signatures that could connect him to the dead guy. A pair on plastic pistols with extended clips and silencers attached made him smile. He grabbed the twenty grand in loose cash, the jewelry and turned to leave. He remembered his manners as he stepped over the corpse and nodded.

"Thanks for donating to the Dolla and Dyme get rich or die trying fund," he said and stepped from the house. Dyme was bundled up in the blanket with a blank look on her face. "You good?"

"Huh?" she asked and came back to the present. "You straight? We straight?"

"A little. Son keeps his bread in the bank. We got some traveling money, tho."

"Well, let's travel then!" she laughed and off they went. Next stop was the ATL.

Chapter Seven

Dolla walked out and took a deep breath to inhale the sweet Brooklyn aroma for the last time. It's a mix of curry, good weed, arroz con pollo, pretty women, and new sneakers. His face scrunched when another scent that invaded his melancholy. He scanned the streets and saw the cause. Chattie was two and a half blocks away and closing in. He turned to escape but heard his name.

"Yo, Dolla! Dolla, you hear me!" she said and rushed in his direction.

"Sup, ma?" he asked and turned into the wind so it would carry the funk two blocks up.

"I heard about April. She foul," she said as if she wasn't foul herself.

"Yeah," was all Dolla had since he didn't do gossip. He turned to finish his mission of getting breakfast for the road while Dyme went to the weed spot. Neither had left New York before, so they figured they would load up on green before they got ghost.

"Where Dyme?" Chattie asked after a scan up and down the block didn't produce her.

"At the whatchamacallit," he said which means none of your business.

"Shit, so come up for a second?" she asked and batted her eyes. She was pretty, but pretty funky too, so his head shook before his mouth opened.

"I'm good, ma. I'll tell Dyme you asked about her," he said and turned into the bodega. He ordered beef pastrami, egg, and cheese sandwiches on Kaiser rolls and grabbed her favorite orange-pineapple juice.

Dolla couldn't believe the people around Dyme who claimed to love her yet harmed her. Her mother put herself over her daughter and allowed a man to touch her. Her cousin steals all her money and clothes, while her funk box friend just tried to fuck him.

His chin lifted in pride knowing he was the one who would love her and protect her. Verses from the Qur'an always seemed to pop in his mind when he needed them. He could hear his father saying, *"Men are the protectors and maintainers of women"*. Dyme was his woman and that's what he planned to do. She was all he had and vice versa until death did them.

*****

"Welcome to Atlanta!" Dyme cheered and cheesed as she read the sign welcoming them to their new city. They made the 13-hour drive in two days and five hours because they had to stop and fuck several times on the side of 95 south, motels and once while he drove. Each was a new toy to the other and neither could get enough.

"Now what?" Dolla heard himself say. She knew he wasn't asking her since she picked up on his habit of vocalizing his thoughts. She also knew he would have an answer. He would lead and she would follow. She could only hope he didn't lead them over a cliff because again, she would follow. Dyme turned the radio on while the wheels turned in his head.

"Join us at Chaos, the ATL's hottest new club! Special invited guest include..."

"That's where she gonna be!" Dolla said it at the exact second it popped in her head. Her head nodded in agreement.

"Word. She gonna find the hottest club in the city. I just hope we ain't too late!" she said as she checked her cousin's Instagram feed. She could have at least blocked her if she was going to stunt with their stolen money. April was balling out of control on their dime.

"Too late for what?" Dolla asked since he never expected to see a dime of that money back. Thieves never return what they steal no matter what.

"Before she..." Dyme began until she caught on, too. She shrugged her shoulders at what she knew was to come. "Oh well."

"I'll do it since she family," he offered since they were now on the same page.

"And that's exactly why I'ma do it. I can't believe she would do me like this! She always be wanting whatever I get!" she pouted as a lifetime of indiscretions flooded her mine. "This is on me. I got her."

Dolla wasn't surprised by Dyme 's sudden change of mind. The one thing he taught her was to never allow anyone to snake you, family or not. Dyme was learning well which made Dolla proud. He had a pretty chick that was a go getta and wouldn't hesitate to leave a bitch stinkin'. That to Dolla was definitely worth bragging about.

"That's prolly why she offered to blow me last week," he guessed. He didn't have to share that since April was already as good as dead. He just wanted it to be brutal. The low growl emanating from the passenger seat said it would be brutal indeed.

They drove through the city of Atlanta and settled in the northern suburb of Marietta. It was twenty minutes away from the action yet busy enough to blend in. Dyme went to the restaurant next door while he registered and got their room.

"Need some help?" she offered when he began to unload the car.

"I got it, ma. Set that food out. I'm starving!" he said and passed her the key card.

"I got something you can eat," she purred seductively. He twisted his lips into a frown just like the last time she suggested it. Just like he did whenever she suggested him going down on him, especially since she was practicing on him every day. She always heard April and Chattie telling their blow job tales about driving dudes wild and couldn't wait to have a man of her own to try it out on. Her cousin and friends may suck stray dicks like stray cats, but she waited for a man of her own and now she had one.

She heard some dudes would wait awhile before going down on a chick to put some distance between them and the last dick. Also to ensure that it's their pussy before they eat it. None of those things applied to them and it was definitely his pussy. They had the rest of their lives, so she would wait before asking again. Like maybe give him another week.

"I need some clothes," Dyme pouted when he sat the bags down. He still had all of his clothes while she had none. She would only bring an overnight bag each night when she spent nights with Dolla.

April even stole her dirty clothes from the hamper. Her fault for showing off matching bra and panty sets to a chick whose bras and panties never matched. A lone tear slipped and her lip began to quiver as she got emotional.

"We'll go tomorrow," Dolla said to comfort her. He wanted her angry not sad, so he scooped her up and planted some kisses on her face.

"The food gonna get cold," she warned since she was getting hot. Dolla nodded his head toward the microwave and walked her over to the bed. The young couple made love like a couple of young people in love. The food would have to wait.

*****

"Let's go out, check out the city," Dolla suggested after they awoke from a nap. Three rounds of sex, followed by dinner put them to sleep like a baby in a car seat on the highway.

"Un uh, I'm good," she moaned and flipped over in the bed. A smirk spread on his face knowing he dicked her down so well, she couldn't get back up.

"Well, I'm going for a ride," he said and rolled out of bed. He slipped under the shower to wash away the residue left behind from her juice box.

Dolla was a goon at heart but allowed his woman to buy some fancy clothes she wanted to see him in. He pulled on a pair of the designer jeans and loafers and matched them with a tasteful button down shirt.

"Eh," he chuckled at his well dressed reflection in the mirror. He looked like one of those fancy dudes he liked to rob, but he liked the look on him.

He snuck a kiss on Dyme's cheek, then moved up and placed another on the cheeks on her face. His mission was to learn his surroundings so he turned the GPS off and felt his way around. They arrived here on 75 north, so he reversed course and pulled onto 75 south.

Once he reached downtown Atlanta, he navigated the surface streets. The scenery went from swank to dank when he reached MLK Boulevard. He shook his head when he realized that if a tourist to any city in any state wanted to buy weed, crack or pussy, all they had to do was find MLK. He was pretty sure this wasn't the dream he had.

"Humph?" Dolla wondered when he drove past a well-lit building with a parking lot packed with luxury cars. He had to pull a U-turn to come around for a closer look. The sign above read "Dimes", so he pulled in to check out the scenery.

"Twenty dollars!" a pretty, yet ratchet hostess demanded and stuck her palm out the window. Dolla was slow moving, so she left her news feed long enough to look up at him. Her face changed when she saw the new face. One look told her the pretty thug wasn't from around here. "Heyyy"

"Um, hey?" he repeated. He would soon get used to the down south version of "sup yo". He reached into his pocket and pulled out a large roll of cash. "Twenty?"

"Nuh uh, go on in!" she smiled, blushed, and batted her eyes. He nodded his thanks and stepped inside.

Dolla stopped dead in his tracks when he reached the bowels of the establishment. He squinted his eyes to decipher the smells rushing towards him. This was a strip club, so he quickly recognized pussy and baby oil. Then perfume, cologne, alcohol, weed and tobacco, but through it all he smelled cash. Lots and lots of cash.

Cash rained from several sources throughout the club. One dude actually had a gun that spit cash out the end. It was a virtual gold mine or mint. He knew right then he was going to rob the place. He followed his nose and ended up at a velvet rope that separated regular people from very important people.

"A hunnid for VIP section, my nigga," a large bouncer boomed down at him. Dolla almost laughed at him as he went back into his pocket.

"All I got is a hundred," he said deliberately to correct him as well as show him he didn't intimidate him. He stepped aside and Dolla entered. All the booths were loaded with dudes who were loaded.

One dude wore so many diamonds his whole booth twinkled like little stars. He flicked dollars in the air towards two dancers he barely even looked at. A scan of the dimly lit club showed several more dudes flossing and spending.

Nah, I ain't robbing the club. I'm robbing all y'all niggas, he thought and nodded.

"You tryna get a dance, handsome?" a voice asked, disturbing his thoughts.

"Huh?" Dolla asked as he looked at the woman standing over him. She leaned her crotch towards him like a good salesman does when trying to sell something. He couldn't tell if she was good looking or not, because she had quite a few aftermarket parts. God is perfect and would not have put her together like that. Her breast, lips, and ass were all spare parts and extras.

"Dance? Strip club? I'm a stripper," she smiled and showed a diamond laced front tooth. He scanned her from head to camel toe to toes and back to the camel toe.

"Sure. Why not?" he shrugged.

"Twenty dollars a song," she said and unhooked her bra. The custom made titties didn't budge when she did.

"Hope the DJ ain't playing the mixed tape," he laughed, and scanned the room once more. The dancer looked back and saw he wasn't paying her much attention. Either way, he was paying her so she kept shaking what the doctor gave her.

"Instead of paying by the song, why not just give me a grand after we close and I'll show you how the south was won," she offered with everything that came along with it.

"Some other time maybe," he said after the song. He paid for the next song and stood to leave. He left, but planned to return. Soon and he was bringing Dyme back next time.

Chapter Eight

"Guess we can go shopping now," Dolla gave in after Dyme put it on him real, real good. He had been a little stubborn after her cousin made off with their money. After all, April stole from them, not just him.

"I know that's right," she giggled since she knew she just put it on him. She thought she knew the power of the pussy, but she had no clue just how powerful it was. Many men had been corrupted or ruined from the pursuit of pussy.

They dressed and set out to the nearest mall in search of much needed clothing. Dolla was straight since his stuff hadn't been in Dyme's closet. If so, April would have run off with it, too. The grimy broad even scooped up the loose change she found so she wouldn't leave her cousin anything. It was payback for being prettier, smarter, and cleaner than her.

They ended up in the huge mall of Georgia and took in all the strange sounds and sights. Mainly the people.

"We ain't in New York no more," Dolla remarked as they took in the dress and talk of the natives.

"Why they won't finish they words? Why they ta' li' thi'?" Dyme frowned as if it irritated her, then cracked up as she imitated them.

Luckily for Dolla, she wasn't one of those perpetually angry women and was still able to laugh. Despite the rough hand that she'd been dealt by others. She could be blamed for the way she played some of those hands too, though. Dolla reminded her that there was much more to life than what was directly in front of her.

"I'on know. They just talk funny down here, yo. Naw'mean?" he replied like New Yorkers don't speak funny themselves.

"Word up, yo," she said and dipped into a store. She racked up on jeans and designer tees, while Dolla browsed through the women's negligees.

47

"Can I help you?" a salesclerk asked so seductively, Dyme snapped her head from across the room. Dolla stifled a laugh when she came rushing over.

"Naw, he 'ont need no help, or herpes or whatever else you got!" she said as she rushed over. "I can smell the yeast coming out your shit now!"

"Dyme, get help, ma," Dolla cracked up. He laughed so hard and so loud, Dyme had to repeat her question.

"I said, what you doing over here anyway? Dang freak!" she laughed. He was an old fashion T-shirt and panties type of dude, so she didn't understand his sudden interest in the fancy stuff. She was about to find out, though.

"Oh, nothing. Just grab a few things just in case. You never know. You know?"

"Mmhm," she said and side eyed him skeptically. She grabbed a few boy short and bra sets and put them with the rest.

"Don't forget something for the club. We going out tonight!" he reminded.

"That's right, Chaos!" she smiled wickedly. She planned to bring some chaos to April's life when they caught up with her.

*****

"Yeah, y'all broke bishes. This is how rich bishes stunt!" April said as she went live on her IG.

"This chick wearing my shit and it don't even fit her!" Dyme moaned as she watched the feed. April didn't even bother to block her so she could stunt on her. She wanted to cry seeing her fancy clothes stretched beyond capacity.

"Man, she done spent all our little bread!" Dolla said when he saw the big bag of fluffy buds on the glass table. The weed was a hundred dollars a quarter ounce and the apartment ran a grand a month. April paid her rent up and furnished the joint with the stolen money. She wasn't worried about a job for monthly bills since she had a vagina for that.

She would just sling that salty pussy far and wide like a boomerang and let it bring in some money. That was her plans for the night at the club. Meet some big ballers and shot callers to help pay the bills. She went live to show off for the rest of the G.M.Gs back at home but one M.D.C was watching right there in Georgia. Dyme was one Mad, Dangerous Chick.

"A bitch went from the block in Brooklyn to the good life!" April said as she scanned her surroundings.

"Dummy!" Dyme announced when the sign of her apartment complex came into view. She snatched Dolla's phone to check it so she didn't have to cut the live feed.

"Yo!" Dolla protested at the rude interruption.

"Bruh, you looking at pictures of pussy? Wait, that's mine!" she laughed then pulled up the complex. "Concept 21, Norcross."

"Got her?" he asked hopefully. He knew the money was lost the second she ran off with it. All that was left was revenge and he wanted all of it.

"I got her!" she said as the Google earth popped on the screen. She had the whole layout to the whole complex except her apartment number.

"Guess we still going to the club, huh?" he asked.

"Yeah, but we can't go in. She gone take flight if she see us," she sighed.

"We'll, just lay on her in the parking lot then. We can check out the club some other time. I got another spot we can go..." he said, putting her on their next move.

*****

April arrived by Uber but knew how she was getting home when she saw the parking lot to the club. It was loaded with fully loaded luxury cars. She was hoping for the owner of one of the several Bentleys out front but would settle for a Benz if push came to shove. She was still balling off Dolla and Dyme's dimes, so she bypassed the line and used the VIP entrance. She knew good and well the only time she came close to being a VIP is when she got burned and had a very, infected pussy.

These Atl dudes didn't know any better and she was new pussy. New pussy has a new car smell the first time you get it. Now April had a new city of dudes to get ran through.

"Dang, shawty," a gold tooth player said and reached for her arm as she neared to bar. "Let me buy you a drank."

"Naw, cuz you gonna want me to sit here while I drink it," she declined. There was too much money in the club to get sidetracked by a drink.

"Fuck you then, ole lame ass, fuck ass, bitch ass..." the man spat as she walked away. Atlanta people sure now how to curse you out. April wasn't shit, but you couldn't tell from the naked eye. She turned heads as she strolled through the club. She spotted her target for the night and headed his way. He was dressed to impress in silk, diamonds and platinum and was about to get some pussy for it.

"Whoa, lil' mama!" he said when she sashayed by. He too reached for her wrist but didn't get dissed.

"Excuse you?" April said minus the venom as she turned like she was seeing him for the first time. Little did he know, she calculated his net worth just by what he was wearing. He had two lumps in his pants, so she hoped one was cash and the other one dick because she wanted some of both.

"My bad, shawty! I'on mean no harm. My name is Nino, but you can call me Nino," he greeted.

"Yes!" she cheered because a name like Nino explained one of the lumps. He removed a large roll of cash from the other and paid for the bottle of bubbles that just arrived.

"My name is Dyme," she decided. Why not use her name too since she had Dyme's clothes on her body, and Dyme's money in her purse. Only thing she didn't have was Dyme's pussy in the panties she was wearing.

"Well, Dyme, what you say we get out of here?" Nino said since he knew a freak when he saw one when he saw how she eyed the money. The couple grand she salivated over was just play dough, so he didn't mind using it to play in some pussy.

"I say hell yeah," she said and stood. He grabbed the bottle of champagne for the road and led her outside.

"She just came out," Dolla announced and regretted it instantly. Dyme abandoned the blowjob she was giving so she could get a look, too.

"Grrrr," Dyme growled when she saw her cousin wearing her outfit that didn't fit. It was supposed to be tight, just not that tight. April was a whole size bigger and packed in the clothing like a sausage.

"You picked the wrong trick, homie," Dolla said to Nino who couldn't hear him. Dude was about to be a casualty of war and didn't even know it.

"Who you stay with?" Nino asked since he couldn't bring her to his house.

"I stay by myself!" April said with the pride that should be reserved for chicks who stayed by themselves because they worked hard or smart and paid their bills. Not for them who stole from their family and left them high and dry. She gave the address which he entered into the GPS.

Nino tied her up and whipped out his dick for the ride. He got some expert head as he followed the turn-by-turn directions to her complex. Sucking dick in the whip can actually work for or against a chick. It can be an appetizer to show what's to come when they reach their destination or sometimes not.

"Shit!" Nino grunted and filled her mouth with baby Ninos just as they reached her complex. The night was young and he was a freak, so he decided to see what else he could get into.

"Here we are," she said with come on her breath and went right back to chewing her gum.

"I'ma have to take a rain check. Here," he said and handed her half the cash and the half bottle of champagne.

"That's what's up," April agreed because she was up almost a grand already. Plus, the night was young and she too was a freak so she planned to head back out as well.

April rushed upstairs to put her cash up and call for another car. She left her door ajar since she was coming right back but heard it close from her room.

"Came back for some of this pussy, huh?" she smiled as she came back out. The smile disappeared in an instant when she saw a nine-millimeter instead on Nino.

"I wouldn't touch that funk box if it was the last pussy on the planet," Dolla growled.

"Yes you would, my nigga. Stop fronting," April laughed. She knew this could go either way, so either way she wasn't scared.

"Where my money at, April?" Dyme asked rather calmly. Her cousin knew then which way it would go. Only killers are that calm. She never knew her little cousin to be a killer but the demeanor was unmistakable.

"Gone, yo. I spent that shit," she said, waving her hands around to show her purchases. "Now, it's plenty bread down this bitch. I know how yall get down. We can..."

No one knew what was coming next because Dolla swung the gun so hard, it broke her jaw. Dyme rushed over, grabbed the designer scarf around her neck, and pulled it tight. Pulled so hard, the silk burned her hands. Pulled so hard, April forgot about the pain of her broken jaw. She let out a gasp that would have to go down as her last words. She and Dolla locked eyes while Dyme squeezed. He saw the flicker of life just before the lights went out.

"She ain't in there no more," he told Dyme, but she kept on squeezing. He had to come over and pry the scarf from her hands. "She gone, yo."

"Bitch!" Dyme said and stopped just short of spitting in her lifeless face. That would have left DNA that would tie her to a murder scene.

"Find whatever cash we can find and get your clothes!" Dolla said as he collected the bag of weed off the table.

"She can keep them clothes," Dyme frowned. She found the money April just sucked out of Nino's dick and they fled the apartment complex.

"Let's make a stop before we go back to the room," Dolla said. It wasn't a question, so Dyme sat back for the ride. She felt nothing after just killing her kin since she deserved it.

*****

"What is this place?" Dyme frowned when Dolla pulled into the parking lot.

"What's the sign say?" he said and braced himself for the pop that always came when he answered a question with a question.

"Boy!" came with the pop. "I can read but what this got to do with us?"

Dolla didn't reply, instead he sat back and let her figure it out on her own. She looked at the packed parking lot and nodded. Her pretty head kept nodding when a Lamborghini pulled up to the valet. A man got out dripping gold and diamonds tipped the attendant from a large roll of cash before he stepped inside. She watched the valet pull the four hundred thousand dollar car into a separate area full of other exotic cars.

"Yo, this place is a fucking gold mine, yo!" she gushed. "Only what's our way in here? Just run in, guns blazing and... nah. So how do we get to the money?"

"Well, it is a strip club. I mean if it was a male joint I would dance, but it's a gentlemen's club, so..." he said and let her finish that part, too.

"Oh boy!" Dyme sighed when she filled in the blanks.

*****

"Hey there, handsome," Diamond greeted Dolla when he returned with Dyme. Meanwhile, Diamond was busy scanning Dyme from head to toe. If she had a dick, it would have been hard. "Who dis?"

"My girl, Me—" he started, but she jumped in to finish.

"Meoshi!" Dyme cut in before he gave her real name. Besides, she always wanted to be a Meoshi and now she was.

"Well hey, Meoshi. Can you dance?" she asked into the cleavage poking out the top of her shirt.

"Can I! Y'all do the Bruck up down here?" she asked but her brain caught up and she realized that's not what she meant. "Dance, dance? No. I don't have the body for all that."

"Say what! Girl, stand up!" Diamond demanded. Dyme did and she checked her out, then spun her around to look at her ass. Dolla was almost jealous at the way she was eyeing his woman. He realized he would have to get used to it for Dyme to dance in the club. She would have to dance for them to get the inside track on all the ballers who frequented the place. "Chile, you fine as hell!"

"You think so?" Dyme giggled and cooed, almost making Dolla bust out laughing at her act.

"Girl, you gone make a band a night easy just working the pole and table dances. Even more if you get up in VIP. Even more if..." Diamond was saying but caught herself before telling her about all the money to be made turning tricks with customers since she was with her man.

"Okay," Dyme giggled again and batted her eyes. Dolla was impressed by her acting skills.

"Come on. I'm finna take you up to meet Ant. He the owner," she said and looked to Dolla. He gave his permission with a nod and off they went.

"Who?" Ant yelled from behind his desk. Diamond didn't respond since she didn't have much respect for the man. Instead, she opened the door and walked in.

"Ant, this Meoshi. She finna dance here," she practically demanded.

"You know she gotta audition!" he said, blinking in Dyme's stunning beauty

She was nothing like nothing he'd ever seen before. He got rock hard in an instance at the prospect of auditioning her. That meant free pussy for him since he couldn't care if a girl could dance or not. He was more concerned with what that mouth do.

"Naw, she ain't here for all that! Plus, her man down stairs right now. You know ain't nothing like her in here, so quit playing!" she demanded like it was her club. She was a star, so he let her have her way. For now, because he was gonna get to Miss Meoshi one way or another.

With that, they were in.

Chapter Nine

Dolla and Dyme knew this club was the ticket to their mil ticket. Their million dollar goal, so they could go where ever and do whatever they liked. Neither had an invention or patent, so they planned to steal it.

They knew these dope boys were sitting on plenty of cash to donate to their cause. They started from zero and didn't plan to stop until they reached a million.

The Dolla and Dyme get rich or die trying fund, but who was first?

"Is that him?" Dolla asked, squinting through the dimly lit club. The ice on the target's neck illuminated him, putting him on his radar from all the way across the room. The dancer in front of him looked in the direction he was looking while still popping her caramel ass cheeks in his face.

"He shole look like the one," his equally ambitious partner Dyme said, licking her lips at the tasty lick in front of them. A good lick has a taste, and it's sweet. After wearing a three-thousand-dollar designer outfit and another ten around his neck, they were going to need a shot of insulin after this one. "It sure looks like him."

The mark must have wanted to get robbed when he pulled out a wad of cash and made it rain on the two dancers dancing in front of him. It was mainly ones and fives, but he still wouldn't have been doing it if he weren't caked the fuck up. He could be charged as an accessory to his own robbery for flossing so hard. His Instagram post could be used against him in a court of law or holding court in the street.

"Yeah, that's him, daddy," she purred like she does when her kitty is stroked. He wasn't supposed to be touching it since the club had a no touching policy but it was his pussy, so he would touch it when and where he wanted. "See, if I bust a nut on your hand, you gone swear I did you wrong."

"You do and I'm gonna bend you over this table and give you the business. All of it!" he warned and lolled his head back in laughter. His bright smile contrasted brilliantly against his dark skin and turned heads. The same heads quickly turned back away since Dyme was quick to beat a bitch up over her man. He felt the same way and stopped fondling her when some locals watched him play in her pussy from a few tables over. He used the liquid she leaked to smooth the thick waves on his head since it worked better than Murrays.

"I'm down," she dared and would have done it if he wanted. Dolla was the first man to treat her right, so she was down for whatever he wanted. What he wanted now was to relieve all the cities clowns of their money.

Dyme was what's known as a fine muthafucka. She stood five foot six inches and had an athletic body, as in an ass as round as a basketball and firm breast the size a regulation soft balls. What set her apart from most of the highly made up strippers was she was naturally pretty. As pretty as she was, she was as rough as a dirt road.

Her round face needed little embellishments to turn heads. A little lip-gloss on the thick lips beat all the beat faces in the club. She further drove the value of her vagina up by not tricking with the ballers. Now they chunked bands at her to get her home and fuck. She accepted a few times but they were the ones who got fucked. Fucked out of their money, drugs, and jewels that is. Not one lived to tell about it.

"Nah, can't lose sight of buddy. Sic him," he laughed and sent her on her way with a slap on her ass. The low budget ballers laughed at the display and earned and angry scowl from Dolla .

He knew they were a problem when they kept staring at them in his native Brooklyn, New York eye contact which was considered a challenge. Staring could get you killed in the blink of an eye. An Atlanta, Georgia stare was slightly slower, so it took two blinks. They proved his point when one of them reached for Dyme as she walked by. He could hear the music from The Omen when dude grabbed her wrist.

"Let us get a dance!" the spokesman insisted and tried to pull her close. She used a martial arts move and twisted herself out of his grip. Dolla knew his girl could handle it but stood just in case. He didn't bring a gun in but knew how to use a beer bottle as a club and knife if need be.

"Unhand me, nigga!" she fussed as she came free. She saw Dolla rise and knew she had seconds to defuse the situation before he lost his mind and blew the lick. "First of all, if all y'all malt liquor drinking niggas need one bitch for a table dance, you can't afford me!"

"Ooh!" his partners jeered, trying to get him to turn up. These were the type of broke goons who got into some shit everywhere they went. They got into more fights than into a woman, so the strip club was as close as they came to some pussy. Dyme beat her feet and put some distance between them before security or Dolla intervened. Security would have evicted their asses from the club. Dolla would have evicted their souls from their bodies.

"Fuck you looking at?" the spokesman dared when he saw Dolla looking their way.

"My bad, shawty," he said like a local and raised his hand in surrender. This wasn't the time or place for confrontation, so he put it in reverse. He summoned a waitress with his hand and sent them a round of drinks on him. It was the least he could do for the condemned men. They didn't know it yet, but their last meal was their last meal.

"Damn! Who the fuck is that bitch?" Po-boy asked the stripper working in front of him when Dyme sashayed through the VIP section. Her round ass did its little dance as she walked without even trying. She had a naturally nasty walk that she couldn't turn off if she wanted to. It could turn up, down a little, but never off.

Po-boy got his name as a skinny child but never changed it even he got his weight. His financial weight that is because the six-footer was still rail thin with large eyes that made him look like a cartoon character. He really was poor coming up and couldn't afford to keep a chick. He made up for it now by tricking almost every night.

"Her name is Meoshi, but she ain't gone fuck," Diamond replied and shook her ass a little harder. She couldn't stand Dyme's pretty ass since should had to fuck and suck these salty dicks to compete with what the pretty girl could make just from dancing. She had to wear so much makeup and wigs to fake being pretty that she resembled a transvestite. A few guys actually thought she was a dude when they took her home only to be disappointed she was really a girl in boy shorts and not a boy. This was Atlanta after all.

"All bitches fuck if the price right! Call her over here," he said and shoved some cash at her to send her on her way.

"Bitch ass nigga," she fussed as she went to carry out her mission. She stepped back into her boy shorts and rushed to catch up. "Yo, Dyme. That nigga with the ice want you. We can take this nigga to the motel and work a band out his ass!"

"We?" Dyme laughed at the attempt to be down. The veteran stripper made it known she wanted a taste when Dyme first started working here. Either her or the owner Ant got to sample all the products. All except Dyme, that is.

"I'm saying, though. You know these trick niggas be wantin' to see some freaky shit! They spend more money to see two gals," she explained. She and Ant had a standing bet to see who fucked her first so she wouldn't take no for answer.

"Hell naw," she said since the regular no didn't get it. She looked over at Po-boy and scrunched her face up like he was ugly then turned away. The snub drove her stock even higher.

"Told you she be on that bullshit. Shit, I'll grab any other one of these hoes to come with us. We'll freak yo' skinny ass out!" Diamond dared and lolled out her tongue to show off her well-used tongue ring. It touched as much pussy as dicks since she went both ways and sideways. She was a true tri-sexual who would try almost anything sexual.

"Her!" Po-boy cheered, pointing at Desire. She was his first choice until Dyme sauntered by. He may not have gotten her tonight but vowed he had to have her.

Dyme threw up one finger towards her man as she entered the dressing room. He understood it to mean "one minute" as she dressed in her street clothes. He hoped it didn't take much longer since the club was closing and he had one last thing to do before they retired for the night.

"You ready?" Dyme asked as if it were she who had been waiting on him. She looked just as sexy in the short skirt as she did in stripper clothes.

"Yeah, come on!" he urged and rushed her towards the exit. He spotted who he was looking for just as they pulled from the parking lot. Dyme saw them too and smiled. People always talk about the murder but not the fuck shit that prompted it. These dudes were disrespectful and were about um get disrespected in the worse way.

"You drive!" Dolla said and went to retrieve the long bag from the trunk. He came around to the passenger seat but Dyme had beat him to it. He could only shake his head and handed her the bag. "Here."

Dolla came back around and jumped behind the wheel. She pointed left in the direction of their prey and he pulled out after them. Meanwhile, she got the grill ready for the cookout.

He smiled at the sexy sound of her racking a round into the AR 15 submachine gun. It had a modified stock that let it rip almost fully automatic. It could empty the 100 round clip in seconds. She removed the safety and waited on her shot to take shots.

"We'll catch 'em on Griffin Street," he said as they bent a corner. She rolled down her window as he closed the distance between them. They made it easy when the driver pulled to sudden stop when he saw Rabbit waving at cars. Her head game was the stuff of legend. She could make quick work of the four dicks in four minutes and get another blast.

"Suck a nigga dick or something," the driver proposed. It was his car which meant he had first on her tongue. Rabbit opened her mouth to name her price until she saw Dyme rolled out the passenger window and up the rifle. The men all turned to see whatever made her eyes go wide as a hit of the city's finest dope. None of them liked what they saw.

"Oh," would be the last words the driver got to utter in this life before she blasted him into the next. The shit that was to follow would have to wait until he got to hell.

The gun looked more like a flamethrower as it threw round after round into the car. The men in back tried um duck behind the door but the heavy 5.56 rounds didn't give a fuck about a car door. They ripped through it them and out the other side. The front passenger made a break for it but didn't get far. He only made it a few feet before a shot to his back knocked a lung out his chest. She gunned Rabbit down as an afterthought so she could never testify.

"Yo, that shit was dope!" Dolla said as he pulled from the curb. He mashed the gas and put some distance between them and the murder scene. That shit made my dick hard!

"Nuh uh!" Dyme dared and reached for his crotch. Sure enough, it was as hard as a scorned woman's heart. She knew just what to do with a hard dick and leaned in to do it.

"Shit," Dolla said as her hot mouth welcomed him inside. Her slow stroke, kiss, lick, suck, had him fucked up and he knew they wouldn't make it good.

He reached under her skirt and played and played in her puddle and they both knew they wouldn't make it to their suburban hide-away. Dyme giggled when he snatched the car to a dark on a dark street. He pulled her on top of him and slid her thong aside. She shoved her whole tongue his mouth as he wriggled himself inside of her.

"Shit!" she cussed from the pain his pleasure always brought. She decided to make him feel it took and bit his bottom lip.

"Grrr," he growled from the taste of blood in his mouth. He palmed the basketball-sized cheeks and bounced them up and down on his dick. The smell of fresh gunpowder mixed with the sounds of her splashing juice box and drove the both wild.

"Mm, that's it. Get it," she urged even though he was hurting her. His guttural grunts signaled the end was near. She gripped the head-rest and threw her hips into overdrive.

Dolla 's whole body seized and shivered when he began sending a torrent of semen into her. He leaned up and matched her kisses un-til the spasms of orgasms subsided.

"Whew!" he exclaimed when his breathing returned to normal. He patted her ass signaling her to get up. She did and fell over into the passenger seat. His dick was still too hard to put up so he drove off with it still out.

"You know I ain't done, right?" she said wickedly.

"I'll pull over again if you want," he dared. Would have to, but she declined.

"Nah, I need some space," she said and leaned back for the ride. She rode him backwards once they got back to the room.

They made love until the crack of dawn and finally got some rest. They were going to need for their next lick.

Chapter Ten

"Look, this nigga a real trick. He gonna break us off real good for a private show," Diamond explained to Desire in the dressing room.

"How much? Like a hundred?" she asked with her eyes wide. The young thot just graduated from fucking for blunts, chicken and beer to tricking for clothes and weaves. The goons from the club didn't mind parting with a c-note for some ass, so that's what she was used to.

"Um, yeah. A hunnid, but we gotta split it," Diamond decided. She didn't get a break when she was young, so why should she give her one? She knew Po-boy would peel off a band for a freak show. "Girl, you can get you some new bundles!"

"I need me some," she said patting her head. They quickly dressed and hurried out to catch Po-boy before one of the other girls got him.

"Un uh, y'all hoes beat it!" Diamond said and shooed another young stripper away. "You ready, daddy?"

"Hell yeah! Let's ride," he said and led the way out to his tricked out SUV. He had way more money than class and proved it by putting the big ass rims on the brand new truck. He drove out to his house in the suburbs since he was forced to move away from his childhood hood. He had to because his childhood friends broke into his house every chance they got.

"Dang, you live way out here!" Desire said from the backseat as they rode. Diamond jumped in to shut her up before she fucked up her money.

"Yeah girl, all ballers stay out here. Ludacris, Big Boi," she said, making up names as she went along. They made it out to his modest house and went inside. Diamond wasn't at all surprised to see the stripper pole in his living room but Desire sure was.

"Dang, he got a pole in his house!" she cheered and rushed over and did a twirl.

"She young," Diamond explained. "That's why you gotta pay me and I'll take care of her. A band will get you the whole show!"

"I want the whole show, too!" he insisted as he parted with the cash. She tucked it into her purse and went to get Desire off the pole.

"Un uh, girl. That's not why we here," she explained and took her by the hand. They followed him upstairs and into his master bedroom. Diamond steered her into the bathroom to get her ready.

"Wash up,"

"Okay," the young girls said and got undressed. She washed between her legs as Diamond stripped down to thong and bra. They returned to find Po-boy next to naked on his bed, looking like a young Snoop Dogg.

"You ready to get fucked? You freak ass nigga!" Diamond demanded, taking control like a pro-hoe. Desire looked at her to follow her lead.

"Shole is!" he said and pressed the record button on his phone.

"Wait, I mean, huh?" Desire asked as Diamond placed her on the bed and crawled between her legs. She figured out what was happening when Diamond flicked her serpentine tongue across her clit. "Oooh! Mmm. Ssss."

"Hell yeah!" Po-boy cheered happily as he recorded the freak show. After Desire busted a nut, he wanted in. He dropped his droopy drawers and stuck his erection in Diamond's face. She politely guided it into Desire's mouth and slid back. She was the queen of turning a trick with the next chick's pussy.

"Give me the camera," she said and took over the filming. She recorded the action while not participating. Po-boy fucked the young girl every way until he was spent. He then wisely called them a car service so he didn't fall asleep with them in his house. That was a four thousand dollar lesson the last time he fell asleep with a dancer in his house. He was going to get himself in trouble bringing girls into his home.

"Did we get paid?" Desire finally asked when they arrived back at the club. Her weave was a mess and her vagina was sore or full of come, so she earned it.

"Oh, yeah. Cheap ass shorted us, though. He only gave me fifty bucks, but I'ma split it with you fifty, fifty," she said and gave her twenty-five dollars.

*****

"What you doing, Lil Lo?" a beat cop asked as he rolled up on the twelve-year old, trying to remove the 30 inch rims from the Chevy. The police twisted his lips at the barrage of bullet holes and broken windows but didn't see the occupants slumped inside.

"Shit, tryna get paid!" he shot back at the silly question. He damn sure didn't have a car, so he planned to sell the rims and tires for next to nothing. Just enough for weed and food for the next couple of days.

"Oh yeah and what you gonna do when the owner come out and put a foot in yo' ass? Call the cops?" the cop laughed.

"Man, these dead nigga ain't gonna do shit," he laughed and went back to the futile attempt at removing the rims with a pair of pliers.

"Dead?" he asked and noticed the dried blood that had ran from the car onto the Atlanta street. He hopped out and saw the bodies slumped all over the car. He came around and saw Rabbit lying on the sidewalk next to the car. "Oh shit! Move away from the car!"

The officer made a call on his radio to summon more cops and the homicide unit. The murder happened hours earlier so the crime scene was as contaminated as it could possibly be. The vehicle had been pilfered for valuables before the sun came up. An hour later, backup and homicide finally arrived. Dead niggas never has and never would be a priority in this city.

"What we got here?" Detective Helms said as he took a peep in the vehicle. He made a facial shrug and came around and saw Rabbit stretched out. He removed his hat and lowered his head in mourning of the loss of some good head. Good head is something to be mourned. "Damn shame."

"Yeah," his partner Goodwin nodded. He grimaced at the large holes in the car and bodies and shook his head. "They don't call it a chopper for nothing."

"A/R, I'd say," he guessed correctly when he spotted a stray shell casing on the ground. The neighborhood children had collected most of them already. He picked it up, looked and tossed it aside.

"No one seen shit, right?" Goodwin called out to the gathering crowd. As expected, no one said shit. Even if they did know, they wouldn't say it in front of a crowd.

Chapter Eleven

"Damn, I wanna run this dick up in that pretty lil' bitch!" Ant complained and squeezed his dick as he watched Dyme on stage. The one-way glass allowed him to keep watch over his domain while no one could see in. Good thing since she had his dick so hard, he had to remove it from his slacks. He gave it a couple of good strokes until he caught himself.

"Wish I would," he chuckled and checked himself. He had almost one hundred girls on payroll, so he had no business jacking his own dick. He spotted one of the new girls and radioed his security to bring her to the office.

"It's me, boss," Miles said as he tapped on the office door. The six foot five man weighed 325 but took orders from a man half his size.

"Come on," Ant called. The door opened and Miles escorted Desire in. They both spotted his still exposed dick at the same time and knew what he wanted. The security guard averted his eyes and backed out while Desire twisted her lips.

"You gonna pay me this time?" she asked and placed her hands on her ample hips. Last time she was up here was for her audition, she left with a mouthful of cum and a job. Ant couldn't care if a dancer could dance or not when he hired them. The auditions he asked for was simply to see what that mouth did.

"Yeah, lil' mama. Come on around my desk," he said, giving his dick a few pulls to keep it erect. The cognac he sipped also helped but he still enjoyed giving it a pull.

"Like this?" she asked and bent over his glass desk like her audition. Last time he hit her from the back on his desk and used her mouth as a condom.

"Just like this," he growled and parted her vagina lips. She was still young enough to be tight, despite being loose. Sooner or later, all the fucking would catch up with her walls and she wouldn't be able to even grip a tampon.

"Ssss," she hissed when he pushed inside of her. He grabbed a name tattooed on each round ass cheek and got his stroke going. Love is needed to make love and Ant didn't love these hoes. Instead, he thrusted his hips with all he had and fucked the daylights out of her.

The older man didn't last long in the good young pussy. Nor did he want to since all he wanted was a nut. It snuck up on him so quickly, he didn't have time to get in her mouth. Instead, he pulled out and jacked himself dry on the names on her ass cheeks. He slapped her ass with his deflating dick a few times before reaching in the drawer for the baby wipes. He kept a fresh supply for situations just like this.

"You said you was gonna pay me," she whined and extended her palm.

"I did," he agreed and parted with a crisp hundred dollar bill from a stack in his pocket. She cocked her head curiously at it as the twenty-five bucks Diamond gave her last night came to mind. "Go on now,"

"Oh okay," she said, snapping from her thoughts as she collected her fee and rushed back out to make more. Ironically, that same hundred was coming back to him when she paid her rent for the night. This was a win/win for Ant, but he had a huge loss in his near future.

"Hey, girl," Dyme greeted when Desire came into the dressing room to wash the cum off her ass and change her thong. Dyme genuinely liked the girl who was only a few years younger than herself.

"Hey, Meoshi!" Desire shot back happily. Dyme didn't mess with many of the girls in the club, but she always had a kind word for the kid.

"I heard y'all went home with Po-boy last night," she said and looked around to make sure no one overheard their conversation.

"Girl, yeah. Me and Diamond went home with his cheap ass!" she said, pursing her lips to show her displeasure.

"Cheap? The man paying fifty bucks a song for table dances," Dyme reminded her.

"I know he broke bread to fuck!"

"Girl, yeah!" she lied. She wasn't the brightest girl but realized she got, got. She shrugged it off since she did get her pussy ate and now had enough for her bundles.

"So, where he stay?" Dyme asked offhandedly, yet took note of every word she spoke as Desire told all she knew. In turn she relayed it back to Dolla. Po-boy was one step closer to getting robbed.

*****

"What that fake bitch talm'bout?" Diamond demanded of Desire when Dyme left the dressing room.

"She cool! Why you say she fake?" Desire whined in defense of the only girl who treated her nicely.

"Cuz she bougie. Acting like she too good to trick with a nigga. Fake ass!" she fussed, batting her false eyelashes, flipping her weave out of her face, and adjusting her silicone breast. She was put together like a jigsaw puzzle with a tummy tuck and butt shots but had the audacity to call her fake because she wouldn't fuck.

"Cuz she got a man maybe?" she asked since she wasn't quite sure. She once had a dude she called her man, but he let his friends have her from time to time, so she wasn't really sure what that meant.

"Puh-leeze! I will take that pretty black boy whenever I want. I'm letting her keep him warm until I come for him," Diamond said and really did believe it herself. She had her eye on Dolla since they showed up a few months back. Dyme too and couldn't decide which one she wanted to fuck first.

"Wow!" Desire exclaimed. She was way out of her league and would be lucky to make it out in one piece. It was a lose/lose situation where she would either end up dead or even worse, like Diamond.

Diamond put the rat in hood rat. A lot of girls were homegrown Atl-aliens but Diamond was the worse of the worse.

*****

"You must not like getting yo puppy ate," Diamond cracked when she had caught Dyme alone in the dressing room. "When the last time you had that thang sucked proper?"

"Ummm," Dyme replied when she was caught off guard by the question. Dolla laid some mean pipe but never went down on her. He never did and she never asked because again, he laid some mean pipe. She slipped into her mind and flashed back to the last time someone did go down on her.

Here we go again, Dyme complained mentally as her bedroom door eased open. James silently slid in her room and crept over to the bed. Her mother's boyfriend had stepped up from staring and flirting, to sneaking in her room. The only reason she didn't tell her mother what happened was because she was scared to hurt her. Men weren't beating down the large woman's door, so she was delighted to have a live-in boyfriend. So delighted she worked hard to support them all while he stayed home. There was another reason, but Dyme would never admit to enjoying what he did to her.

"You ain't sleep, girl," James said as he pulled the thin sheets from her thick legs. She proved him right by slightly lifting her hips when he slid her panties off. He kissed around her thighs before giving her young vagina a long lick like an ice cream cone.

Dyme managed not to hiss but couldn't stop her body from bucking when he got to work. Her mother Danielle was way too big to go down on, so he took it out on her sweet sixteen-year old box.

"You like this?" he asked, while twirling his tongue around and inside of her. He didn't know she was fucking already or he would have

done that too. Instead, he reached down and tugged on his swollen manhood while he ate her.

"Mmhmm," she lied and shook her head. She gripped her sheets and pressed her lips together tightly to prevent moans of pleasure from escaping.

"Yeah, you, do," he said as he worked his lips and tongue. She could say what she wanted, but her body couldn't lie. His mouth filled with nectar from the sweet young box. Some of it was some cum deposited by her seventeen-year old boyfriend during an after school romp. She proved him right once more when her whole body seized from an orgasm. Her and KC had just started having sex, but she never came close to cumming until James starting coming into her room. He lifted up and rubbed himself on her warm legs and bust an even warmer nut all over them.

"I'ma put it in you next time," he vowed as he stood. He shook, shivered, then eased out her room as quietly as he eased in. He entered her mother's room and slid back in bed next to her...

"That long?" Diamond asked and snapped her back to the present. "Don't tell me that pretty black man you got ain't eating that pussy!"

"Yeah, he do!" she shot back in his defense as if it was something that needed to be defended.

"You need to quit playing and let me get that. You know I'ma break you off. Ain't shit free," she said, appealing to her greed. Women only stripped in strip clubs for money and most would do extras for extra money. Dyme was the only chick that had yet to turn a trick. As a result, her stock had went way up. Diamond figured if she could get her to trick with her, she could get her to trick with the customers.

"I keep telling you I don't get down like that," she fussed and rushed out of the dressing room. She made a beeline over to Dolla 's table and filled him in.

"How much?" he laughed, making her pout. "I'm just kidding, baby."

"Well it's not funny!" she said, crossing her arms and poking her lip out.

"I bet ole girl sitting on some bread," Dolla guessed as he watched Diamond stepped regally from the dressing room. She wore quite a few diamonds on her expensively made body and drove a brand new luxury car so it wasn't a very hard guess. Her body was put together piece by piece like a Barbie doll.

"Yeah and as much as she be tricking these broads out they coochie..." she added and filled him in on what Desire told her about Po-boy.

"Hmph," he said as the wheels turned. Po-boy was next on their list but it may be worthwhile to take a closer look at Diamond, as well. Ratchet chicks like her didn't do banks, so chances were she might be sitting on something other than her artificial booty.

"Speak of the devil," Dyme said, seeing Po-boy walk in the club. He headed straight to the VIP to be treated like a VIP.

*****

"Baby?" Dyme asked between well placed licks and kisses below his belly button. The thick erection in her hand was just the reaction she expected. Perfect timing to ask anything of any man.

"Huh?" Dolla asked sharply. This wasn't the time to be talking. There was something much better she could be doing with her mouth at the moment.

"Why you don't never go down on me?" she asked with a lick and twirl of her tongue.

"Huh?" he asked and slipped inside his past for the answer.

Dolla AKA Malik ibn Samir was born into a pious Muslim family on the planet of Brooklyn. His father was a popular prayer leader of the mosque and his mother was a fashionable Muslimah loved by all.

Dolla was a very well behaved child who loved reciting Qur'an just as much as his PlayStation. His parents instilled in him a love of his Lord as well as fear of the hell fire. He didn't lie, steal, or disobey his parents for fear of falling into it

Fate took his loving parents away in a car crash and he was sent to live with his mother's older sister. The childless spinster did her best to erase all traces of Islam from the boy but once faith enters the heart, it never leaves. It can go up or down, but it never leaves. Young Dolla still behaved himself out of fear of the fire. His parents didn't live long enough to instill the hope that should accompany that fear. To fear punishment while having hope for mercy.

She chipped away at his morals by the day. First, by having him help her boost from the stores. Soon he was a world class thief able to steal the smirk off of Mona Lisa.

Next, the two hundred eighty pound woman rarely wore clothes around the house. She got a kick out of him trying to lower his gaze around her. When he turned ten, she took it further by masturbating in the same room as him. He would try to leave, but she demanded he stay until she got her rocks off.

When he turned thirteen, she demanded even more from the boy.

"Shit!" she fussed when she rubbed and rubbed but couldn't get off. She had squeezed the life out of her vibrator the last time she used it and now it wouldn't come back on.

Dolla tried not to laugh at her dilemma as he played his video games. He knew once she finished her daily exhibition, he would be allowed to go outside. Dolla was well liked but didn't have any close friends. He saw too many so-called friends betray and backstab each other to want one. Still, he found the sights and sounds of the block entertaining.

"You think it's funny, huh?" Aunt Cynthia snapped when she heard a giggle escape.

"No," he said quickly. *The large woman bullied and beat him since he arrived. Even though he now stood six feet tall he was still afraid of her.*

"Come here. You gone help me with this," she demanded. *Dolla turned and saw her large, bushy vagina looking back at him. She rubbed the big black lips exposing its dark pink interior. Curiosity made him look before he caught himself and looked away.*

"Can I go outside now?" he asked as she played in her pussy.

"Sss, if you, mmm, help me with, sss, this," she said. "Come here. I'ma give you some ice cream money, too."

"Here?" he asked and inched one inch closer. *He didn't want to get too close between her legs. The inside of her thighs were black and burned from years of friction. He could feel the heat emitting from it when he got closer.*

"Closer, sss, closer," she said, drawing him near and nearer. *She was coiled like a Venus flytrap, ready to strike. As soon as he was in range, she struck. She grabbed him by the back of his head and snatched him face first into her pussy.*

Cynthia grinded her muff on his mouth and muffled his protest. She pulled him deeper into her abyss and kicked her large legs in the air. This was as close as she ever came to having a man eat her out except, Dolla was just a boy and this was rape.

"I'm... cum, cum, cumming!" she shouted and did just that, *Soaking the poor boy with musty pussy juice. He didn't know it though since he collapsed between her legs. She released her grip and he fell limply below.* "Uh oh."

Uh oh was right because how could she possibly explained pussy asphyxiation? Death by vagina, drowned in pussy juice.

Luckily for her and him, he began to stir back to life once he could breathe. He came to and saw the huge, wet vagina in front of him. A feeling of dread overwhelmed him for what he had done. He figured he committed a sin and was doomed to the hell fire. Too much fear and not enough hope, but his innocence was lost. All the sins he would go on to commit stemmed from this day. She would be a party to his crimes from that day on.

"You okay, baby?" she asked between gasps of air. The intense orgasm set off one of her asthma attacks.

"Are you?" he asked with a sinister smirk.

"Get me my.inhaler,." she pleaded. He shook his head no since that wasn't part of the deal. She said he could go outside and promised him ice cream money when he was done. He was done, but so was she. He went into her purse, bypassed the inhaler, and came out with a few dollars. She was still searching to breath when he walked outside. She still hadn't found it when he returned hours later.

Dolla came home and took his shower like he would do every other day and went to bed. The next morning he called to report his dead aunt. He'd been with quite a few chicks and all asked the same question as Dyme just asked. He was able to answer them, that they weren't his girl. He couldn't say that to her so he just said... "One day, I will. I promise," he vowed.

He'd long ago lost his religion, but his word was just as good. If Dolla said it, he meant it. Dyme knew it too and continued doing what she did.

Chapter Twelve

"Yo, that's enough," Dolla warned and tried to pull the glass from Dyme 's hand before she could down yet another shot of straight vodka.

"Un uh!" she protested and spun away from him. She used the separation to toss back the whole glass.

"You bugging!" he said loud enough for those closest to hear. The same men and women who were hoping and praying for the beautiful couple to become beautiful singles.

"And you ain't my daddy!" she reminded sharply. Ant watched from his office perch and hoped his day was near. He'd wanted to bed and bag the bad bitch the day she stepped into his club.

Likewise, the strippers wanted a taste of him or her if they could get some. The argument escalated until Dolla stood and stomped out of the club. Dyme was suddenly bombarded with request for table dances. Like anything else in life, pussy goes to the highest bidder.

"I got a hunnid just fo' you to bring the bitch to my table!" Po-boy declared and shoved a c-note in the waitresses face. She took off like she had been shot out of a cannon and caught Dyme by her arm before anyone else could get to her.

"Ayo, you better let me go before I—" she growled before the woman spoke up.

"Here, twenty bucks just for me to introduce you to dude," she said. The smart woman didn't mind investing twenty of the hundred free dollars she'd just made. The remaining eighty bucks could pay her phone bill for the month.

"Just meet?" Dyme asked before touching the money.

"Just meet!" she assured her since that's what Po-boy paid for. Anything beyond that was beyond her.

"A'ight," she said and took the money. She made that much every three minutes during table dances anyway. Her shifting hips and bouncing breast had a lot of attention as she sashayed up to the VIP section. Technically, she hadn't earned the right to work to coveted piece of real estate but was requested.

All VIP dancers had to be hand selected by Ant himself. He claimed he had to make sure the head was extra special for extra special clientele. True, but he was still a freak. The only exception to the rule was if a customer requested a certain girl. Jackie had just been selected.

"Humph," Ant huffed since she got around his dick and made it to the VIP section. Once the girls made it there, they could make enough money to keep him out of their mouth.

"Here you go!" the waitress said to them both and got ghost. She did what she was paid for and didn't wait around to see what happened.

"My name Po-boy," Po-boy said and pointed at himself. He flashed his platinum and diamond smile because chicks dug them

"Dyme," Dyme nodded and turned away. She turned enough for him to see all that ass and he couldn't let her get away.

"Hole up, hole up, hole up!" he said and grabbed her arm. The look on Dyme's face made him unhand her but he still took his shot. "Look, I'll give you a band to come home with me."

"An Uber is a lot cheaper if you looking for a ride home," she informed him and drove her value up when she put a hand on her curvy hip.

"Nah, shawty. I'm tryna fuck something. Shit, I got whatever on it. I'm sitting on a hunnid bands at my crib right now!" he bragged. That got a smile out the pretty girl.

"I don't rock like that. I just broke up with my man," she sighed.

"Then you need you a new man. I know I wouldn't have you in no club if I was yo' man. Look, come home with me. We gone have some fun. I'ma put five grand in yo' pocket, too," he said and sealed the deal.

"I'll have to follow you. Cuz I'on want these niggas thinking I'ma trick," Dyme said and looked around to see who was looking at her. Everyone was, all eyes were on them.

"Okay. Meet me at the gas station up the block!" he said and tossed back his drink.

"Better yet, the corner," Dyme suggested and turned to leave. All eyes watched Po-boy leave alone and Dyme went to give another table dance. Halfway through the song she started crying.

"What's wrong, lil' mama? Here!" Diamond asked as she rushed to her rescue. She handed the man back his money for the dance and led her into the dressing room.

"Me and my man got into it," she pouted once they were alone.

"Fuck him," Diamond said since that's exactly what she wanted to do. She wanted to fuck her too, so she took her shot "Let me take you home so we can talk."

"I'on know..." she paused to think. Diamond thought she had her until her head slowly began to shake left to right. "Maybe some other time. I just wanna get some rest."

"Rain check?" she asked and raised her eyebrows.

"Rain check," Dyme nodded and got dressed. She walked out the front door to make sure everyone saw her. This was important since chances were nobody would ever see Po-boy alive again. She got into the play car and met him on the corner instead of the gas station. The gas station had too many cameras, the corner had none.

"Uh oh," a dancer said when Dolla walked in a few minutes after Dyme walked out. He looked around while around looked back at him. They knew who he was looking for and knew she was gone.

"Looking for Dyme?" Desire asked as she came bouncing over. She was patting her new weave like a new pet. Out of all the girls and women in the club, she was the only one who didn't want to fuck him. Not that he wasn't cute, but because she looked up to Dyme.

"Nah, just here for a drink," he said and raised his hand for a waitress. He ordered a beer and gave her a tip.

"You want me to dance for you? You ain't gotta pay me. I won't pop my coochie," she promised. Dolla cracked a soft smile in the corner of his mouth. He knew she was trying to protect him from the she wolves waiting for her to step away.

"A'ight, shorty," he agreed and nodded. "I'll pay you but no coochie popping."

Dolla ran his eyes up and down the sexy, young thing and shook his head.

She was in over her head and out of her league. If he was in the business of saving hoes, he would save her. He wasn't though. He was a jack boy. His girl was a jack girl and that's exactly what she was doing while his alibi shook her shapely ass in front of him.

*****

"Dang, you live way our here!" Dyme exclaimed when they finally pulled into Po-boy's drive way. She made sure to keep her face down so her weave would obscure her face if he had any cameras. He didn't, but she wasn't in the business of taking chances.

"Yeah, had to move out to the burbs cuz niggas will rob you if they get a chance," he explained as he led her toward the front door. He wondered what was in the large tote bag she toted with her. He started to ask but didn't. Should have, but didn't.

"Nice place!" she lied when they stepped inside. She almost laughed at the striper pole in the living room but held her tongue. She learned dudes are sensitive and since she was here rob him, there was no need to insult him.

"Sho nuff," he said, meaning thanks and went to telling her how much each thing cost. He obvious had more money than taste since nothing matched anything else.

"Can I see the rest of the house?" Dyme asked since she didn't see a safe in here.

"You can see this dick!" he snickered. She didn't laugh, so he began the tour. It started in the kitchen and ended in his bedroom but still no safe.

"So, where's all this money you was talm'bout in the club? This hundred bands?" she asked plainly.

"Shoot, I done showed you two hundred already! Ten grand on the TV. Twenty for the pool table. That fish tank was another twenty." Dyme got madder and madder when she realized he was flexing about how much he was holding. She was really getting tired of dudes bragging on cash they don't have and a stroke they can't match. He had a booming dope spot and had good money coming in. His problem was he was spending it as fast as he made it.

"So where this five grand you said you was gonna give me?" she asked, ready to dig in her bag and pull out his surprise.

"I got that!" he bragged and showed her into his closet. A small safe sat on the self with a fingerprint reader. She scanned the closet and admired his taste in sneakers. The safe opened and showed off its insides like the girls bussing it open at the club. He separated five grand from the thirty and snapped it closed before he could stop him.

"Here."

"Shit! I mean, thanks," she said and took the money. He was all hands as soon as she accepted his money. He just paid for some pussy, so he wanted some pussy. "Whoa, son! Can we get out the closet?"

"Oh yeah," he laughed and walked out the walk-in closet. He began to strip as she bent over to dig in her bag. The panty lines tracing her round ass distracted him while she came out with his surprise.

"Surprise!" she sang like the gun in her hand was a gift. "Now, open the safe so I can be on my way."

"You got me fucked all the way up!" Po-boy laughed. A wicked laugh that didn't match the mask of anger on his face. "Bitch, I'm finna take that gun, take that pussy and put this dick down your damn throat!"

Dyme was almost scared when his crazy came to the surface. She may have underestimated the skinny man. It was her decision to hit the lick on her own, but it looked like it was about to backfire. Then she remembered the gun in her hand and fired.

"Bitch, you shot me!" he said and stumbled backwards from the impact. He grabbed the hole in his leg and tried to stop the leaking.

"Next one going in your head!" she warned. "Ain't enough money in that safe to die for?"

"And you ain't getting it!" he screamed defiantly and turned to limp away.

"Bruh, how you tryna run with one leg?" Dyme asked, following behind him. He wouldn't stop, so she put a slug in his other leg. The shot to his calf muscle dropped him but he just started crawling. Dyme followed him all the way down the stairs and towards the door. "Last warning. Don't touch that door!"

"Fuck you!" he shouted and reached for the door handle. A shot to the back of his head knocked that thought right out of his mind.

"Shoot!" Dyme fussed when she tried to pull his body away from the door. She could barely clear the door, so she knew there was no way was she dragging him all the way back upstairs. She was determined not to fail. This was her idea and she would not come back empty handed. A wicked smile crossed her face and she went back into the kitchen.

This is why dudes have to be careful showing off their houses to random chicks. You never know when one of those chicks will use that fancy knife set you showed them to chop your hand off and open your safe. Luckily for Po-boy, she didn't have to cut off his whole hand. Well, it probably didn't matter one way or the other to him since he was dead.

"Just like chicken," Dyme told herself as she used the shears to take off his middle finger. She rushed upstairs and placed the displaced digit on the scanner. Good plan, but wrong finger. "Shoot!" Dyme let out a frustrated sigh and went back down the stairs. A moment later, she returned with his index finger. The safe opened and parted ways with its content. In all, it was thirty grand, some jewelry, and some really good weed.

She went shopping through his closet and selected all the latest sneakers for her man. Po-boy was laid out with his mouth open to remind her of the fifty grand in Platinum and diamonds in his grill. Lucky for her, this time they were the kind that popped in and out. It saved her the work of pulling them out one by one. She loaded the haul and hauled ass back to the club.

"Eh-em," a dancer cleared her throat to alert Desire when Dyme walked back in. Desire stopped shaking her booty in his face as she came over.

"Hey, Dolla . I'm sorry," she pouted publicly and wrapped him up.

"How'd it go? No problems?" he asked in Dyme 's ear.

"Easy peasy," she smiled. "Let's get out of here."

"I love you guys! Can I come live with you?" Desire pouted as her favorite couple walked out hand in hand.

Chapter Thirteen

"Mmhm," Diamond hummed when she caught Dyme looking at her again in the dressing room. She thought she was tripping at first but caught her red handed this time.

"Yeah you got me," Dyme confessed. She was staring at the bionic stripper made up of extra pieces. Like a thot version of Mr. Potato head.

"Mmhm," she repeated since she misread the signals. She assumed the girl had finally considered her many, many come-ons and propositions to eat her pussy.

"Yup," Dyme nodded with a whole 'nother agenda. "I'm saying, though. I'on do nuffin without my man."

"Good, cuz I been wanting a lil' taste of that chocolate myself," Diamond confessed. She remembered the first time the cool man breezed into the club. She was mad at herself for hitting him up for a band to take her home. Now she was ready to fuck him for free. Maybe even throw him a buck or two since she was sitting on plenty of bread, from sitting on plenty of faces and plenty of dicks.

"So how's this supposed to work? I'on want nobody from the club seeing us all leave together. These hoes talk entirely too much!" Dyme said. She was right since Desire and just gave up the goods on Po-boy and look how that turned out.

"Shit, y'all can just fall through my condo whenever. Tonight if you want?" she said eagerly. She was just as eager to get her mouth on either one of them. Or have him inside of her while she sat on her face. Sex was her business but this was personal.

"Gimme the address," Dyme said with a naughty smile. "One thing."

"Anything," Diamond shot back, ready to overcome whatever obstacle stood between her and sexing the sexy New Yorkers.

"Can you teach my man, how to eat pussy?" she asked sheepishly. Everything up to then had been an act. Now, she was serious.

"Chile he 'bout to learn from the best!" she declared and lolled out her lizard length tongue. Dyme felt her pussy jump when it touched the tip of her tongue. Dyme rushed from the dressing room to fill Dolla in.

"Beat it," she fussed at White Chocolate as she shimmied her botox buttocks in front of him.

"No it's cool, babe. It's on the house! A donation," Dolla laughed. The girls always offered him free table dances when he came into the club. Some did to piss her off but most did it to bag him up. Only because they didn't have x-ray vision to see how deep was their love. It could be seen on the surface but went deeper than a Keith Sweat song.

"I'ma donate my foot up that white girl's ass I catch it in front of you!" she barked at him but loud enough for her. "Anyway, ole girl gave me her address."

"Good, so no one can say they saw us leave together."

"Mmhm," she said, knowing Diamond was about to join Po-boy. "Let me change so we can get up out of here."

*****

"Look, you have to go along with whatever she say until we can peep her stash," Dyme said as she drove.

"Okay," he said reluctantly and side eyed her from the passenger seat. The time they had been together felt like a lifetime, so he knew her well enough to hear something under the surface. She was up to something, he just didn't know what.

"What?" she giggled when she glanced over at him. He twisted his lips and cracked her up.

You have arrived at your destination, the GPS announced. Both scanned the area for witnesses and cameras before stepping out of the disposable car. Dolla remembered his mother making him change from good clothes to his play clothes before going outside to play. That's why he kept the Lexus parked and used play cars to do his dirt.

"Camera," she nodded up towards the building.

"And there and there," he said pointing out a couple more. Both donned their hoods and glasses to hide from the cameras and got out. Both tucked their "his and hers" silenced pistols and made their way to the door.

"Lawd, yes!" Diamond cheered when she saw the couple at her door. She quickly snatched it open and bust a pose.

"I see you ready!" Dyme said since all she wore was a pair of stilettos and belly chain.

"Ready and waiting!" she said and stepped aside to let them in. "Last room on the left."

Dolla was on high alert as he led the love of his life down the hall to the master bedroom. Diamond grabbed a tray of party favorites and came in behind them.

"Remember, go along with whatever she say," Dyme fussed in her whisper.

"Okay," he said and handed her his gun so she could tuck them aside.

"I'on know what y'all like, so I bought a lil' of err thing," Diamond said like a good hostess and sat the tray in front of her guest. Dyme frowned her face up since she couldn't even recognize most of the pills and powders on the mirrored tray.

"I'll take this right here," Dolla said and plucked a blunt from the middle.

"Me too," Dyme said since neither messed with the Molly, X, coke, or opioids left over. Diamond did and popped a few pills.

"You first!" Diamond said and knelt before Dolla and went for his zipper. Dyme opened her mouth to protest but he raised an eyebrow to remind her of her own words. She could only pout when Diamond removed his dick and gave it a lick. She twirled her tongue around the head as he lit the blunt. Dyme couldn't watch the woman suck her dick, so she glanced around the room for treasure.

An easy twenty grand worth of jewelry adorned the white lacquer dresser. That was going in the bag but where was the cash? She kept scanning the room while Diamond literally gagged herself on his dick. She was doing all kinds of tricks and techniques while Dolla laid back and enjoyed it. When Diamond threw her hands behind her back and just worked her neck, Dyme had seen enough. She pouted and kept searching. He grunted loudly and she swallowed even louder when he erupted.

"Mmmm, taste like chocolate!" Diamond said, licking her lips. "Come on, girl. Your turn."

"Her turn, what?" Dolla asked when he saw the devious look on Dyme's face.

"Time for you to learn how to eat some pussy, young man!" Diamond replied as Dyme stepped out her panties. She could have hung them on the shower rod since they were soaked from anticipation.

"Huh? You, told her...I mean..." he stuttered and stammered. He looked to Dyme for help but found none.

She paused to give him the same look he gave her to remind him to go along with whatever Diamond said do. If they showed their hand too soon, they wouldn't get anything out of the woman.

Dolla changed his tone when Dyme laid back and spread her legs. He'd seen quite a few vaginas in his life, but hers was by far the prettiest. She kept it clean, tight and freshly trimmed at all time. His aunt tried to invade his memory, but he shook it away.

"Damn, that thang is pretty!" Diamond exclaimed and leaned in for a closer look. She leaned in a little more for a lick. "I'll show you how to work it..."

"Nooo!" Dyme shouted and almost blew it.

"Me first!" he said and slid in between her legs.

"Just give it a lick and watch it blossom," Diamond ordered. Dolla complied and gave the pretty lips a long lick like a fresh soft serve cone. "Now watch!"

Dolla pulled back and marveled as her vagina bloomed and blossomed like a spring flower. Diamond pushed his head and he began to work his tongue. Good thing for both, eating pussy is pretty much self explanatory. You don't need a tutorial or YouTube it. Just listen to the moans and body movements.

"Ssss, mmmm," Dyme moaned and arched her back off the bed. Dolla got a kick out of pleasing his woman and went to town.

Dyme managed to lift one eyelid when Diamond stepped into her closet. She cast a glance back at them before dipping down to remove more pills from a small safe. Dyme tried to alert Dolla but decided not to interrupt him. Not now with electric butterflies fluttering around her body.

Dolla felt the difference and twirled his tongue around her swollen clit. He plunged it inside of her and held on while she bust a shivering, quivering nut all over his tongue.

"Like that?" he asked. He smiled up at Diamond with his wet face, looking for approval. His thick lips looked like a glazed donut and that's exactly how it should look.

"Just like that," she said and patted him on his head. "Let me take it for a spin. You slide that dick up in me from behind."

"Nah ma, party over," Dyme said and rolled off the bed. She wobbled on her rubbery legs but caught herself. She retrieved the "his and hers" pistols and handed his to him.

"Shole nuff?" Diamond said when she realized what was happening. "Y'all doing it like that?"

"Just like that," Dyme assured her and went into the closet where she saw the safe. She realized that chicks who love pussy are just like dudes who love pussy and put themselves in harm's way to get it.

"I ain't going out bad. Y'all gone have to kill me 'fo I just let y'all just take all my bread," she warned. Dolla shrugged and raised his gun to comply.

"Wait!" Dyme said just before he pressed the elevator to take her to the upper room.

"Huh?" he asked since there was no way Diamond was going to live through this. She was about to join Po-boy and all the rest. There would be plenty more to follow because they had a million on their mind and wouldn't stop until they got it up.

"She's right. She probably knows somebody who got more dough than she do. We can just rob them instead.

"What! I know plenty niggas with bread! Ant, dude who own the club is strapped! He run a cash business, so you know what he sitting on. He don't wanna pay tax on it, so it ain't in the bank," she said. They listened and got more information about the man who was already on their list.

"Cool, but we gone save him for last," Dolla said. In the meanwhile, they would keep using the strip club as their personal pond until all the big fish was gone.

"Y'all ain't shit!" Diamond shouted when she figured out she just got played a second time.

The couple nodded in agreement and aimed their weapons. Both fired their silencer equipped guns sounding like *psst, psst, psst.* The guns whispered as they spit like chicks telling secrets.

"Who next?" Dolla asked as they collected their haul. Diamond made plenty of cash but blew a lot on clothes, drugs, and pussy. They got thirty thousand dollars and another twenty grand worth of diamonds.

"I'm next. You gotta do that again as soon as we get back!" she insisted.

"Okay," he smiled like Mikey since he tried it and he liked it.

Chapter Fourteen

"You heard about Diamond?" Desire asked when Dyme came into the dressing room to get undressed for work.

"Arrested for prostitution?" she guessed. It would have been a good guess since she turned more tricks than a magician. A phony guess since she knew exactly where Diamond was because she sent her there.

"Un-uh, she got kilt!" she said wide-eyed with shock. Not that she cared since she found out that Diamond beat her out of her money for tricking with Po-boy. All the other girls who went home with him got enough for a whole head full of weave instead of just one track.

"Hmph," Dyme shrugged. "Any ballers out there?"

"Girl, yes! Lil Thug is in the VIP right now!" Desire cheered and started rapping his latest song.

"Oh!" Dyme said when she recognized the song that was on the radio every couple of minutes. If he was in rotation like that, he had to have some bread. It was time for him to donate to their cause.

Dyme undressed and dressed in her stripper clothes and heels. It was time to go out and get a closer look at this Lil Thug.

*****

"Yo, I think I got us one. Dude in the VIP right now. With all the ice," Dyme said over her shoulder as she began dancing.

"Ice, huh?" Dolla said skeptically. He knew a little about diamonds and they looked a little cloudy from here. "Do ya thing, ma. Sic 'em."

"Grrrr," Dyme growled and sashayed her fine ass up to the VIP. Lil Thug stopped in mid-sentence when he saw Dyme. He was surrounded by women but they didn't look like her.

"Hole da fuck up! Who da fuck is dat?" Lil Thug asked and shoved White Chocolate out of his line of vision. He had seen her talking to Dolla a minute ago but now had his chance.

"Dyme, he wanna meet you" Desire said and pulled her over. "This is Lil Thug! He sing that song, 'Drop low'!"

"Sup, yo," she said and nodded as the DJ put his song on.

"You, shawty. Y'all 'scuse me," he said and shooed the other dancers away. He patted the seat next to him as an invitation and passed her a glass of champagne. Once she accepted both he got to what was really on his mind. "Who is dat?"

"Who is who?" Dyme asked. She tried to see where he was pointing but Dolla was the only one over there.

"Dude you was just dancing for. Don't get me wrong, You's a bad bitch, but shawty is right! He get down?" Lil Thug asked. Dyme had a blank stare as she tried to process what was going on. This was Atlanta though, one of the gayest cities on the planet. She figured it and realized he was the gayest rapper in the city.

"I'on know? Want me to ask him?" she asked but wasn't sure how he would react. Dude looked like money so she went to find out. The gay rapper still watched her booty as it wiggled away.

"What son talking 'bout?" Dolla asked when she returned.

"You? He wants to meet you," she relayed.

"Me?" he frowned and tried to figure out why. He couldn't and asked, "Why?"

"Prolly cuz you a pretty, black boy," Dyme said and tried not to laugh. She couldn't help it when he blinked as he processed it.

"Nah! Say word!" he laughed, assuming she was joking. He peered over and Lil Thug raised his glass to him. "Oh well. I guess son gets a pass."

"Why? If he got some dough to donate, we needs to get that. Just like we did when you sent me home with Po-boy," she reminded.

"But..." he said and looked for a but, but couldn't find one. She was right and he had to take one for the team. "A'ight yo, but if son touches me—"

"I already know," Dyme giggled and led him up to the VIP. Lil Thug still checked her out again when she returned. "Dolla, meet Lil Thug. Lil Thug—"

"Oh, you the one that sing, 'Drop Low,'" he said like he knew the song. He loved everything about the south except the rap music.

"Sho nuff. Sit, have a glass," Lil Thug invited. Dolla shrugged and sat. Dyme excused herself but he didn't hear him since he was so busy looking Dolla up and down.

Dolla nodded and pretended to care about whatever the rapper was talking about. The champagne was good and kept flowing so he didn't complain. He only half listened and scanned his conversation for hints of where the cash was. He was flexing real good about platinum sales so he had to have cash. He was paying for bottle after bottle as well as table dances while they spoke.

"You kinda remind me of my uncle. He lived with me and my mama," Thug said.

"Word?" Dolla said since he didn't care. He did care about this stash of cash and jewels he mentioned.

"I love when y'all New York nigga say 'word'. Word, my Uncle Cat. He used to make me suck his dick while my mama was at work," he said out the blue and made Dolla choke on his champagne.

"Word?" he asked since he didn't know what else he could say to that.

"Word," he giggled and continued. "Yeah, I used to hate that shit. Then I started to like it. Then I started to love that shit. Started sucking errbody dick. How you think I blew up in this rap game!"

"Um, word?" Dolla asked once again.

"Word. You wanna go to my spot? I got a condo on Peachtree. Smoke some weed. And I'll suck your dick," Lil Thug said like a dare.

Dolla tried to keep his composure at the advance. The right side of his brain wanted to beat him up. The left side said, chill and get this money. Then beat him up.

"Check it. Let's go smoke one, and see what happens. I'll meet you in the parking lot I follow you," he said wisely as he stood. Lil Thug waited a few minutes and followed him out. He dealt with enough so called straight men to know why he wouldn't want to be seen leaving with him. At least he thought he did because had his own reasons. Plus, he was 100% straight up and down like six o'clock.

"Follow me," Lil Thug said when Dolla flashed his lights at him in the parking lot. There were no cameras out here, so he wasn't worried. He did pull a baseball cap low on his face and pulled out his dark shades for when they got out. He grabbed the plastic pistol and silencer as well.

Dolla knew they struck gold when they pulled into the underground parking lot of a high-rise building. He donned the shades before getting out and kept his head low.

"You on the down low fa sho!" Lil Thug laughed as they made their way to the elevator.

"Mmhm, down, low," he said. They arrived at the twentieth floor and went inside a plush end unit. Dolla nodded in approval at all the expensive etceteras in the condo. There was no time to waste so out came the heater.

"Fa real, bruh? I invite you to da crib for some dome and you finna rob me," Lil Thug said and twisted his lips when he saw the gun.

"The sooner we do this, the sooner we can go our separate ways. Now where's the bread!" he demanded.

"So, you don't want no head?" the rapper asked again just to make sure.

"Nah, nigga ! I'm here for the bread! Now get them chains of your neck and come off that dough?"

"Okay, but they not real," he shrugged and pulled the fake jewels over his head. Dolla twisted his lips at the glass diamonds and tossed them aside. Thug went into his pocket and came out with a few thousand dollars.

"So, where's all this platinum sales money? The show money?" Dolla whined. He just knew he got, got again by someone flexing.

"My manager keeps it for me. He pays my bills and gives me spending money," he explained.

"Don't tell me y'all fucking, too," he said and shook his head when the rapper nodded. He was getting screwed too many ways by his manager. Dolla lifted the gun and put him out of his misery.

He cussed and fussed the whole way back to the club. The two thousand dollars wasn't worth the gas to drive over to the condo. Dyme would spend that on panties, bras and bagels. Hers was the first face he saw when he walked in. He took a seat and waited for her to finish dancing for a table. They wanted her to keep dancing but she shook her head no and shook her ass over to her man.

"How we do?" she asked eagerly.

"Bagel money. Dude didn't have shit. Fake jewels and knock off clothing," Dolla fussed. The only things of value were too big to carry, so he left empty handed.

"He didn't molest, you did he?" she asked and tried to keep a straight face.

"Ha ha. You got jokes," he said and twisted his lips.

"Don't pout, daddy. We gone be a'ight. Get rich..." she began.

"Or die trying," he finished.

Chapter Fifteen

"Hmph?" Ant asked himself and scratched his head as he surveyed is domain from the office window. Another patron had made the news or newspapers in another violent robbery turned murder.

He looked at the two detectives at his bar and had no doubt that's why they were there. They were soaking up some free pussy and beer but that was an afterthought. The common denominator to several acts of extreme violence was his club.

Was someone casing the joint and picking off the rich ones? Or maybe it was his competition trying to give his place a bad name. No one wants to frequent a place that can get you killed.

"Here we go," he said to himself when he saw the detectives finish their beer. The bartender attempted to comp them but they placed a $20 bill on the bar. it was more than enough to pay for the drinks but it also serve notice of what type of cops they were. Not that they could not be bought. They could it just wasn't going to be cheap.

"Tell Mr. Anthony we would like to have a word," Detective Goodwin told the bartender and looked up at his window. He couldn't see Ant through the tinted glass, but he knew good and well that Ant saw him. The bartender grabbed the house phone and made the call.

"Send them up," Ant said as soon as he took the call. The man relayed the instructions to the cops and off they went.

"We know the way," Helms said and led the way. They passed by Dyme dancing for Dolla and took note of her fat ass. They took notice of the police, as well.

"Po-Po," Dolla said knowingly. He could spot a cop a mile away and these two are only a few feet.

"Going up to the office. They probably in Ant's pocket," she guessed.

"Maybe," he said and began to wonder if they had not worn out their welcome. If they had, Ant would be next on the list because Dolla could add real well. He did the math and the club was doing major numbers seven nights a week. That meant Ant was sitting on a shitload of cash but where, that was the question.

"Come in," Ant said sarcastically when the cops just walked into his office without knocking or getting permission. That was a sign that they didn't give a fuck about him.

"Oh, we will," Helms said. Meanwhile, Goodwin looked around the office. He picked stuff up and moved stuff around like he had a warrant. He did not but knew Ant couldn't stop him.

"What can I help you with, detectives?" Ant asked so he could help them move the fuck along.

"Maybe something, maybe nothing. Could be nothing could be everything," Goodwin said and shrugged his shoulders. Being nosey backfired when he curiously picked up a wadded napkin from there the garbage can. Ant had tried to toss it in earlier but missed. Now he just smiled at the cop unwrapped it like it was something. The look on his face was priceless when he reached the used rubber full of cum.

"Yeah, we had a couple of bodies connect to this dot over the last few weeks," Helms laid out casually. They were all black bodies, so he was less than enthusiastic about solving them. People who live the street life often die the street death and who is he to interfere with that. "We had a quadruple homicide a month who just left your club."

"If I had a dollar for every murder that left this club," Ant said wistfully.

"Eh, I bet you do," Goodwin tossed in since it was his turn. Ant nodded and turned to his partner since it was his turn to speak.

"Martha worked here, didn't she?" he asked.

"Who? Oh, Diamond! I keep forgetting they had regular names before they come here to dance. Ain't no mama going to name her blonde-headed, blue-eyed child white chocolate, are they? Have you seen my white girls? Got one on days and another on nights. Both will suck the black off a dick," Ant said since he knew it would get under the racist cop skin.

Helms turned beet-red at the thought since he had once had a wayward daughter of his own. He had sent her to college for a degree but all she came back was with a mulatto baby in her belly and clipping the ends off of words. She left home speaking perfect English and now she, "ta' li' thi', too.

"Well, if you hear something, I'm sure you won't give us a call," Goodwin said out of turn.

"Sure won't," Ant assured them. He was from the fuck the police school of thought, so fuck the police.

"Well, were going to check out your private rooms. So send me one of those white girls in the bottle of Jack," Helms ordered like it was on the menu.

*****

"Psss," Dyme hissed when she saw the name on her vibrating phone. She swiped right to ignore it but it just vibrated again when they called right back.

"Who is that?" Dolla asked when she ignored the next call, then turned it off when they called again.

"My Aunt Lynn. I ain't tryna talk to her. She probably still bugging cuz I didn't come to April's funeral," she guessed.

"Yeah, well that would have been awkward," he said and stifled a laugh. He still got a kick out of her killing her cousin. He would have done it himself but she insisted.

"You so silly!" Dyme laughed at the goofy face he made from trying not to laugh. She turned the phone back and saw the voice mails. After debating for a second she decided to listen and put in on speaker.

"Yo Dyme , I know you don't like funerals and all since you ain't come to your cousin's, but yo' moms just passed. The funeral is Friday, so whatever'

"Wow, I'm sorry, ma," Dolla said and came to comfort her. He wrapped and arm around his stunned girlfriend who just went stiff.

"I don't know what to feel. She put me out over some nigga. Same nigga who was sneaking in my room at night. She ain't mind until he started buying me shit ," she reminisced.

Dolla hadn't heard about this chapter of her life and didn't know what to feel. He watched her face vacillate between sorrow and anger. She went from sad, to mad and back to sad. The lone tear that escaped seemed to make her angry again. She angrily knocked it away and made her decision.

"I'm going to New York. Alone, I need to handle some business," she announced and stuck her chin up defiantly.

"I need to keep an eye on Ant anyway. Need to peep how he handling this bread," Dolla replied. He wanted to go with her to have her back but knew this was something she had to deal with on her own.

"Thank you," she sighed and kissed his cheek. "Now, I need some bread. May as well shop while I'm up there."

"May as well," he agreed and dug some cash from the stash. Meanwhile she grabbed her phone to make a few calls.

"Sup, Auntie. I got your message. I'm on my way. Huh? Because she was a foul snake who stole from me that's why," she finally answered. Lynn wanted to know why Dyme didn't come to see her daughter off and now she knew. Her next call went to Desire to make sure Dolla was in good hands. She couldn't, wouldn't trust anyone else in the club.

"Hey, sis!" Desire sang happily. Dyme didn't call anywhere near enough for her liking, so she was excited to have her on the phone.

"Sup, Desire. Look, I need a favor. I gotta go up top for a minute. I need you to look out for Dolla . Make sure he gets whatever he needs. Give him whatever he want and keep them trifling hoes away from my man!"

"I got you! Whatever he needs. No hoes! I got you!" she repeated to make sure she had it.

"Thanks. I'ma bring you something back from New York," Dyme said and hung up. Not having a bank account meant having to go to the airport to buy a ticket.

*****

"I hollered at the brother Yusuf. He got you a ride and a burner," Dolla advised when he and Dyme neared the security gates. He left out telling him to watch her back.

"Thanks babes," Dyme sighed. She was still wrestling with her emotions. Her mother just passed and all she could manage was one tear. Most of their kisses lasted several minutes, but this one was a quick peck and Dyme turned to leave. Dolla watched her booty shift from side to side until it was out of sight.

"Now what?" he asked out loud. Dyme had been a constant in his life since they met. He shrugged his shoulders and walked out of the airport. He still needed to keep an eye on Ant and figure out where he was stashing this cash.

Dolla stopped at a diner for dinner before heading back to the room to dress. He now liked his slacks, button down shirts and loafers. He nodded approvingly at his reflection and was set. He cracked a sly smile at the Lexus when he stepped outside. It would be traded for a Bentley once they reached their goal.

"Get rich or die trying," he told his reflection in the rearview mirror once he sat behind the wheel. A press of a button made the Lexus roar to life. "On second thought, I'ma keep you. I'll just have a Lexus and a Bentley!"

They had quite a ways to go before reaching their million-dollar mark. They hit licks totaling a hundred grand but they spent it as soon as it came in. Dyme took ten thousand dollars just for a funeral. He had a thousand dollars in his pocket for the night. He was playing the role of rich dope boy in the club so he had to floss a little.

"Uh oh!" White Chocolate said when she saw Dolla entered the club without Dyme on his arm. She waited a few minutes as he took a seat but Dyme never came in behind him. "Oh, I got you now, pretty black man!"

Desire was twerking up a storm for a table full of thugs paying the minimum for a table dance. This allowed three of the four men to look at some free ass. She was just about to drop it like it's hot when she saw White Chocolate rushing across the club.

"Oh, hell naw!" she insisted when she saw him approach Dolla 's table. She grabbed her top and tried to rush over.

"Hole up, lil' mama. Song ain't done yet!" one of the men said and grabbed her wrist.

"Turn me loose, nigga !" she snapped and snatched her hand free. The movement caught the eye of security and he made his way over.

"Here go yo ten dollars back!" she said and gladly tossed his money back. She was dancing for four for the price of one and no extra tips. She pulled her top back on and made a beeline to Dolla as Miles reached the table.

"Y'all rise up and push!" Miles demanded and hoped they bucked. It had been a while since he got to gets hands on anyone and the four men would be fun.

"We don't want no smoke," one said and raised his hands. He was their leader, so they stood when he stood.

Miles turned his massive frame so they could get by. The leader looked over at where Desire went and took note of Dolla. Dolla's diamonds glistened in the strobe lights and caught their attention.

"So, where we going now Todd?" one of them asked.

"Not far. We finna lay on this nigga," he said, scheming on Dolla who was too busy tossing a shot back and watching White Chocolate shaking her white ass to notice.

"Un-uh, move! Get away from him!" Desire fussed when she made to over to Dolla . "Dyme told me to watch him!"

"Watch me? What am I, a toddler?" he laughed and raised his hand for another drink. He tipped the white girl for the whole song even though she only got halfway through it.

"Hey, Dolla!" Desire sang and waved. She jumped right in on the other half of the song and started dancing.

"Hey yo self, Desire," he said and admired her young girl curves. She probably could have ran track or played volleyball with an athletic frame like that. His head snapped to the left when someone sat down beside him.

"What's good. Dolla, right?" Ant said as he sat. He raised his hand and two waitresses came rushing over like they had been shot out of a cannon.

"Yeah Ant, what's happening?" he replied to show he knew who he was too, and tossed back another drink.

"That's what I'm tryna ascertain. Hey Desire, take a break," he dismissed so they could speak candidly.

"I'll be right over here!" she told Dolla forcefully. She was obviously taking her babysitting duties very seriously.

"A'ight," he said and turned back to Ant. The conversation was paused by the waitress arriving with the bottle of Hennessey he was buying shots from. She poured two glasses and got a pat on the ass for a tip. "So, what's up."

"That's what I'm tryna get to. I mean you show up a couple months ago with the baddest chick in the joint. She dance mainly for you but still pay her bar fee at the end of the night. All these hoes turning tricks and flips and shit but ole girl won't buss a grape. Then, a few of my choice customers go missing. They ain't breathing no more when get found. Now, how that sound to you?" Ant laid out.

"Hmph? Well, ain't no such thing as coincidence so..." he began. They both paused to down their glasses and refill them before resuming. "If I was the cause of this strange phenomenon, I certainly wouldn't be talking about to..."

"Someone on the plate. I feel you. You probably thinking I'm sitting on a nice lil' stash and you right. I am, but it ain't duffle bag money. It's washed and pressed waiting for me to go to it. Now, you look like a smart man. You could run a joint like this and be sitting on a mil of your own in no time. Come up with a quarter and take it over. I might even point you in the direction of where you can get it. Lawd knows Diamond ain't have nothing but some expensive weaves and dope."

"I'm listening," Dolla said and turned to face him face to face. The man knew he was a jacker and knew he was on his list. He respected the game and stepped to Dolla like a G. Plus, he knew where two hundred and fifty grand was waiting for the taking.

"We'll talk tomorrow, or the next day. Enjoy your night. The bottles on me," Ant said and stood. Dolla stood too and offered his hand. They locked eyes and squeezed hands like men do. If there's any bitch in a man, it'll ooze out at moments like this. Both nodded when none did and parted ways.

"You okay?" Desire asked when she came rushing back over. Dolla's glass was empty again so she hurried to fill it.

"Yeah, I'm good. Real good," he said, thinking about his proposition. Sure he could run the club. This was right up his alley.

"Want me to take my top off?" Desire asked when she started dancing again. It was a strip club after all and this was a table dance.

"Sure. Why not," he said and leaned back. It could have been the Henny talking but someone said, "Take the bottom off, too."

A few hours later Dolla stood and wobbled from drinking half a bottle of Hennessey. His vision was blurred from the alcohol, plus the raging erection in his pants.

"Un-uh! I'm finna drive you home!" she insisted and ducked under his arm to escort him to his car. Dyme would never forgive her if he wrecked or got a DUI, so she took his keys. Dolla was too drunk to argue, so he staggered out using her as a crutch.

"Here he come!" Todd announced when he spotted Dolla. Dolla saw them approaching and reached for the gun he kept in his waist. Only problem was it was in the car and that was a problem.

Dolla swung on the first to reach them. He caught the man on his chin but was so off balance, he fell too. The rest of them jumped in and jumped on him, while digging in his pockets and removing his jewelry and cash. Desire ran for Miles but the attack was over by the time they arrived.

"You a'ight?" Miles asked and extended his large hand to help him up. He saw Ant talking to him and knew they must be cool.

"Oh No! Your eye!" Desire fussed as it puffed up rapidly.

"I'm good," he said. He really wasn't, so they helped him inside the car. Good thing she took his keys from his hand or they would have taken the car, too. It was all he could do to give turn-by-turn directions back to the hotel.

"Okay, here we go!" Desire grunted as she helped him up. She scooped under his arm again and escorted him to the door. She propped him against the wall and used the key card to open the room. She managed to get him to the bed and pushed him down.

"Messed up your dang clothes!" she pouted and began to take them off. She stripped him down to his boxer briefs and wife beater as he began to snore. Desire snickered at the thought of taking a peek at his dick but shook the thought away. She laid down on the opposite direction like you do when your cousin spends the night and went to sleep.

Dolla awoke late the next morning. His head hurt from the Hennessey and getting beat up. As usual, his morning erection throbbed below. He felt the warm body next to him and reached for her. He pulled her up with one hand and pulled out his dick with the other.

Give him anything he wants, Dyme 's voice rang as Desire came face to face with his dick. It was so pretty, she gave it a big kiss before taking it into her mouth.

"Huh?" Dolla asked when he felt the foreign mouth engulf him. It was just as hot as Dyme's mouth but the technique was different. Dyme was all lips, tongue and neck. This was a combination hand/blow job. She tugged the shaft while vigorously slurping and sucking the top.

One eye was swollen shut, but he still didn't want to look down. He tried to recall the events of last night, but they wouldn't come just yet. The thoughts didn't come but he was about to. He reached down and gripped the head full of tracks and exploded.

"Shit!" he shouted and pumped her mouth full of more kids than an elementary school. Desire clamped her lips and took every drop like Maxwell house coffee. She felt his hand release but waited until his dick stopped spasming before letting it go.

"You want breakfast?" Desire asked when she popped her head up.

"Um, sure?" he said and wondered how that just happened. She rushed over to the Waffle House as the events of the nights trickled in. His phone began playing Mary J and Method Man classic collab and he reached to answer.

"Hello," he croaked since it took a couple attempts to get out.

"What's wrong with you?" she asked with worry in her voice.

"I got my ass kicked. Leaving the club last night," he admitted.

"I'm on my way!" she shouted, ready to skip the funeral and everything else.

"Nah, it's all good. Check it though..." he said and laid out the conversation he had with Ant.

"You think he had you jumped?" Dyme asked. She was excited about the proposition but wondered if it was connected.

"Nah, he would have just had me killed," he reasoned. It also stood to reason that the lick he had for them was personal. He would just wait and see.

"Yo, did Desire take care of you?" Dyme wanted to know.

"You told her to do that?" he asked, assuming she was meaning the blowjob.

"Sure did!" she said proudly but she wasn't talking about the blowjob. "Told her to give you whatever you need."

"That's what's up. What time is the service?" he asked.

"Soon. Let me get off this phone so I can get ready. Love you," she said and blew him a kiss.

"Love you more," he replied and returned the kiss just as Desire returned.

"Who was that? Better been Dyme!" Desire demanded when she heard him blowing kisses.

"It was. She said what's good," he said and accepted his food. She watched him scarf it down before moving again.

"I gotta go home. Need anything else before I go?" she asked and stood.

Dolla opened his to decline then had another thought.

"As a matter of fact I do," he said and pulled his dick back out. She gladly gave him some more head to please Dyme. It was about to be recess in her belly because more kids were on the way.

Chapter Sixteen

Dyme arrived in New York after midnight. She may have assigned a sitter for her man she didn't want a babysitter herself. She was still glad to see Yusuf waiting when she got off the plane. She didn't want to have to deal with family any sooner or any longer than necessary.

"Sup, ma. Dolla told me to scoop you," he explained with his hands up in surrender from the murda mommy scowl on her face.

"My bad, yo. Long day. I appreciate you coming," she softened and offered half a smile. She fell in step behind him to leave the terminal.

"I feel you. Check I got you a room uptown near Yankee Stadium," he said, handing her the key card and a key fob for a car. "Check the glove box. I'm number two in the speed dial."

He led her out to the parking lot and stopped at a blacked out BMW. She smiled hopefully that it was her whip for the week. When she pressed the button on the remote, the pretty car chirped and flashed it's lights to holla back.

"Word," Dyme nodded approvingly and opened the door.

"Yo, he said be easy in Brooklyn. Yayo may be gone but he ain't forgotten," Yusuf warned.

"Understood," she nodded. That explained why he rented her a hotel two boroughs away in the Bronx. They nodded their goodbyes and got into separate vehicles and went their separate ways.

Dyme remembered his words and checked the glove box. She smiled at the plastic pistol, extra clips, and throw away cell phone. She used her own to call Dolla to let him know she landed safely. It went unanswered so she called Desire.

"Hey, sis!" Desire yelled over the music.

"Where my man? I thought I told you to keep an eye on him!" she fussed.

"Girl, I got two eyes on him!" she shot back and told him they were in the club and he was chatting with the owner. "Oh, and let me tell you about White Chocolate!"

"Good job," Dyme laughed when she told her about running her off. Dyme still wanted a word with the white girl so she could inquire about the cops. She knew what the detectives put in her mouth. She wanted to know what they put in her ear. "A'ight, let me get some rest. I'll call in the morning."

Dyme was too tired to shower but too classy not to. She settled for a quick rinse under the hot water and washed her goodies. After all, a steady flow of soap and water is what keeps goodies good. She dried off and crashed on the bed.

*****

"What the—" Dyme nearly panicked when she woke up alone. She looked around and got her bearings and calmed down. Her man was just a phone call away, so she reached for her phone. She reached Dolla just after Desire gave him his first blow job of the day. She inadvertently gave them permission, so he got another one before she went home.

Once she hung up she got up and took a proper shower. She brought cash but no clothes, so her first stop was shopping. Since she was in the Bronx she headed up to Fordham road. A few hours later, she had clothes for a week, even though she was only staying a few days.

"Shoot, what I'm supposed to do now?" Dyme asked out loud. Her mother's funeral was another day away and she really wasn't trying to see any family until then. "Guess I'll just get me a bag of weed and binge watch Yolo."

That was a good plan as she passed by her hotel and crossed over into Harlem. This was where some of the best weed on the planet could be found but she didn't stop. Not until she crossed the next bridge and entered the borough of Brooklyn. The same Brooklyn she was told to stay away from. Brooklyn was bigger than most cities so the whole borough wasn't the problem. The problem was she went right back to her old hood.

The fancy car turned all heads on the block. The jack boys perked up when it slowed down near the group of girls sitting on the stoop. The girls were just as treacherous as the dudes. So treacherous they were dubbed the Get Money Girls. Most were so proficient in keeping blades in their mouths they could tongue kiss or give head without taking them out. Legs spread to advertise pussy prints when the black car came to a stop and the black window slowly lowered.

"Any y'all bitches know some bitch called Dyme ? Bad bitch, pretty face, fat ass?" she asked from the window.

"Yo!" her old crew all cheered when they saw who it was. Most closed their legs except Chattie because her box needed some air.

"You doing it like that?" Rosa asked and checked out the borrowed whip.

"Doing it just like that!" she shot back and posed so they could check out her new outfit.

"Dang, ma! You done moved down south and came up!" another girl cheered. Dyme was naive enough to believe they were happy for them. Why would they be when most would never leave the brownstone stairs they posted on every day?

"You know we doing our thing," she bragged.

"So, why y'all ain't come up for April funeral? How y'all let that happen to her down there anyway?" Venus wanted to know. She and April were close, so she knew she stole from them before she took off. And then she come home in a body bag soon after they go down.

"Yo, my cousin was doing the same shit down there as she did up here. One of them dudes got at her. Me and Dolla had business and couldn't make it. That cool with you or you tryna do something else?"

she dared. Dyme ain't never scared but sometimes that's not a good thing.

"I feel you. Smoke something then, ma!" she shot back. Chattie frowned at the switch since Venus never gave up that easy.

"Now you talking, ma. Who got that gas?" Dyme said. Then pulled out a roll of cash like she didn't already have enough problems.

"Lil Milk got it good. A buck for a quarter," she said and extended her hand. These were the same chicks who had to chip in on a dime bag of brown weed that were now talking about a quarter ounce of the good shit. Dyme parted with a hundred and Venus rushed off to get it.

"Yo Dyme, shoot me around the corner real quick!" Chattie asked urgently.

"I just gave her a yard for the weed!" she shot back.

"Yo, it's mad important!" she pleaded, while the rest of the crew squinted to see what she had going on.

"Yo, y'all roll up. We'll be right back," Dyme said and led the way to the car. Once they were seated, she started the car and turned. "Where to?"

"Anywhere but here! Venus scheming, yo. She been talking about what she gone do when she see you again," she warned.

"Say word," Dyme sighed. She didn't mind fighting, but Venus was known for cutting. What would she tell Dolla when she wasn't even supposed to be here? "A'ight, ma. Good looking out. Still need some weed, though."

"Swing over to Marcy. They got it good," she said. Once they arrived, Chattie ran into the spot and copped a whole ounce since Dyme was splurging.

"Thanks mama, here," she said and pulled a handful of buds out and passing it over. She dug out a couple of twenties and passed them over, too.

"What's this for?" Chattie asked as she accepted the cash.

"Cuz you my girl and you looked out for me. Now, I'm looking out for you. Go buy some vinegar and water, some Summer, some Eve, something. Girl, your pussy stinks! You fogging up the damn windows!"

The girls cracked up and hugged. Chattie knew she had a funk box but dudes still hollered, so she didn't care. Dyme dropped her off at the end of the block before driving by the Get Money Girls without stopping. She lowered the window enough to shoot them a bird as she sped by. She wanted to try the glock out but didn't. She still needed it for the funeral.

*****

Friday came right after Thursday like always but Dyme still wasn't ready. Her mother sucked at motherhood but she was her mother. Now she had to put her in the ground.

She grabbed her phone to call her man but a drop on her phone caught her attention. She wasn't sure what is was until the floodgates opened and the tears streamed down her face. Dyme didn't try to stop them this time. Instead, she sobbed, rocked, and moaned with snot bubbles coming out of her nose. It took several minutes to get it all out and required another shower.

"A'ight, get it together, chica," Dyme told her reflection in the bathroom mirror. She squirted some Visine in each eye to get the red out and put some gloss on her thick lips. She lifted her head high and set off to bury her mother.

Dyme sighed when she entered the borough of Brooklyn once again. She patted the pistol on her lap like a rich chick with one of those loud ass little lap dogs. She wished Venus would try her today so she could make it a double funeral.

She pulled up to the same church the whole family attended back when they were still a family. Grandma died and they all lost their damn minds. Dyme 's mother eventually moved in her much younger boyfriend when he came home.

James was content with his older, larger woman until Dyme started getting round and curvy. He started sneaking in her room and licking her clit like a little lollipop. He had just got up the nerve to fuck her but her mother put her out before he could. He was the first face she saw when she walked into church.

Dyme cracked a smirk when she saw James and then her Aunt Lynn at the front of the church. He misunderstood and smiled back. He was looking forward to seeing her again since he had been hearing how fine she had gotten. The tight black dress she wore proved them right.

"Damn dress is inappropriate," Lynn muttered under her breath. No one was paying the pastor much attention as he delivered the eulogy. James was scheming on some ass but so was Lynn. Dyme moved past the rough patch in life and remembered the good about her mother. She wasn't the best mother but she wasn't the worse either.

The procession moved out to the graveyard but no listened then either. Soon the woman was in the ground and the party was over. Or, just beginning.

"I'm sorry about your mother," Lynn said and gave Dyme a hug so cold, it sent a shiver through Dyme's whole soul. "Come out to the house. We cooked."

"Um, okay. Thank you, auntie," she said and squeezed her back. She watched her aunt leave and make a call on her way to the car. Dyme felt someone walking up behind her and already knew who it was.

"Guess who?" James said and covered her eyes like he did before she grew breast.

"Um, let's see," she sang and leaned her round ass into his crotch. She felt him grow stiff instantly. "Mandingo?"

"Not even!" James laughed and spun her around to face him.

"James!" she shouted and rushed into his arms. She pressed her whole body against him until his dick began to throb.

"So, um what's up. What's good? Where you staying now?" he asked.

"I moved," she said but didn't say where. "Leaving tomorrow, though."

"Well come hang out. Let me eat that pussy like I used to do," he said and took his shot.

"That's all you gonna do to it?" Dyme asked so sultrily, his knees buckled.

"Girl, I'ma tear that ass up! Come on, I'll get us a room," he shouted like they weren't a few feet away from her mother's grave.

"I'll follow you!" she and had to jog to keep up with him. They reached their cars and zigzagged through traffic. He pulled into the first motel he found and parked. He rushed inside and rented a room.

"Sorry about this," he apologized for the rundown room as he led her inside the room.

"We cool. Go shower so I can return the favor. Can I be on top if we 69?" she asked.

"Hell yeah!" he shouted again and rushed into the bathroom and under the water. Meanwhile ,she stripped and got ready on the bed.

"Oh wow!" James proclaimed when he saw Dyme naked on the bed. His dick already stuck straight out in front of him but quivered like a diving board.

He crawled between her legs just like the good old days.

"Damn!" Dyme said when his tongue touched her love button just like the bad old days. She reached back under the pillow and gripped the glock. She started to pull it but damn he was eating that pussy. She lifted her legs into invisible stirrups so he could get it all. Dolla was eating pussy now but not like this.

"Mmhm!" James hummed proudly when Dyme shivered and filled his mouth with her juice when she came. He lifted up with his mouth glistening like a glazed donut. He gripped his dick while she gripped the glock. "You ready to get fucked?"

"Nah, are you?" she asked and fired. James looked so shocked when the bullet socked him right between his eyes. His eyes fluttered for a moment, then went dim as he fell over. Dyme felt guilty for letting him eat her but that was the plan to get him alone. She really felt guilty for coming so hard because that wasn't part of the plan. Her legs were still shaking when she climbed off the bed and got dressed again.

She decided to go to Lynn 's house and make amends. They were in mourning after all. If she cooked all that food in her mother's honor, the least she could do was show up. She might have made some of that macaroni and cheese Dyme loved so much. She pulled her phone and call to the house.

"Hey auntie, I'm—" she began but got cut off.

"Hey baby! Where you at? We miss you so much sugar!" Lynn sang sweetly. Too sweetly since she was never that nice.

"Um, yeah. I'm close. I'll be there in a second," Dyme said wearily and hung up. Her next call went to Chattie who could almost be trusted. Her pussy stank and she would fuck your dude but other than that she was good people.

"Yo, where you at?" Chattie whispered into her phone.

"On the way. I'm close—" she offered and waited for her reply.

"Don't come over here, ma. Yo' aunt got Venus and the whole crew ready to jump you. Got dudes and errthing,"

"Say no more. Good looking out,'" Dyme said and whipped the car around. She headed back up to the Bronx for one last night alone before heading back to her man and new life in Atlanta. She couldn't resist calling her aunt back from the throwaway phone. She disguised her voice and asked, "Dyme came yet?"

"No, but she on the way! Hurry before she get here. I want that bitch dead!" Lynn growled.

"That bitch want you dead, too," she said in her own voice. "See you soon, or later. Just know I'ma see you."

Chapter Seventeen

"Mm-mm-mph," Dolla said as he enjoyed one last blow job before Dyme returned. In fact, he needed to shoot down to the airport as soon as she finished.

Poor Desire went down on him twice a day, every day that Dyme was gone. She wanted to please her only friend, so she made sure her man was straight. She made sure Dolla ate and made sure no chicks came anywhere near him. Most nights he sat in the room and smoked, and watched movies. She would bring food and blowjobs in the morning and evening.

"School's out!" Dolla cheered and exploded on her tonsils. It was a good one but he couldn't wait to get ahold of his woman.

"So, I took good care of you, right? I did good, didn't I?" she asked eagerly.

"You did great," he said and stopped just short of patting her on her head. "You riding with me to pick her up?"

"Can I?" she asked and bounced happily as she raised up from going down.

"You can," he said and went to shower the saliva and semen away. He dressed nice and spiffy like Dyme liked and led Desire out to the car. The girl bantered the entire way to the airport. He only half listened and nodded. His mind was on his baby. He never wanted to go this long without being together. He reached down and played their theme song on his phone.

'You're all, I need to get by...' Mary J sang. She was still singing when he pulled onto the concourse and saw Dyme standing by the curb. She smiled brightly when she saw the Lexus pull up. The smile grew even wider when she heard their theme song playing.

Dolla slammed the car in park and hopped out to hug his woman. He hugged her off her feet as she shoved her tongue down his throat. Desire hopped out the front seat so Dyme could have it.

"Yay!" the girl clapped watching the happy reunion. She jumped in the back seat as they broke off the kiss and got in.

"Sup, lil' mama," Dyme said into the back seat.

"You! Have fun? Oops, I forgot," she said when she remembered she went to bury her mom.

"It's okay. I handled my business," she said. She answered Desire but was talking to Dolla, too. She planned to tell him about James later. Tell him all of it including letting him eat her out but decided to fuck him first though. Bad news always goes down better after a good nut.

Desire yapped about the happenings in the club as they rode back out to their room. Dolla decided it was time to get a spot in the city once they hit this next lick. They would be business owners, so it was time to go legit. She was still yapping when they arrived and started to follow them inside the room.

"Um, excuse me, but I need to fuck my man. I'll see you later," Dyme said.

"Oh! Okay, yeah. I'll see you later then. You coming to the club?" she asked. Dyme looked to Dolla before she answered.

"Sure," she replied when he gave a slight nod. They rushed inside and she got into her car and pulled away.

Inside, Dolla and Dyme stripped like it was a race. Dolla won and laid on the bed to watch the show. It hadn't even been a week but it seemed like he was seeing her body for the first time. His dick stretched out and throbbed in anticipation.

"Un-uh," he said when she tried to go down on him. He pulled her on top and put his tongue in her mouth. Meanwhile, she reached down and inserted the head of his dick between her slippery lips. She sank slowly downward as their tongues danced in each other's mouths. They started off slow and easy, then ended up fucking fast and furious. A simultaneous orgasm rocked the room and put them both asleep. They woke up hours later in each other's arms and traded soft kisses.

"So, how was the trip?" Dolla asked. She paused for a second to see where to begin. She decided to save James for later and started with Venus.

"Yo, ole girl Venus was bugging! Tried to get at me twice! First time when I went to smoke with them and—"

"You went to Brooklyn even when I told you not to? I'm tryna keep you safe but you going to the danger!" Dolla fussed.

"I'm sorry, daddy," she whined. "I was just mad bored up there in the Bronx!"

"Mmhm," he sighed and listened to the rest of the story. He cracked up about the part about Chattie but was grateful she showed some loyalty. He was hotter than a hand me down 380 when she told him about her aunt trying to set her up. "We gotta go see about her one day. First, let's ride down to the club. I need to holla at Ant and see about this lick."

"First, I need to ride this dick. The rest of that can wait!" she proclaimed. The rest did wait until after she mounted the dick backwards and rode off in search of a nut. She ended up finding two one for him and one for her.

*****

Ant saw the couple when they walked into the club. He focused on Dyme as she kissed his lips and headed into the dressing room. He left the window and rushed over to his desk to watch the monitor. The camera he secretly installed at Dyme's locker gave him a clear view when she began to undress. He grew rock hard watching her change from street clothes to stripper clothes. He stroked himself vigorously when her breast came out then blew his load when she removed her panties.

"Shit, shit!" he cursed twice. Once for the nut and the next because the nut landed on some important papers on his desk. Then the house phone rang and he cursed again. "Shit !"

"Boss, Dolla is here," the bartender announced like he was told.

"Give me five minutes and send him up," he said and scrambled to clean up. He wiped his dick with a napkin and put it away. He wiped as much nut off the papers as he could before Dolla came knocking.

"Come in!" Ant called out from behind his desk. He noticed the monitor was still on Dyme as her man walked into the office and changed the feed to the camera over the door.

"What's good. Ready to talk about that biz?" Dolla announced as he entered. This was a business meeting, so he extended his hand.

"Okay, okay," Ant said and shook his hand with the same hand he just jacked off with. "Have a seat."

"Thanks," Dolla said to the seat and shot of Hennessey he poured them both. "Just one. Last time I got drunk didn't work out so well for me."

"Yeah I heard. I also got names and where them clowns stay. That's on me," he said, proving he had nothing to do with him getting jumped and robbed. "Now, about this lick. They sitting on half a mil in cash. Like I said, three will get this joint signed over to you and you can rake in some legal money."

"Three? You said a quarter," he reminded.

"I did but you can't buy a business with duffle bag money. It'll cost fifty to wash all that bread. Going rate is twenty percent, so you catching a deal!" he shot back. Dolla realized he was in the big leagues now when he heard about money laundering. He pressed his lips tightly so they wouldn't open and took in every word. The lick was almost too good to be true. Too easy, too. A man and woman sitting on half a million dollars in a bedroom safe with no security.

"Why no guards?" Dolla wanted to know. Had to know since it was so easy.

"No need. No one knows they sitting on that kind of cash. They got plenty in the bank. Plus, they ain't in the game. Easy money!" he cheered.

"Who are they? This couple that no one knows, but you do. Plus, you know how these things end. No witnesses. So, who are they?" the Dolla asked wisely.

"Nobody!" Ant shot back hotly like he touched a nerve. "Now you want this lick or not? Wanna buy this club so your girl don't gotta dance in it or not? If not, then I can find someone else. Oh and forget about trying me because my dough is safe and secure!"

"A'ight homie. Don't get yourself all worked up. Give me the info and I'm on it. Next week you'll be retired somewhere and I'll be sitting behind that desk."

"Now you talking!" Ant cheered and gave up the info on the future victims. Then gave the names and address for Todd. He was about to be a victim, too.

*****

"Did Dolla tell you how good care of took of him while you was gone?" Desire asked and bounced like a puppy in search of a treat.

"Yeah girl, he did. He asked me if I told you to do all that like he couldn't believe it. Of course I did! Shoot I want my man happy at all times!" she shot back.

"He was, too. I brought him breakfast, lunch, and dinner. Rolled his blunts, sucked his dick, washed the clothes," she said. Dyme frowned when she caught up with what she said.

"You fucked my man?" she asked incredulously.

"Of course not! You my big sister! I would never do you dirty! You said give him whatever he wants," she explained. Dyme listened to her life story before and knew she was used to men taking advantage of her. She really didn't know any better or mean any harm.

"I know, chica. You did good. Plus, that makes us even!" she said and planned to take what happened with James to her grave. "Big mama is home now, so I'll take over now."

"Okay, sis. I love you!" Desire sang and stole a hug.

"Love you too, little mama. We family now."

Chapter Eighteen

Dolla and Dyme split up to handle the separate missions at the same time. He went in search of the half million dollar score while she set off to settle a score. Not that it would even when she finished. He went down to the southern suburb on Fayetteville while she hit the hood of Adamsville.

"Get the door, fuck boy," Todd snapped when he heard the bell ring.

"I'm playing the game!" George complained since he was up on the PlayStation. He didn't complain about being called a fuck boy and that's why they kept calling him that. If a man won't fight about being called a fuck boy, it's only because he is a fuck boy.

"Pause the shit !" Todd snapped. George knew what came next, so he paused it and went to see who it could be. The small circle of friends were all present since they didn't have any other friends and couldn't get girlfriends.

"Who?" George demanded but didn't get a reply. He did get another ring of the bell and pulled it open before he got in trouble. He stood there blinking at the bad chick wearing a trench coat. The front of the coat was open showing the matching bra and panty set. Plump breast protruded from the top, over a flat, hard stomach, over a fat vagina .

"You just gonna stand there or let me in?" Dyme asked. He answered the silly question with a silly grin and pulled her inside. He happily led her into the den where the crew awaited.

"Look!" he announced excitedly.

"Damn, George! Where you get her from?" Todd asked and came for closer inspection.

"I'on know? She was at the door!" George said as Dyme looked around.

"Who else here?" Dyme finally spoke. Her hands eased behind her back as if she was about to take the coat off. All she wanted was the greenlight to set it off.

"No one. We here alone!" Todd said and gave her the green light she was waiting for. She whipped her hands out of her coat with a tech 9 in each. Each spit flames as she gunned the men down. Body shots laid them all out in front of her. Two taps to the temple made sure they never got back up again.

"Dolla said what's up," she told the corpses over her shoulder as she left the room. "One down and one more to go!"

*****

"Too easy," Dolla repeated when he drove passed the targets house a second time. He had come by earlier in another car just to peep the surroundings. This was suburbia at its finest. Children played on manicured lawns in front of well-maintained homes. Homes, not houses. Places where families were raised instead of where people stayed. He wondered again who this couple was and how they got put on Ant's shit list.

Still, a lick is a lick and he was a jack boy. This was the lick that would set him and his woman straight for life. He hoped the couple lived a good life because it ended badly for them tonight. He grabbed the pizza delivery bag and marched towards the door.

"Who is it?" a sweet voice called out in reply to the doorbell.

"Pizza," Dolla said as the door came open. He blinked when he saw the beautiful older woman smiling back at him. She looked to be in her mid-fifties but was just as fine as any twenty five year old. In a tasteful way though, but the spread of her hips and large breast couldn't be hidden.

"I didn't know William ordered a pizza. Come in," she directed and stepped aside so he could enter. Dolla watched her round ass wiggle beneath her dress as she led him into the kitchen and called for her husband. "William, your pizza has arrived!"

"Pizza? I didn't order a pizza," he said as he came into the kitchen. The man looked to be around the same age with a splash of grey in the temples. He took one look at Dolla and knew what time it was. "Oh shit!"

"Nuh uh. No, you don't!" Dolla warned and whipped a sawed off shit gun from inside the pizza delivery bag.

"Anthony sent you, didn't he?" the woman asked and lifted her head in dignity like she accepted her fate.

"Sure he did," the man nodded. "Told you we had half a million in the safe, huh? We do but no witnesses, right?"

"That's right. Now, let's get to it," he ordered. The couple held hands as they led him up to their room. He pulled the woman next to him and pressed the gun to the back of her head. "Open it. No games because you know what this does."

"No games. We knew he was sending someone again someday," William said and kneeled in front of the safe. Dolla heard a loud gasp when he saw what a half million dollars looks like. They both saw it before, so he knew it came from him. "One favor? Just me. She won't say a word."

"No! I'm going with you. Anthony will get his one day. Me first, please. So I don't have to watch my husband die," she insisted.

"Who are you people?" Dolla demanded. This whole thing didn't sit right with him and he just had to know.

"My name is Melody. I was once married to Anthony. I helped him start that club. With my own money. It was supposed to be a good investment. It was until he started investing himself into all the dancers. More and more until I didn't exist anymore. I took back what I put in and divorced him," she explained.

"And I married her. He's had a grudge ever since. He vowed revenge and now you're here," William added. Dolla twisted his lips as he contemplated. He hated being taken advantage of but he was in too deep now.

"You're a nice young man. Your manners prove you were loved," Melody said. "Why don't we just give you the money? Then it's not a robbery. Then there's no need for what comes next."

"Or, I have a better idea. It's our money but we'll hire you. To do a job," William offered.

"I'm listening," Dolla said and listened to the change of plans.

*****

"How'd it go?" Anthony asked eagerly when Dolla came back to the club. He had been watching the news for a report of the murdered couple but saw nothing.

"Like a charm!" Dolla said and placed the bank check for two hundred and fifty thousand dollars on the desk. "My people were able to wash it for me."

"What about Melody? And William?" he asked eagerly. "Nothing on the news about them?"

"That's because they won't be found any time soon. When they do show up, they won't look the same," he assured him. Ant smiled and nodded as they signed the papers that transferred ownership of the club to Dolla and Dyme .

"My man!" Ant cheered and shook hands to confirm the deal. He smiled as he turned the keys over. As soon as he left, Ant made a call. "Hey, Detective Goodwin. I got word on a couple of bodies. William and Melody Bradshaw. Check them out. I'll give you the name from the Bahamas. That's where I'll be living!"

Ant walked out of his office and found Dolla and Dyme involved in a nasty argument. He smiled and listened as she fussed him out about sleeping around while she danced for dollars.

"It's my dick and I'll put it in whoever I want. You dancing in the club but bitch, I own the club!" he shot back and dangled the keys in her face.

"Fuck you and this club! I'm going back to New York!" she shouted in his face and stomped into the dressing room to change.

"Bye!" he laughed and stepped out of the club. He hopped in his car and took off.

Ant clapped and rushed into the dressing room behind her. He was already happy but seeing her topless and in panties made him even happier. He couldn't even look her in the face as he spoke. His eyes went back and forth from the large brown nipples, the hard stomach, and the fat mound of flesh in her panties.

"What do you want!" Dyme snapped as he looked her up and down.

"You!" he said and finally found her pupils. "I want you. I got a house in the Bahamas. Plenty of money so you never have to work or dance or do anything you don't want to do."

"Except you," she said and felt bad when the diss registered on his face. "I'm sorry. He just makes me so angry. Plus, he gone come looking for me. For us."

"Trust me, we ain't never gotta worry about him no more. You don't need anything. I'll buy you everything. Just come," he begged her. The whole dressing room got quiet and waited for her answer. Every girl present would have gladly said yes if she said no. Dyme didn't say anything but her head began to nod. Ant snatched her hand and drug her straight to the airport.

*****

"We're home," Ant said when they reached his beach house in the Bahamas. It was so breathtaking Dyme almost forgot how to breath.

"We live here?" she asked and twirled around on the marble floor.

"Yup. My ex and I built this place many years ago. The judge made us share it, but she just passed away, so it's mine now," he snickered.

"That's not funny," Dolla laughed as he stepped in behind them like a Lifetime movie.

"What are you doing here?" Ant frowned at him and the gun in his hand.

"I'm here for my lady," he said as Dyme rushed to his side.

"Oh, this won't be so funny when police find my ex and her husband. That ass is going to jail!" he laughed. He laughed loud but wouldn't get to laugh long.

"Not quite," Melody announced as she and William stepped from the bedroom. They wiped the smile right of his face.

"So, what now? Y'all gonna kill me?" he asked, looking back and forth between the two couples.

"We're not," William assured him, so he turned to Dolla and Dyme.

"We ain't either," he answered as more men entered the room.

"We are, Mon," A dread locked Bahamian said, holding a cutlass. All the men held long, sharp machetes in their hands. Dyme picked up the overnight bag he had containing fifty of the two hundred and fifty thousand dollars and tossed it to him. The man nodded and they drug Ant out the back door.

"He does need to be found please so our daughter can get what he has in the bank. And I'll get this house," Melody explained.

"Everyone say bye to Ant!" Dyme announced as he was taken away.

"Bye Ant!" the two couples sang and waved until he was gone.

"So now what?" William asked Dolla.

"Now we enjoy the weekend then go back to Atlanta. I have a club to run!" he said triumphantly.

"Run it, don't let it run you!" Melody warned. She knew what they didn't. Running the club was more trouble they could ever imagine. They were about to find out though. The hard way.

Chapter Nineteen

"Give me another!" Dyme's aunt Lynn demanded and slapped her palm on the bar.

"You ain't had enough?" the bartender asked as he poured her another shot of cheap liquor. The woman was way past drunk but she was paying so he kept pouring.

"I can't never get enough liquor or dick!" she said loud enough to be heard throughout the neighborhood bar. She looked around to she if her lonely old vagina had any takers.

Lynn had never been shit and never will be shit but she did love her trifling ass daughter April. She had been a wreck every since her funeral a few months earlier. The woman had become a fixture in the bar drinking until drunk and looking for love. She gave up on love after the first week or so now she just wanted some dick.

Lynn came close to getting laid one night when a desperate dude plucked her from her perch on a barstool. He would have taken her home and rocked her old lady box but she peed her pants on the way to the door. She fell out in the lobby of her building and slept til morning.

"Last one. We closing up," the bartender said and began closing out his register. A last minute patron caught his full attention since his hat was pulled low and large shades obscured his face. He reached under the bar and gripped his heat in case dude wanted some smoke.

"What's up ma?" the young man asked as she slid next to Lynn on the adjacent barstool.

"What's up with choo," Lynn slurred and almost fell off her stool. She frowned trying to bring the face into focus but had far too much gin in her to see straight. Not that it mattered since he was a man and men have dick.

"You live near here?" he asked and helped her off the stool. She tossed her drink back as she stood.

"Right up the block. You want some of this good old pussy ? Huh, some of this well seasoned, marinated pussy ?" she dared.

"Mmhm," he said and directed her towards the door. The bartender nodded in approval since she finally found a taker for her beat up old box.

Lynn's young suitor shot a wayward glance up and down the block when they stepped out of the bar. It was late enough for the city that never sleeps to at least take a nap. A few stray crack heads scurry about looking for anything to steal, suck, borrow or beg in exchange for one last blast. That one last hit they will covet until death comes for them. The same one last one hit they had been chasing since they hit that first one.

He locked eyes with a chick in passing and gave a nod. She nodded and watched them walk down the block and into the building. Lynn led the man up to the third floor. She looked both ways like she was about to cross the street and spotted her apartment by the doormat. The neighbors were getting tired of her attempting to get into their apartments in the wee hours of the night. Then falling asleep on their doorstep when she couldn't get in. Especially since she kept peeing her pants on their doormats. They bought her a bright red doormat of her own to help them all out.

"Let me get that for you," the man offered when Lynn struggled to get the key in the keyhole.

"Mmm, you put that right in that hole," Lynn slurred as seductively as an inebriated old woman can. A loud burp slipped out and made the man wince from the sharp smell of gin and stale peanuts.

"Mmhm," he said and shoved her into the apartment. She stumbled inside and landed on her backside. He stepped in behind her but didn't bother closing the door behind them. She squinted up at him when he removed his hat and glasses.

"I know you!" Lynn declared and tried to place the face with a name or place. When it came to her but it was too late to do anything about it.

"Hey auntie!" Dyme sang as she walked in and closed the door behind her.

"Girl you bit that from Black Panther!" Lynn griped as if it mattered. Dyme did get it from the movie but that had no bearing on why she was there.

"Never mind all that," she said with a brutal back hand that knocked her back down.

"Do ya thing mama," Dolla encouraged and took a seat on the plastic covered sofa to watch the show. Dyme did her thing too and beat her aunt like a runaway slave at a trump rally.

"Tried, to, set, me, up!" she demanded with each punch, kick and stomp. Her aunt was drunk and punch drunk when Dyme drug her over to the cat's litter box. She shoved her face into the filthy sand and put her entire body weight on her.

"Ooh that's cold!" Dolla laughed as she suffocated the woman in cat piss and shit. Once Lynn's legs and arms stopped flailing he stood so they could leave.

"Can we get some bagels before we go back down south?" Dyme whined. She missed her favorite snack and those box bagel stores in Atlanta had nothing on a good old fashion Jewish bakery.

"Sure and some cream of wheat too. I still ain't eating no grits!" he declared. They left Lynn face down in the kitty litter and left the apartment. The cat bolted from the open door like he was tired of the woman too.

Dolla and Dyme went back to their motel room and slept the rest of the night away. They made love in the morning before heading out for bagels for breakfast. Then it was off to the airport so they could return to Atlanta. They had a club to run.

Chapter Twenty

"Hey sis!" Desire sang and clapped when she saw Dolla and Dyme emerging from the airport.

"Hey lil mama. How's everything?" she asked and gave her a hug. They had to fly in and out of New York in a day since they didn't want to close the club. Neither trusted Sam to hold it down in their absence. A wise choice because the man could not be trusted.

"Fine! Hey Dolla!" she replied and greeted him too. Dyme almost made the trip to see her auntie alone but didn't have anyone to watch her man. She certainly wasn't letting Desire babysit him again.

"Sup yo," he answered and looked around the airport. He may not be in Brooklyn anymore but there was still plenty of Brooklyn left in him. He always scanned his surroundings in any surrounding he found himself in.

The couple followed Desire out to her car since had been their ride to and from the airport. He squeezed into the backseat of the cramped chick car smelling like weave glue and assorted beauty accessories while Dyme got in the passenger seat. He stared off into space and tuned out the banal banter coming from the front of the vehicle.

Dolla had his sights firmly set on his million dollar milestone. Buying the club put them back to zero and they needed a quick influx of cash. The club was doing decent numbers under Ant but it was yet to be determined under its new management.

"So what you want for your birthday big bruh?" Desire asked, snapping him from inside his head and back in the backseat.

"I um..." he began to tell her that he didn't celebrate birthdays. He wasn't practicing his faith anymore but still held on to many of its precepts. Dolla didn't eat pork or celebrate any holidays even if he did drink and smoke weed. He still awoke just before dawn as if his body wanted to make the prayers he made when his parents were alive. His deen was still deep down inside of him but his mind was on his money.

"Well, I got a surprise for him!" Dyme snickered wickedly. Dolla knew her well enough to know it would be nasty and he was with it.

"Whatever is fine with me," he related without letting on this would be the first birthday gift he ever got. Dyme's born day wasn't far behind his so he would return the favor.

"I'll see you guys in the morning!" Desire cheered as she pulled up to their new apartment. It was closer to the club and would do until they could find a place to buy.

"OK," Dyme sang and hugged her across the center console. She got out and watched Dolla struggle to extricate himself from the backseat made for purses, not people.

"See you in the morning," Dolla said over his shoulder as he walked away. They had a busy day and even busier week ahead as they took over the club. All he could remember was the look on Melody's face when she said, 'Run it, don't let in run you'.

"You OK?" Dyme asked when she saw the faraway look on Dolla's face.

"I'm gonna be OK!" he assured him. The rest of the day was spent relaxing for the first day as business owners.

******

"We should change the sign," Dyme stated plainly when they pulled into the parking lot of Club Dimes.

"I would have thought you liked the name?" he shot back since it was her name.

"Dyme with a 'y', yes but, I was thinking about a Dolla and a Dyme. How that sound?"

"Like one of them corny ass urban romance books!" he laughed even though he loved the name. Not to mention their love story was straight out of one of those same books. Not long ago they were lonely and loveless in the mean streets of Brooklyn. Now they were legit business owners in a new city and in love.

"No, yo ass too cheap to get a new sign!" Dyme nodded. Dolla was frugal and she liked to shop so they they balanced each other out.

"Nah, just wanna generate some dough before we spend some dough," he reminded. They had spent most of what they made off their various licks and she was ready to spend thousands more on a new sign.

"OK baby. I need some more clothes anyway. Can't be a manager wearing the same clothes I wore as a regular person! I'ma need some shoes, some purses, some..." she said all the way into the club.

Dyme was named the new manager of dancers even though she knew very little about dancing and even less about being a manager. She never even had a manager before since she never had a real job before. As a member of the GMGs all she did was sit on a stoop and look cute.

Dolla was the manager of the whole club and had no idea what he was doing either. He had a manger once when he worked in a warehouse out in Queens but that man did was sxly harass the girls and sleep in his office. He could do neither with Dyme around. Not that he wanted to since he had his mind on his money.

"Hmph?" Dolla huffed when he noticed just how quiet the joint was when empty. Of course he had never been inside when it was empty until now. The club usually opened around eleven so they could service the midday freaks. The men who loved looking at pussy so much they came over during their lunch hour. Then there were self employed and independently wealthy who punched their own clock when and how they wanted to.

"Where all the girls?" Dyme wondered since the day shift usually came around ten thirty so they could be ready when the doors opened.

Most of the day shift girls were bored housewives, in search of excitement or helping make ends meet. A few single moms worked it like a regular job and were home by the time the school buses brought their children home.

"Hey sis!" Desire sang as she rushed inside. She worked nights but came early to help out in any way she could. Dolla and Dyme were the only family she had and there wasn't anything she wouldn't do for them.

"Where is everyone at?" Dyme asked again since she had her ear to most of what went on in the club.

"Ooh, they probably went with Newberry!" Desire said wide eyed with drama.

"A what?" she shot back. She had heard of blueberry, strawberries, blackberries and even boysenberry, but "What the heck is a Newberry?"

"Not a what, a who!" Desire said and stopped to giggle. "He owns the Hoe-down club over on Memorial drive."

"Hoe, down?" Dyme asked and scrunched her face up to show what she thought of the crass name. She was expressive like that any time she spoke. A conversation with Dyme was like a game of show and tell, complete with frowns, scrunches, grimaces and giggles.

"Yeah he nasty," the young girl said and scrunched hers as well. She looked up to Dyme and was taking on more of her mannerisms and habits by the day. She was now a nickel to her Dyme.

Saying Newberry was nasty was equivalent to saying the Titanic was a boat. He was miles past nasty and had zero respect for anyone with a vagina. Women weren't the weaker vessel they were simply a place to come in.

Ant often turned tricks with his own dancers but Newberry took it to the extreme. He would humiliate them in exchange for the right to his exclusive clientele. While Dimes was known with hood celebrities and rap stars, Hoe-down catered to real stars with real money. If the girls wanted to be in proximity to that type of money and power they had to submit to his whims.

"I'm telling Dolla!" was all Dyme could think to say. She took off and ran to the office to file a report with her man. "Baby!"

"Yo, look at this shit!" Dolla interrupted when she rushed in. He turned the security monitor around so she could see.

"The fuck? That's my locker!" Dyme shouted and pointed at the locker she used when she used to dance. Those days were over now that they owned the place.

"That explains this," he laughed and picked up a bottle of hand lube from the drawer. He frowned and tossed it in the trash when he felt how sticky it was.

Dolla played with the system and pulled up cameras all over the club. There was one on each door, the stage, and two behind the bar. One was zoomed in on the cash registered so Ant could keep more than just his mind on his money. He kept his eyes on it as well.

"Well we ain't gonna have nothing to put in that register! We lost most of the girls!" she said and filled him in on Desire had told him.

"Hmph?" Dolla said and leaned back to process the information. A slight smile parted his lips when a solution came to mind. He whipped out his phone and swiped his way to what he was looking for. "Look-it."

"What, thots-r-us?" Dyme fussed at the young girls on his Instagram. "Chicks shaking ass for Cash-app. How that help us?"

"Sht if they'll shake it for Cash-app they'll shake it for cash!" he said and started hopping in Damns.

"Here," Dyme said and pulled the lube out the trash. "In case you get worked up!"

"Ha ha. If I get worked up I'll call for you," he called after her as she left the office. Dyme was relieved to see a couple of girls began to show up.

"Hey Chanel!" she greeted and hugged the woman. "You stayed with us!"

"Nah I wasn't going over there with that guy!" she fussed. But not for the same reasons as Desire. Chanel was dancing her way through law school and didn't want to dance in front of the men who would one day be her colleagues. Instead she shook her round, brown ass for their dudes who would one day be her clients. The dope boys who would inevitably catch dope or MDR charges. The irony only helped her shake her ass a little harder.

"That man tried to recruit me too!" Claire frowned in disgust as she came in. The man wanted way more than she could give him since she her husband thought she was working part-time in a day care. In a way she was.

"Well, I'm glad you girls stayed down. No bar fee today," Dyme decided on her own. The announcement brought cheers all over the dressing room but Dolla wasn't pleased when he heard about it.

"You did what? Why? We need cash baby! We need money asap!" he fussed.

"Well when your Insta-hoes come work we'll make it up!" she shot back.

The first day was one disaster after the other. Dolla went from manager, to host, to waiter and even the DJ. They ended up owing money by the end of the night.

Chapter Twenty-one

"Sup for the day?" Dyme asked when Dolla pulled up to the club the next day. Only half the night shift showed up last night so it wasn't a good day. Even the bar had dismal sales since there wasn't enough booties shaking to keep customers spending.

"Auditions. I talked to a few of the girls of the Gram. Talked them into coming down," he replied.

"OK. You won't need me for that so, me and Desire have some shopping to do," she said and held out her hand.

"Man..." Dolla pouted but came off them dollars. He understood the girl never had money before so she was having a ball. Besides it gave him a chance to get some work done.

"Hey sis. Big bruh," Desire said when they came inside.

"Did Andy show?" Dolla wanted to know. The man was a no show yesterday and he had to DJ himself. He didn't know how to work the equipment so he just changed the CD and let it play out.

"No. He over at club Dynamite," Desire replied. She got all her news in real-time straight off social media.

"Cool. I got someone coming in for that too," Dolla said. He was getting the hang of this manager thing already. Ant's old bartenders both stayed on so he wouldn't have to fill those positions just yet.

"Well, come on. We going shopping!" Dyme announced. Desire clapped and cheered before following her out to the car.

"Morning," Sam greeted as he entered the club and headed straight for the bar.

"Morning," Dolla replied with a curious frown. The man always avoided eye contact when he spoke and that spoke volumes. Dolla thought back to his dad and how he used to make him look at him when he spoke.

'The truth is in the eyes son' he used to say. 'Eyes can't lie'.

Dolla didn't force eye contact on the bartender but he did take note of it and went up to the DJ booth and put in a mix tape CD. He headed up to his office and tried to make heads or tails of the paperwork until the dancers arrived.

*****

"We gonna need you to dance still," Dyme announced as they rode towards the mall. "We need you on the floor to keep an eye on the girls."

"I got you but, what girls?" Desire wondered without a hint of sarcasm.

"Dolla got some chicks coming to audition today," Dyme said without a care. The loud gasp from the passenger seat caused her to snap her head in that direction. "What?"

"You know how these owners audition chicks don't you?" Desire asked wearily. She could still taste Ant's salty semen on her tongue from her audition a few months back.

"Yeah, they dan..." she began until she remembered how Diamond had to shut Ant down when she brought her in. The tires screeched loudly as she pulled a reckless u-turn in the middle of the street.

'Whoop-whoop' a police car chirped as it pulled the same maneuver and pulled behind her.

"Shit! I ain't got time for this shit right now! These hoes ain't gonna be sucking my man dick!" she fussed and pulled over. She gathered her info as the cop in the rearview ran the tags.

"I know that's right!" Desire protested even though she sucked it herself. She was just following orders though, so she saw nothing wrong with it.

The cop verified that the car wasn't stolen and had no outstanding warrants associated with it. He got out and arrived at the drivers side window at the same time the first dancer arrived at the club.

"I'm looking for Dolla?" the sassy young thing demanded as she stepped up to the bar.

"Over there," Sam said and hooked his thumb over to where Dolla was sitting. He watched her large ass shift from side to side as she walked over.

"Dolla?" she asked even though she recognized him from the pictures he posted to his IG. Dyme was in most of them but these hoes don't care. She put her hands on her wide hips and leaned in with her crotch.

"Yeah, I um..." Dolla said when he looked up from the paperwork. He knew what he wanted to say but the closeup camel toe made him lose his train of thought.

"I'm Mzladi from the Gram. I'm here for the audition," she said with a giggle at his reaction.

"Oh, OK," he said and shook it off. "OK, get to it."

"Here?" she shrieked like she was surprised.

"Sure," he shrugged since this was one of the tables she would be giving table dances at. The music was playing so, why not here he wondered. He got his answer when she kneeled before him and went for his zipper. "Whoa!"

"What's wrong?" Mzladi asked when he knocked her hand away.

"Nah mama. I just need to see if you can dance? You ain't gotta do all that," he said. He still let out a sigh in mourning of the blow job that got away.

"You already know I can dance?" she reminded since Dolla said he liked the way she danced when he hopped in her Damn.

"Oh yeah, so you hired! Can you stay now or you wanna work nights?" Dolla asked.

"Nights. When them ballers be up in here!" she said with a shimmy. That's exactly how Dyme saw her when she rushed in and rushed over.

"What you doing?" she demanded and looked down to make sure his dick was still put up where it was supposed to be.

"Auditioning dancers. Like I said?" he asked and frowned to match the frowns on her and Desire's faces.

"Mmhm," they both hummed and looked Mzladi up and down.

"Well I'll see you tonight boss man," the new hire said and turned to leave.

"Don't forget boss lady. Me. The dancer manager," Dyme insisted. The girl looked her up and down with a frown then flipped it.

"OK then boss lady," Mzladi smiled. She liked girls as much as she liked boys so it didn't matter to her. The girl pulled her phone as soon as she stepped and made a call. "I'm in!"

"Thought you were going shopping?" Dolla asked as Dyme took a seat beside him.

"Nah I'ma stay here and help you audition these girls," she decided.

"Well I'm finna change so I can handle some of these tables," Desire said and waited for an answer. Both nodded so she took off for the dressing room.

"Hey y'all," White Chocolate greeted as she came in. She had a weary look on her face, not knowing what to expect.

She quit on the couple as well in favor of Newberry and the Hoedown. Until she found out she would be the hoe down on her knees in front of the cameras. Newberry had real white girls on staff and didn't have much use for a wannabe white, black girl. He stuck her in a closet with a hole cut in the wall. VIP customers could step into an old fashion phone booth and get some quick relief. The woman didn't have many morals but was a step above being treated like a come urinal.

"Hey um..." Dyme said as if she couldn't remember her name. White Chocolate had been rejected her whole life and was used to it. She twisted her lips and turned to leave.

"Wait. Go change. You can work days," Dolla said. She smiled, bounced and clapped before rushing into the dressing room.

"What you do that for?" Dyme wondered. "She ain't got no loyalty."

"Sure she do. That's why she back. And she gonna tell you all about what they got going on over at the Hoedown. Dyme smiled and nodded as she put it all together.

They auditioned a few more dancers and by the end of the day were almost fully staffed. A young DJ named Hood got the nod and went behind the booth. The club was on its way to more trouble.

*****

"This can't be right?" Dolla asked when he went over the days receipts. The bar was booming so it should have done twice what he actually it did. The twenty dancers paid a hundred dollars each for two grand but the bar only made a grand.

"Yeah well, we had a special, and then the sale, and..." Sam explained down to the ground, over at the wall and up to the ceiling.

"Hmph?" Dolla huffed and walked off. He headed over to the bank to make the deposit since the business account was already established.

"Hello?" the pretty teller flirted when Dolla arrived at her station.

"Huh, oh hello," he greeted still in a fog of confusion. The tally wasn't adding up. It would take a year of three thousand dollar days to reach their million dollar goal. Even more when he added in bills and overhead. Then there was Dyme's shopping and added another few years.

"Oh you're new?" she asked when she pulled up the account on the deposit slip. She blinked at the amount since it was far short of the usual receipts. She saw first hand how much pussy was worth. Far more than she was making working in the bank. Her moral compass just wouldn't lead her in that direction so she would stay right there

"Yeah we just bought the place," he said with an aire of pride.

"You did?" the woman shot back since that revelation came with a host of questions. The account had been opened for years but was drained when Ant decided to move to the Bahamas. "Will you be changing the account over?"

"Nah, it's cool," Dolla decided since Humpty Dumpty couldn't put Ant back together enough to come take money from the account.

"Are you sure?" the woman frowned.

"Yeah, I'm good," he insisted. She shrugged like, 'oh well' and made the deposit. Dolla waltzed out as if he didn't have a care in the world when he actually had plenty.

*****

"Now that's what I'm talking about!" Dolla beamed as he peered out his office window. It was just like Ant used to do minus the hand lube and hand job. The club wasn't back to full steam yet but, it was a heck of a lot better than the first week.

Even the bar was busy pumping out drinks and beer so he knew it would do more than the couple grand it had been doing. Likewise the addition of the new dancers was a boost in revenue as well.

Mzladi worked her social media platforms and had tables wanting for her to come dance. She also had a few more chicks who followed her all clamouring for auditions.

"Let's see what's happening in here," Dolla said aloud and checked the monitor that monitored the dressing room. He felt slightly stalkerish peeping into the heram but did it anyway. Desire had taken over Dyme's old locker so her round, brown was the first thing he saw. "Damn, she fine!"

"Hey babes, I..."

"Nothing!" Dolla declared when he heard his woman come in behind him. He quickly switched to the camera over the bar. Dyme squinted at him and his sudden movement then moved on.

"Anyway, weirdo. Look at who we got in the VIP!" she said and led the way back over to the window. Dolla joined her and watched a stud dripping in diamonds make it rain a flurry of ones.

"Who is he, she? He?" he asked since he wasn't quite sure from this distance.

"He is a she. A rough ass dyke from Cobb county. Somehow she got a plug so all the dope boys gotta go through her," Dyme explained. Dolla nodded proudly since she had done her homework.

Chicks who like pussy are pretty much the same as dudes who like pussy. They will brag and boast in hopes of impressing their way into some pussy. Dyme could sic Desire on them and she would come back and make a full report.

"She sitting on some dough?" Dolla wondered. He was all for going legit but the slow money had him in search of a lick.

"Ion know yet. I may just have to suite up and see what she talking bout?" Dyme said, seeking approval.

"Get 'em girl," he said and granted it.

"Grrrr," Dyme growled and quickly stripped. She no longer had to dress and undress in front of a bunch of chicks like high school gym class.

"Wow!" he exclaimed at seeing how fine his woman was. He may have seen her naked a hundred times but she always amazed him with her amazing body.

"I can't tell. You ain't touched me in a week," she pouted as she slipped into a pair a white boy shorts.

"It ain't been no week? Damn! It has been a week!" he said when he realized it had been a full seven days since he had been inside of her. A few of those days were necessity since she had her cycle but he had just been so busy after he would come in and go straight to sleep.

"Well, play your cards right and you might just get lucky tonight," she vowed and set out to bag a stud.

"Ain't no such thing as luck. We fucking tonight!" he assured her as she left. She gave her own ass cheek a slap to show him how she wanted it.

"Uh,uh,uh!" Lil Pop grunted as she flicked ones at the booties shaking in front of her. She stopped dead in her tracks when Dyme sashayed by. Tried to anyway because the stud grabbed her hand and pulled her over.

"Really?" Dyme fussed and looked down at hand in Lil Pop's clutched. She used to smack dudes for that but now she just played along. "How can I help you?"

"By letting me get a sip of that juice," she shot back and licked her thick lips as a preview of how she would lick Dyme's.

"Seems like that would help you," she shot back, hard to get. The harder the pussy is to get the more it's worth.

"Yeah but I can help you too. You in school?" Lil Pop asked, trying to figure her out. She certainly wasn't like the thots shaking and shimmying in front of her.

"Um yeah College..." she said and followed her lead. She agreed to everything the stud offered except when she invited her home. The value of her vagina shot up and the stud settled for some bargain box and took a stray home for the evening.

"How did we do?" Dolla asked when the bartender brought his receipts up once they closed.

"About the same. One thousand, two hundred and thirty bucks," he said to the ground and handed over the cash. Dyme came in with the bar tabs from the dancers and the man rushed out.

"Hmphh?" Dolla said and cued up the video. He and Dyme both watched as Sam pocketed more than he put in the register.

"Yo, this nigga killing us!" Dyme snapped, ready to kill him back.

"Yeah he is, and we going to get our bread!" Dolla vowed. It could wait since he had some more pressing matters to tend to.

Chapter Twenty-two

"Right, there!" Dyme moaned when Dolla's tongue found that magic spot. She could conquer the world if he just stayed right there. Maybe not conquer the world but at least bust a good nut.

She got one too and Dolla didn't let up. He went from not eating pussy at all to wanting to eat it every chance he got. Dyme pulled him up around into a perfect sixynine with him on top. She opened her mouth and he lowered himself inside. She let out a slight gag when he reached her throat.

Dolla slow stroked her face while twirling his tongue between her lips. She came again and he kept right on going. No telling his long he would have stayed in it if she hadn't pulled him off.

"I need you inside of me!" she declared urgently and scrambled to get him inside of her.

Dolla probed and pumped until he found a stroke that was good for the both of them. He focused on her moans and hisses and let them be his guide. They directed him to her next rgsm like a human GPS. Come to find out his nut wasn't far off and he bust inside of her. The couple shook and shivered then basked in the warm aftermath of a mutual climax. No one wanted to ruin the moment with talk but there was plenty to discuss.

"So what we gonna do about ole Sam?" Dyme asked. Dolla twisted his lips up knowing she knew the answer to that question. "Well yeah, but how?"

They could just press charges on him since they were legitimate business. But ole Sam wasn't stealing from the police, he was stealing from Dolla and Dyme. What they would do wasn't the question. All that was left was how, because ole Sam was about to be dead Sam.

"We gotta get him at home. Then we can get the money he stole," Dolla suggested with a yawn. Dyme caressed him affectionately since he had a long day. First at the club and now he just rocked her world real good.

!Yeah baby," she said and watched him blink himself to sleep.

*****

"Hey Desire. Didn't you say Sam tried to holla at you?" Dyme casually asked when she caught up with her in the dressing.

"Yeah with his bad body and stretch marks on his booty," the young girl said and inadvertently told on herself. She wouldn't have known he had stretch marks on his booty if she hadn't seen his booty.

"Ha-ha-ha. He-he," she giggled and continued to pry. "So where he stay? He live alone?"

Desire rattled on for the next ten minutes spilling every bit of tea she had on the man. Dyme was sure glad they were close so she wouldn't one day give up all her goods.

Meanwhile Dolla peeped from his perch and saw the man cuff at least half of what he took in. Sam sold one drink for the club and one drink for himself. One beer for the club and two beers for himself. By the end of the night he had made more than the club. It was cool since it was his last night. Not just in the club, it was his last night period.

Dolla turned his gaze over to the VIP when another flurry of bills floated in the air. Lil Pop was putting on a real show. She was stunting on most of the dope boys with their own money. Dolla took note of the hate on their faces and knew if he didn't get her one of them would.

"What you looking at babes?" Dyme asked as she came in the office. She rushed over and peered over his shoulder to see for herself.

"Ma at it again. She dropped five grand just tonight. She gotta be sitting pretty at the house," Dolla surmised since dealers don't keep dirty money in the clean banks.

"We may have to pay her a visit?" Dyme asked hopefully. Dolla had shut her shopping down lately so she was down for a lick.

"We might, but Sam first," he growled. They say speak of the devil and he'll appear and Sam knocked on the door.

"Receipts!" the bartender sang happily as he entered.

"Good night?" Dolla asked even thought he already knew the answer. He looked down and saw both pockets bulging more than the bank pouch he turned in.

"Great night!" Sam cheered. He was doing good to skim a hundred or two when Ant was in one piece. Now he just went to the extreme and stole half of what he took in.

Dyme twisted her lips when she saw a familiar twitch of his lips. She grew up around enough junkies to spot one a mile off so she easily recognized him from up close. Dolla shook his head when her mouth began to open and in snapped shut once again. He knew how this ended once it began and didn't need that in his club.

"You guys OK?" Sam asked since it was obvious something just happened.

"Yeah, thanks. See you in the morning!" Dolla said and escorted him out before Dyme lost her cool.

"Um, OK. Yeah, see you guys in the morning," he said and scurried off. In his heart he knew he was caught and should run. He should take the money he had and went somewhere, anywhere but here. Greed and lust whispered softly in his ear and told him everything would be OK. He smiled, nodded and walked out the office.

"On God I was about to..." Dyme growled and punched her palm.

"Chill ma!" Dolla urged.

"Chill? That nigga been robbing us blind and you talmbout chill!" she fussed.

"Yeah cuz you turn me on when you get mad and we ain't got time to handle that right now," he explained and cocked that smirk that got him so much pussy in the past. The look on Dyme's face suggested it was about to get him some pussy in the near future.

"OK daddy. Once we handle that, you need to handle this," she said and placed his hand under her short skirt. He bypassed her panties and palmed the plump pussy behind it. Sam's book of life just swiped to the last page.

*****

"Bet they got about a 'huned racks in there!" a goon snarled as Dolla and Dyme exited the club. The way Dolla clutched the bank pouch was a dead giveaway.

"Chill!" the dancer in his passenger seat said when Dolla scanned his surroundings. A habit he picked up from the streets of Brooklyn since he always had to be on the lookout for cops and robbers. The girl ducked her head as if about to give some head when he looked in their directions.

"I guess no tricking in the club don't transfer to the parking lot?" Dyme fussed when she saw the same thing he just saw.

"Nah. We closed. Buddy tryna get straight before he go home to his girl," Dolla said in their defense.

"What, he can't get his dick sucked at home?" she shot back as if it were a crime. It actually should be at least a misdemeanor punishable by a fine or a couple days in jail.

"Dm shame," Dolla said and lowered his head in sorrow. He finished locking up and headed over to their car.

"They gone yet?" the dancer asked from the mans lap.

"Naw, they standing there talking," he said as Dolla pulled out the parking lot and pulled out his dick. "Sht you may as well hook me up while we wait."

The woman grumbled something but he couldn't make it out with her mouth full of meat. He leaned back and enjoyed her lips, tongue and tonsils while plotting on robbing the robbers. The dancer licking him down was down with the lick to jack the jackers.

"Here," Dyme said when they reached Sam's block. She had turn by turn directions courtesy of Desire and they parked right in front of his house.

"He's home," Dolla said, looking at his car in the driveway. He looked up and down the block to check if the coast was clear. It was so he hopped out and headed up the walk.

"We gonna just knock?" Dyme whispered as they crept forward.

"Nah. I got a key," Dolla said and lifted his size twelve. The flimsy door spread quicker than a thots legs after Burger king and a blunt.

Sam's eyes were already wide from the hit of crack he was sucking from the business end of a straighter shooter. They went even wider when he saw the straight shooter pointing a pistl at his face.

"Budge and I'ma erased your whole face right off your head!" Dyme said through clenched teeth.

"See that's the shit I'm talking 'bout! When you clench yo teeth like that! Mph!" Dolla laughed and grabbed a handful of the handfuls of ass Dyme toted around at at times.

Sam held the smoke he had just inhaled for as long as he could before blowing it back out. He shrugged mentally since he was caught. If he lived through it, or died from it at least he would be high. He blew a plume of noxious crack exhaust towards the ceiling before he spoke.

"Guess y'all here about the money?" he said to all three of his unwanted guest. He made sure to look Dolla, Dyme and the gun in the eye as he spoke.

"That would he a good guess," Dyme said all sassy and turned her man on even more.

"My guess is that he smoked most of it," Dolla said with a nod and Sam nodded along with him.

"You know you cain't never put no crack head over no money," Sam said like it was their fault.

"Wait!" Dolla shouted and extended his life a little longer since Dyme was about to squeeze one in his face.

"Wait for what?" she asked and scrunched her face up.

"Bruh you have to have something of value? I ain't tryna leave up out of here empty handed!" he insisted.

"Actually, I do have something of value. Some jewels you can live off. May I?" Sam asked and reached for his pipe.

"No-Yes," Dyme and Dolla said simultaneously just like many of their climaxes.

"Go 'head. I want to get them jewels," Dolla said. Sam picked up a larger than necessary piece and perched it on his pipe. He might just save them a bullet because the hit was large enough to bust his heart.

Dyme twisted her lips in frustration as he put the flame to the end of the pipe. She took a few steps back so she wouldn't breath in any second hand crack. She pulled her man back so he wouldn't either.

"A'ight yo," Dolla demanded when the man inhaled for a whole minute straight. He held the smoke for over a minute while they waited.

"This nigga holding his breath like Aqua man!" she fussed. Once again he blew the smoke towards the ceiling. Once his lungs were empty he sucked in enough air for his last words.

"Here it is 'youngin. Get out now. Take what you got and go. That club ain't worth it. You two ain't built like that. It'll separate you and destroy you," Sam said with a sincerity that touched their souls and senses.

He came on board when Sam and Melody first opened the club. He watched it turn them hard and cold as it went from strictly business, to way too personal. Neither would admit it at the moment but they both felt it already.

Dyme grew up without so the money was turning her out. Dolla was molested as a youth and the licentious environment stirred something in his soul.

The sx, drgs and violence were enough to corrupt the best of souls. The damaged ones didn't stand a chance. The room drew eerily quiet as they processed the truth. The truth as a distinct taste that can't be confused with falsehood.

Dolla opened his mouth to thank the man and take his girl and run. He lost the chance when the room exploded from a single shot. It sounded like a cannon went off in the small room. Poor Sam looked like he had been hit by a cannon and Dyme kept her word and erased his face. Dolla mourned for a split second before turning to leave. They were stuck now and the only choices were get rich or die trying.

Chapter Twenty-three

Dolla and Dyme arrived early enough to interview some new dancers and bartenders. If they were going to keep the club going they needed to be fully staffed. They split duties to save time, and so Dolla wouldn't have to look up all that ass.

"I'll handle the dancers. You find us a couple of bartenders who won't steal from us!" Dyme demanded.

"Yeah," Dolla agreed. He was still slightly taken aback from Sam's last words. He shook his head and shook it off so they could get down to business. "Or I could take the dancers..."

"Um, No!" Dyme laughed and mushed him. The contact reminded them that they were over due to do the do. Both were too shook up to fuck when they got in after sending Sam to the afterlife.

"A'ight. Let's get it. The quicker we get this mil the quicker we can retire to some island somewhere," he said and extended his fist to be bumped.

"Or die trying!" she said and bumped it. No sooner than they did the first of the dancers came in to shake what her mama gave her. In this case what her doctor gave her because God would never create a comically large ass as this first one toted in behind her.

"Dayum! You sure you don't need no help wi..." Dolla tried to asked but got shut down before he could get it out.

"Go!" Dyme fussed and pointed towards the bar. Dolla laughed and slinked away. The joke was on Dyme since the super sized booty could be seen from bar. It could probably be seen from the airport too.

"Hey girl! I'm Cynt . Skraight out dat MIA!" she said proudly. She dipped a hip and caused a slight eclipse with her ass.

"Dyme. Straight outa Brooklyn!" Dyme shot back just and loud and just as proud. She hit the boom box beside her and let the show began. It was just a formality since she was already hired. An ass like that was a definite draw even though most dudes couldn't do anything with it. It was still good to walk through the mall with and show off.

"Excuse me?" a soft voice called from behind Dolla.

"Yeah?" he asked without turning around so he wouldn't miss the show. And what a show it was since Cynt had more control over her ass cheeks than her own mouth. She could make each cheek move individually or together.

"I'm here for the bartender position?" she asked again. Dolla snapped out of his trance and turned around, only to be put in another. The pretty, yellow skinned woman made him do a double take. Her light, sandy hair surrounded her face like a halo and trapped Dolla like flypaper. "The position?"

"Any position is fi, um, the bartender position? Yeah! Can you start today?" he asked. He shook his head to remove the thought of the position that popped in it. She had face to face, missionary position written all over her pretty face. Watching her distort from the dick and...

"Today! I guess? I mean, sure. Yes!" she laughed so sweetly it floated over to Dyme and the bounced off the big booty in front of her. Dyme snapped her head to investigate. She noticed the girls pretty, but also saw she wasn't Dolla's type. She was a good girl, college type who drove with a seatbelt and both hands on the wheel. She knew Dolla liked bad girls who hung out the windows and bust a chopper at niggas.

"OK Cynt . You in. You and that big booty can come back tonight," Dyme said and hired the exotic dancer on the spot.

"How much is the fee?" she asked as she collected her belongings.

"Um, two hundred," she decided to up the price of dancing in Dimes.

"What! This ain't the Rolex! Or Magic city!" she fussed. She wouldn't tell her that she got kicked out of the famous Miami hot spot for stealing. Or that she didn't get hired at Magic city.

"Girl we gonna be bigger than Rolex or Magic city. Plus, the front door ain't locked in case you wanna go to Rolex or Magic city," she said with a curt smile to match her tone.

"So how much y'all be making in here?" Cynt asked to open the door to be talked into it.

"A band easy! I only started a few months ago and now I own the joint," Dyme said since they were only telling half stories. Another frown creased her face when she heard that magic laughter waft from the bar once again. She was ready to wrap this up so she could go cockblock. The girl may not have been his type but Dyme still didn't want Dolla laughing with her.

"A'ight ma," the woman said since she had every intention on turning tricks on the side like a part-time magician. She couldn't pull a rabbit from a hat but could suck come out a cck without a magic wand.

"Cool. See you tonight!" Dyme said and hopped up to rush over to the bar. She only took two steps before the woman shook Dolla's hand and walked out.

"Who was that?" she demanded once she arrived.

"Jamesha. I just hired her," Dolla replied. He could tell by the look on her face that some drama was coming.

"Hmph. She look like she smoke crack too. We'll have to find someone else," Dyme nodded.

"Crack?" Dolla cracked up. "That chick prolly ride with her seat-belt on and both hands on the wheel."

"Hmph," Dyme huffed again because she knew he was right. She was a bad chick in her own right and she knew it. Their revelry was cut short when the next couple of dancers bounced in. A clean cut older man also applied for the bartender spot. More bartenders meant more drinks being sold, and that translated to more money.

So did more dancers especially since Dyme upped the fees. Once they were running full speed they should be pulling in at least ten grand a night. That would be plenty for most people but Dolla and Dyme were everything but, most people.

"So we all set for tonight?" he asked once they were alone once again. Tonight was the grand opening so they had a few hours to kill.

"Yes. We got twenty five girls at two hundred a head!" she revealed.

"Two hundred? Yooooo!" Dolla laughed and high fived her decision.

"Shoot I wanna shop and you keep telling me no!" she pouted.

"A million is a long way off ma. We can't be shopping err five minutes," he reminded. Every hustlers knows you can't stack bread and spend bread at the same time.

"Can't be shopping err five minutes," Dyme mocked in her make believe Dolla voice. "Yo, I know where we can get some shopping money."

"Shopping huh?" he laughed. Dolla knew exactly who she meant and was down. "Set it up."

"Consider it set up. In the meanwhile..." Dyme said and lifted her shirt over her head. Dolla shot a glance around the empty club to make sure it was empty. It would be the last time it would be empty this time of day but today they were fucking.

"Remember that time I threatened to bend you over the time and give you the business?" he asked with that smile again and undid his belt and buckle.

"This table?" Dyme purred, hiked her skirt over her hips and bent over the same table.

"This table," he said and took a seat so he could be face to face with her pussy . He fondled her wetness while giving his hardness a few pulls. Once they were both ready he stood and took position for back shots. Dyme lifted on her tippy toes and arched her back so he could get every centimeter to the cervix.

"Mmm," Dyme moaned as he worked his head in creamy froth between her lips. It felt so good to them both neither wanted to move. They knew it could get better so he slid inside with a "Sss!"

"I know right," Dolla chuckled and got to stroking. Dyme gripped the table and held on. Their mutual moans soon filled the empty club. Neither heard the front door when it opened and closed.

"Ooh," Desire said and crept forward for a closer look. She got close enough to hear the sweet and squishy song Dyme's pussy was singing. The rocking of the table provided a beat while Dolla's groans filled in on bass.

She craned her neck to see if she could see his pretty dick again. Neither knew she marveled at it while he slept when Dyme went to bury her mother. She enjoyed blowing him as much as he enjoyed being blown. Her own panties got squishy watching the action. She now wished it was her bent over that table.

"Sht!" Dolla grunted and rang the alarm. Dyme squeezed and wiggled to help get him where he was trying to go. She led him to his destination better than any GPS on the market.

"Sht!" she cussed to when a nut crept up on her as well. "You, about to, make, me come!"

"Come then!" Dolla demanded and threw the dick into overdrive. He looked down just in time to watch her coat his dick in creamy come. He pushed to the bottom and let go.

Desire poked out her bottom lip as she backed away. She pouted since she didn't have anyone one to have mutual orgsms with. The only time she came when she wasn't by herself was the time time Diamond ate her out over at Po-boy's house. Now they were both gone.

"Someone knocking?" Dolla asked when he heard someone knocking. He was trying to will himself to stay hard so he could go another round but that one took a lot out of him.

"Can't be Desire since she got a key? We supposed to go shopping," Dyme told on herself as she dressed.

"Mmhm," Dolla sighed. She was the monster that he created so he would have to deal with it. He tucked his dick away so whoever was at the door wouldn't see it. An unnecessary precaution since Desire had already seen and tasted it.

"Hey girl! Where your key?" Dyme asked on rubbery legs as her friend came in.

"Huh? Oh, in my purse. You know I be forgetting stuff!" she said, going into airhead mode. Desire wasn't the sharpest tool in the shed but was smart enough to play dumb.

"Girl you would forget your own head if it wasn't attached to your neck!" Dyme teased. Desire laughed along with her but she remembered giving Dolla some neck and head.

"I just came to see if you wanna go shop a lil before y'all open up tonight?" she asked.

"Of course I wanna shop!" she said and off they went while Dolla's head shook from side to side.

"Get rich or die trying. We gone die trying," he sighed.

Chapter Twenty-four

"Grand opening!" Dolla announced as the clock struck eight. He was still short a little help so he pulled double duty as the doorman. That allowed him to keep an eye on the new hostess which allowed him to make sure the cover fees added up to the attendance.

He followed Dyme's lead and upped the price of admission from five to ten bucks a head. That would act as a filter from broke niggs. The low budget dudes who would get as high as possible in the parking lot. Spend five dollars to get in and look at free pussy all night while nursing one beer.

"Sup daddy," Lil Pop snarled a sideways smile to show off her diamond crusted grill.

"Welcome," Dolla greeted. This was the closest he had been to the stud and noticed she was actually quite pretty under the masculine facade. He also noticed the bulge in the front of her jeans. He knew what it was and what it was not. She didn't have a dick and there was a no gun policy in place. "You can't bring that in."

"Gotta stay on guard for these haters," Lil Pop reasoned.

"They ain't bringing no hammers in my joint either," Dolla shot back. The stud twisted her lips as if thinking about it, then pulled the pstl from her pants and handed it to one of her flunkies.

"Put that under my seat Peppa," she said and the girl took off.

"I still gotta pat you down," Dolla advised. Not just because he carried two hammers most times but the stud was still poking out in all the right places despite the baggy britches.

"You tripping," she protested. She didn't like being touched by women so she certainly didn't want to let a man feel her up. It was at that moment she noticed how handsome Dolla was, is and always would be. She still didn't want him rubbing on her. She did want to get in there and look at some of this new pussy so she relented. "Back of the hand shawty. Like they do in the airport!"

"You ain't at the airport, shawty," Dolla said as he grabbed a handful of ass. He spun her around and ran his hand down her leg and back up. All that tough guy shit went right out the window when he reached her crotch.

"Mmph!" the stud grunted and buckled her knees. The panties she wore under her boxers got moist in an instant.

"Yeah, you good," Dolla announced as he gave her softball size breast a squeeze.

"Um..." Lil pop said and looked around in confusion. She looked to one of her entourage for help.

"We finna go in," the woman reminded. She was all girl but hung out with the click of girls because they were getting more money than the boys.

"Yeah. That's right! Finna turn up in this bitch!" Lil Pop remembered as her manhood came back.

"You need to search me?" the sidekick asked and put her hands up.

"Nah, you good," Dolla said since she wasn't wearing enough clothes to conceal a bandaid, let alone a handgun. She looked disappointed and looked him up and down to tell him what he already knew. Dolla pulled his phone and hit Dyme up.

"Yo," she said from inside the dressing room. "How it look out there?"

"Line down the block. Some nice cars in the lot and our donor just made her/his way up to the VIP," he relayed.

"A'ight daddy. I'm on it!" she said and gave Desire the nod. She would sic her on the stud and gleam all the details needed to get close to her.

"What if she try to take me home? And eat my coochie?" Desire asked.

"Go. As for the coochie, that's up to you," she said but made a face that explained her position on it. Desire shook her head at the thought since it was her position on it too, now.

Dyme came out of the dressing room and cast a glance around the club. It was almost as busy as it was when they first arrived. She looked over to the busy bar and nodded. Then scrunched her face up at the pretty, college girl fixing drinks. She could only hope the handsome man working beside her kept her from the handsome man who just came up beside her.

"Looking good!" Dolla said and palmed her ass. He was talking about the club but her ass was looking good too. He hated her constant shopping but had to admit she did stay fly.

"You ain't looking too shabby yo self," she shot back even though she knew he meant the club. It was looking good but so was he.

"Looks like our girl is in," Dolla said when he looked up at the VIP section. Lil Pop had Desire and two other young girls dancing while flicking cash at their shaking asses.

"She extra tonight! Wonder what got into her?" Dyme wondered. Lil Pop had been going harder tonight to prove her manhood since Dolla took it from her.

"I wonder..." Dolla laughed and went over to check on Jamesha and Robert. Dyme was about to follow but Cynt pulled up on her side.

"Look. I know y'all got a no tricking policy but this nigg got a band to fuck! I can go with him now, or..." she started and left a space for Dyme to jump in.

"Or I can say go 'head and handle your business in the private room?" she said and twisted her lips.

"Right?" the stripper laid out in a take it or leave it tone.

"Two huned," Dyme shot back in that exact same tone.

"Two huned? What, you must be finna help me fuck him?" Cynt whined and scrunched up her face.

"Absolutely not. It's gone cost two hundred for me to turn the camera off so my man don't know," she explained. Dyme didn't mean to betray her man but she saw these bad pair of shoes she just had to have. This little side job would prevent her from having to ask him. "Come on with it!" Cynt agreed. Eight hundred bucks to fuck was still a good deal. Especially since these dudes didn't last long with all that ass.

Dyme checked on Dolla and saw he was busy running the joint so she ran up to the office. She made it just as Cynt led the man inside. She scrambled to pause the recording but still stayed to watch. Ant had upgraded recently so she also got to hear the action.

"Let me see that ass!" the baller said and clapped his diamond clustered hands together.

"Let's see that bread my nigga!" Cynt demanded and stuck out her palm.

"I got bread lil mama!" the man bragged and shoved his hand into a pocket. It took some doing getting in and even more coming out with a large stack of money. He began flicking it at her feet to show what he thought of it and her. He didn't care less about the money and even less about a broad. "Uh-uh-uh."

"Dang!" Dyme said when he tossed at least two grand since he had got caught up in his flicking and flossing.

"A'ight, come on. We ain't got all day!" Cynt urged and rushed to scoop up the money before he realized he kicked out double. He unzipped his pants and let his limp meat fall out. "Really?"

"I'm saying shawty," he shrugged. She shrugged too and dipped down low. It took a few minutes of slurping before he got hard enough to get inside of. She pulled her thing aside and bent over while he came around behind her.

Dyme looked at another monitor to monitor what her man was doing. He was still moving around like a boss doing boss stuff around the club. She turned back just in time to see the mans knees buckle.

"Nigga I know yo ass ain't tryna come, in, me!" Cynt fussed and shoved him out of he. He finished skeeting on the floor while she tried to scoop some out of her with her fingers.

"Dang!" Dyme repeated at how quick the act lasted. "Two grand for two minutes! Yo ass is getting robbed!"

*****

"So what's up lil mama? You coming with us or what?" Lil Pop asked when the DJ announced last drink and last song.

That was like the closing bell on Wall street signalling time to make last second deals. Dudes were making deals on some vagina all over the club. Even Cynt had negotiated another rack from another baller to spend the night with. She was up almost three thousand dollars for the night with tips.

"Um..." Desire thought about her dilemma. She was working for Dyme to find out more about the stud but she was also having a ball with the girls. The drinks and smoke was flowing and she wanted to flow with it.

"Come on!" Pumpkin urged. She was a new girl too and wanted someone else from the club to come with her.

"OK, cuz I gotta keep an eye on my girl," Desire decided. Lil Pop shared a conspiratorial glance with her right hand girl Peppa. She did a lot more than just put guns under seats when told. She helped the stud turn out young girls just like these two. Desire gave Dyme a nod when she and Pumpkin rushed to the dressing room to dress in street clothes.

"Why they always get dressed, 'fo they come?" Lil Pop laughed. She knew they would both be naked within the hour.

"Word!" Peppa laughed. She was happy she bagged some pussy to feed her boss to keep her out of hers.

"She in," Dyme told Dolla as she came into the office.

"Was you messing with this?" Dolla asked, frowning at the security monitors.

"Huh? Oh, yeah. I was tryna see into the dressing room..." she replied and trailed off.

"OK?" he said and left it alone. A knock on the door changed the subject before Dyme could.

"Hey boss man!" Jamesha sang as she and Robert came in with their tally from their tills. He gave them separate registers to keep them honest. One had to be close to the other. It was a great plan as long as they both stole.

"How we looking?" he asked and held his breath.

"I did two thousand, eighty five dollars," Robert proclaimed and handed his pouch and receipts over.

"I did Eighteen fifty. Plus two hundred sixty in tips," Jamesha said sounding almost defeated.

"Well you killed me in tips. Then again I'm not as pretty as you," Robert comforted. Dyme liked the way he looked at her like a guy who likes a girl looks.

"Sounds good. Thanks," Dolla said since he had doubled his bar in one night. Paying two bartenders cost more but generated more income too. Dyme watched his eyes to make sure they didn't drop to Jamesha's ass when she walked out. They stayed on the money which was where his mind was. They both were beginning to love the money and that never turns out well.

Chapter Twent-five

"Y'all stay far!" Pumpkin fussed when Lil pop crossed over the Chattahoochee river into Cobb county.

"Where all the bread at!" Peppa popped in to remind them of why they were there. She was like a zoo keeping a tiger and it was feeding time. She would feed the young girls Lil Pop on a daily basis.

"All the bread!" Lil Pop cosigned with a slur from all the flossing. She ran through several bottles of bubbly and was on her second blunt for the ride out to her house.

She was right about Cobb county having the bread because it was a wealthy Atlanta suburb. Most of it was legit money from the legitimate business owners but it also had a booming drg trade. Lil Pop was at the top of the food chain since she had the connect.

The local jack boys didn't dare touch her since she was feeding the local dope boys all their product. That would disrupt the hood's economy and no one would stand for that. Dolla and Dyme weren't from there and didn't share their concern.

"Here we go," Peppa announced and pulled up to a large suburban house. Desire was tipsy but still on her job and took note of the street name and house number. She tapped it into her and got out to follow the leader inside.

"Y'all hoes get naked!" Lil Pop declared like it was an official proclamation when they reached the den.

"Dang!" Pumpkin said when she saw the stripper pole in the middle of the room. Her eyes went wide when she saw the candy jars filled with different drgs on the coffee table. Weed, coke, pills and even coffee. "Dang!"

The two strippers stripped back out of their clothes and joined their host on the sectional sofa. Peppa twisted the exotic weed in fruity blunt wraps while Lil Pop made lines in the coke like a kid playing in sand. She didn't have a flesh and blood dick to worry about not getting hard so she leaned in and took a heaping line up each nostril. Her large variety of strap one stayed hard at all times.

"Hmph," Peppa said and handed a blunt to Desire. She had no problem sparking it up and taking a few pulls before passing it off to Pumpkin. Her problem came when Pop passed her the straw she just used to inhale the coke.

"Ion, um, we don't, I'm saying," Desire stammered, looking for excuses. Meanwhile Pumpkin grabbed it and sucked a line up each nostril and sipped her drink.

Desire had no more excuses so she leaned in and partook. She had to play along so she went along with the program. Only problem was she liked it. The coke awakened the addiction she inherited from her mama along with her brown skin and round ass.

The drgs paved the way for hours of sx with stud. They took drg breaks in between sessions until late into the morning when they finally went to sleep. Peppa would drive them home when they all awoke but they would never be the same again.

*****

"Mmm," Dyme moaned when she awoke to find a thick piece of wood pressed against her backside. She did what every woman would, or should do, and grinded her ass on it.

"A'ight now," Dolla warned when he awoke to find a soft ass rubbing against his morning hardness.

"A'ight, what?" she dared and tooted that booty up. Dolla shrugged like, 'you've been warned', and worked that wood inside of her with a hiss and moan.

"Mmhm," he laughed and laid down the law. Laid down some pipe too and filled the room with sounds of skin slapping and slashing pussy . Her moans joined in and made it a sxual symphony. Dyme felt him coming before he came and squeezed her walls shut around his shaft. She felt vindicated when he began to spasm from the orgsm.

"Mmhm, Mr A'ight now," she giggled. There wasn't much time to cuddle since they had a business to run. They shared a few kisses and a shower before getting ready to start the day.

"I gotta hit the bank." Dolla said when he saw the pouches of money. They almost hit the ten grand mark. He was eager to see what today would bring.

"I need to run by the mall real quick," Dyme said and realized, "We need another car!"

"No, we don't," Dolla frowned. He was steady trying to stack and all she wanted to do was spend. She wanted to grab those shoes she missed in her last visit now that she had some extra money from her side hustle. It had dawned on her that they could rent the private room and make spending cash. She didn't tell Dolla since she knew he would decline. What she did know was that girls had turned more tricks in there than a Vegas magic show.

"Well, I'll just have Desire take me when she come," Dyme huffed and texted her so she would come early. She would have to text a few more times since the girl was still sleeping in Lil Pop's den, with Lil Pop's saliva between her legs.

"Good," were Dolla's last words until they reached the bank. He went inside to make the deposits while she pouted and texted.

*****

"Shoot!" Desire fussed when she saw the time. To make matters worse everyone else was still sound asleep around the room. Peppa was the only one awake but was in another room.

Lil Pop was pooped on the sofa with Pumpkin laying on her leg. She felt a flash of shame and quickly dressed. She felt something else when her eyes fell on the candy jars of nose candy and weed. The other had assorted pills looking more like candy than the destructive force that it was.

The memory of last night whispered in her ear and prompted her to grab a handful of the buds. That was so quick and went so easy she decided to use her acrylic nail to put a little powder in her nose.

"Just a lil" she said and that made it OK. She took a little up each nostril then a little went into her purse. Peppa peeked in and pulled back when she saw what she was doing. All the girls Lil Pop brought home did it, including her so who was she to say anything. Desire grabbed a handful of the pretty opiates from the last jar and woke her friend.

"Huh?" Pumpkin whined since she didn't like to wake up. That's why she chose stripping over college or working.

"Girl it's almost ten o'clock!" she urged in a whisper so not to wake the stud. Especially after she almost sucked an ovary out of her last night.

"Ten! So why you waking me up so early?" Pumpkin complained and flipped over.

Desire sucked her teeth and turned away. She was set to march out to find Peppa but the coke suggested she take another hit. She agreed to just a 'lil more' and took two more bumps up each nose hole.

"Hey lil mama," Peppa said when she walked in. She made sure to speak before entering to give them a chance to stop doing what every they were doing.

"Hey girl. Can you take me to my car? I gotta go," Desire replied.

"Sure. Get ya girl," she said since she was not making two trips back into the city.

"She must be staying, cuz..." Desire huffed. Peppa had seen this before too and knew just what to do. She knew her boss would keep pet hoes around for weeks if she could. That was food off her plate and money out of her pocket and that wouldn't do at all.

"Hey!" Pumpkin protested when Peppa pulled her off the sofa by her leg. Peppa was a pretty girl but could fight pretty well too so she wasn't worried if she didn't like it.

"Get dressed. We finna leave," she said in a tone that left no room for negotiations. Pumpkin sucked her teeth just as hard as Lol Pop had her sucking Desire's box last night and put her clothes on.

Soon they were back in one of Lil Pop's vehicles headed back to the club. They arrived shortly before Dolla and Dyme and got out. Both watched Peppa pull away before speaking.

"Man we 'shoulda got some of that powder! And dem pills!" Pumpkin said.

"Girl you just ratchet!" Desire fussed. "She gave us five 'huned to hang out and you still wanna jack her!"

"I know. My bad," the young girl said and lowered her head in shame. She felt none about eating pussy and letting a girl eat hers for the first time.

"Yeah it's your bad," she scolded as they got into her car. She rushed to get her home so she could get back to the club and hang out with Dyme.

*****

"I been texting you?" Dyme whined when Desire waltzed into the club. They were back open for lunch and knew she couldn't get away now to go shop. Growing up poor can be a curse when one suddenly comes into some money. Some are so used to being broke they spend their money quickly so they can be broke again. Others hold on to it for dear life and don't want to spend a dime. Both stem from the love of money and that is the root of all evil. Not some evil, all of it.

"You did?" Desire asked as if shocked and checked her phone. She had already seen and deleted them so she turned her screen to show, "They ain't come through?"

"Anyway. We ain't gone be able to leave now," she said. "You can dance and get some of this businessman money if you want?"

"I want!" Desire said and rushed into the dressing room to undress. She really wanted a hit of the coke so she did that first.

"Un-uh! No you ain't!" a daytime stripper chimed when she stumbled across Desire in the act.

"Don't tell nobody!" Desire pleaded when she was caught red handed shoving coke up her nose.

"Tell? Chile I wanna hit too!" Chili demanded. Desire handed over her stash and watched as the woman snorted almost half. "Thanks girl! I needed that! All I need now is a xandy bar and I'll be right!"

"One of these?" Desire asked and produced the small batch of various pills.

"Girl!" Chile cheered and almost teared up at the sight of her beloved drgs. The only thing worse than the love of money is the love of drgs. She selected four different pills and plucked them from her palm. Then replaced them with a crisp hundred dollar bill. "Let me know when you get more!"

"Um, OK?" Desire said unsurely since she wasn't sure what just happened. She had just became a dealer is what happened and that just happened to be a problem.

*****

"Not bad," Dolla announced when he checked the tally after the midday shift. "A few more thousand to add to the Dolla and Dyme get rich or die trying fund!"

"What's the fun of making money if we ain't spending none?" Dyme whined. The couple may have been on the cover of the same book but were definitely of different pages. Whole different chapters.

"Here," Dolla grunted and parted with a couple hundred and braced himself for her complaints.

"Thanks," was all she had and took off. She would have had a lot to say about it if she hadn't hit for two hundred dollars on the side last night. Now she could grab a purse to go with her shoes.

"Hey sis. I'm finna go home for a minute and come back tonight," Desire said when Dyme found her in the dressing room. The long night and day had caught up with her and she needed a nap before coming back to dance during the lucrative night shift.

"Un-uh girl, I need you to come to the mall with me!" Dyme protested. She could see her little friend was beat but was selfish like that.

"Oh OK. Just let me use the bathroom first," she sighed. Desire rushed into a stall and inhaled the last of the powder. The euphoric rush that followed had her feeling like Supergirl when she came out. Dyme frowned curiously at the obvious change in her demeanor but didn't care enough to question it.

"Let's ride!" she cheered and led the charge to the mall. Desire bounced animatedly in her seat and filled her in about Lol Pop. She had no knowledge of why she wanted the info but planned to go visit again the first chance she got. Little did she knows the stud was about to get robbed.

Chapter Twenty-six

"Our girl is here again," Dolla said when he saw Lil Pop and her lil crew enter the club. It had been a week and everyone was happy to see her.

Desire was craving more coke while Pumpkin was just turned out. She wanted a reason to eat some more pussy and it just took a seat in the VIP section.

Meanwhile Dolla and Dyme were ready to hit this lick but for different reasons. He planned to stack the proceeds with the rest while she planned to shop with her half. The club was business but jacking was personal so she felt entitled to half.

"Good. Desire gave me the 4-11, but we need to peep the move for ourselves," she said. Dolla nodded because Desire couldn't give them any info on safes or security. One of them needed to get close enough to the woman to see how best rob her.

"I think I can get next to her," Dolla admitted. He wouldn't admit to turning her into a whole chick during the pat down. He caught her looking at him all night then avert her eyes when he looked at her.

"Awe my baby think he can turn studs straight!" Dyme laughed. "Boy you can't get close to her if you don't have a pussy . And this...is not, a pussy !"

"A'ight now?" Dolla warned as she gripped his meat. The club may have been booming but he would bend her over the desk and give her the business. All of it, right there on the spot.

"You always say that but be the first one curled up in a ball. Sucking yo thumb like a baby!" she teased. Dolla and Dyme laughed and joked like they did when they were broke and desperate, living in a beat up motel room. The money wasn't just corrupting them it was separating them and that's even worse. The love of money takes away from the love of everything else.

"One thing for sure, this broad got some dough. We need to move slow and figure out how to get err penny of it!" Dolla said and got back to business.

"Word!" she agreed since she was tired of catching little licks from big ballers. Dudes who flossed all their dough and were next to broke. They died for nothing. At least Lil Pop could die for something. Both plotted on getting close enough to the stud to squeeze her for all she had. They weren't the only ones.

******

"Thanks. I'm finna go over here and..." Desire was telling the man she was dancing in front of. She was so glad when the song ended so she could go to Lil Pop before someone else did. Pumpkin already beat her to her side but she had one side left.

"Hole up shawty! How you finna just bail on me and I'm spending bread?" the dope boy wanted to know. He was trying to let the table dances add up to taken her home for the night. Or at least some head in the parking lot but she was trying to leave.

"Get yo hand off me nigga!" she shouted and snatched away. Dolla took notice and began to come over.

"My bad shawty," he said in surrender and raised his palms. He may have surrendered but didn't forgive her for wasting his time and money. Desire just made an enemy and didn't know it.

"Hey Pop! Where you been?" Desire flirted when she arrived at the table. Pumpkin shot her a crooked glance as if they hadn't known each other all their lives. Like she didn't get her a job dancing in the club.

"Oh hey," Lil Pop nodded dismissively, then went back whispering into Mzladi's ear. It may or may not have been funny but she laughed none the less.

"We'll catch you next time," Peppa said and shooed her away. They had enough pussy for the night. Pumpkin wouldn't even look her way again.

"Oh OK. Yeah, next time," Desire said even though no one was listening. She slinked back over to the dude she ran off from, who had his eye on her the whole way.

"Oh so they got enough hoes so you come back to me huh?" he snarled.

"Boy, I just wanted to say hey. Plus she be having some good pills and powder," Desire admitted.

"Sho nuff? Sht I got the powder the pills, gas, all that!" he said and laid out his menu. He wasn't moving work like Lil Pop and probably indirectly copped from the stud. He only slung dope on the side. His main job was a jack boy. Just like Dolla and Dyme he played the strip clubs looking for ballers with money to donate. "Come chill after you get off?"

"Um..." Desire said and cast a lonely glance up to the VIP. It didn't take a rocket scientist to realize they weren't thinking about her. "Sure."

Meanwhile Dolla made his way up to the VIP section with the next bottle of champagne. Dyme went to change into some stripper clothes so she could push up. Dolla decided not to wait and went to shoot his shot. Lil Pop was a businessman even though she was a she, so that's how he was coming. Besides he had something to prove since Dyme laughed at him. Lil Pop was still a chick and chicks dig Dolla.

"Y'all excuse me for a second," Dolla said and the dancers scattered. They didn't go far though so they wouldn't lose their places. Peppa didn't budge and sat back to prove she wasn't. "You too."

"I..." Peppa began to protest but her boss piped in before she could.

"Spread out for a second," Lil Pop ordered and she hopped to her feet. Dolla smirked at her and poured two glasses. "So you here to feel me up again?"

"Yes and no. Actually I'm here on business. Word is you got that work. I'm trying to get in where I fit in," he explained.

"I'm listening," Lil Pop said. She knew he could move a ton of work through the club and didn't mind a new stream of revenue. Dolla made it up as he went along but started to believe it halfway through his make believe spiel. He realized he might have to invest a little bread to see just how much weight she could get. He would rob her for money, drugs or both if necessary.

"Oh, and as for feeling you up again. Just call me when you ready..." he said and slid her his number when he stood to leave. He knew she would call when her eyes shot down to his crotch.

"What the..." Dyme fussed when she emerged from the dressing room in time to see Dolla stand from the table. She adjusted her halter top and marched over. "Let me show you how this is done!"

"Hey again!" Lil Pop almost cheered when she saw Dyme. Dolla had her so worked up thinking about some dick she needed to hurry up and get her tongue in some pussy. She quickly dismissed the girls again even though they just returned.

"Hey yaself," Dyme shot back seductively and sat down beside her. "What my man wanted?"

"Talking business. We finna get some money together," the stud said and reached for her thigh.

"You move fast," Dyme said and gently removed the hand instead of smacking it away like she normally would do.

"Oh, you don't get down huh? Lil Pop got you curious huh?" the stud laughed. Dyme actually blushed when she peered into her eyes. It was good acting and got the stud wide open. Now she had both Dolla and Dyme on her mind.

*****

Desire frowned and pouted when her new friend pulled into a run-down apartment complex. She wasn't being uppity since she grew up in a similar complex on the other side of town. What bothered her was knowing that Pumpkin and Mzladi were chilling up in Lil Pop's big house out in the burbs. She put the girl on and she beat her out. Mzladi just started and beat her too.

Then she couldn't remember what dude said his name was but there she was pulling up to his apartment. She knew exactly what he expected and planned to give it to him, but it would be nice if she knew his name.

"Sup Tommy," a goon greeted and nodded when they got out of his car. He looked Desire up and down as he gave him a pound.

"Sup shawty. Finna get these guts," he said as if Desire wasn't even there or didn't speak English or didn't have any shame.

She kept it to herself since she now had a name. She just pouted some more as he led her inside. The inside was a lot better than the outside. Tommy obviously invested some of his ill gotten gains into his apartment. Everything was new

"Roll up," Tommy said and passed her some weed and a blunt. She opened her mouth to protest since he said he had coke but he produced a bag of the stuff. No where near as much as Lil Pop set out but it was coke and it was free.

Desire rolled the blunt, lit the blunt, hit the blunt and passed the blunt. All the while watching the lines he made on the glass table. She picked out two thick lines for herself and claimed them.

"That's you lil mama," Tommy said and leaned back to smoke. He had plans for his dick and snorting coke would interfere with those plans.

"Thank, you," she said and greedily inhaled the drgs before he could change his mind. Instead he reached down and fondled her backside. She spread her legs so he could access what he was after. Once he got her wet and slippery he took her in his room and slipped inside of her.

Desire felt some kind of way about sleeping with the man for drgs but the drgs he she parted with as a parting gift made up for it. She was now officially a coke head in training.

*****

"Mmhm," Dyme dared as Dolla drove them home after another good night in the club. Revenues ticked up each day they were in business. They had another heaping deposit to make in the morning.

"What?" Dolla just asked instead of trying to guess what she was 'mmhm-ing' about.

"You tryna beat me to the punch. Bruh I can next to Lil Pop quicker than you!" she challenged.

"Only cuz you got a pussy , but I'm trying to find out how much work and bread she sitting on. We may have to make a buy or two just to see what she working with," he explained. She nodded along and realized they had to work together. A plot was formed, shaped and molded on the ride home. By the time they arrived Lil Pop didn't stand a chance.

Dyme felt guilty about the side money she made on the private room. It stayed on the tip of her tongue but just wouldn't come out. She wanted to shop and he just wanted to stack.

Dolla would never know why he got the best head of his life when they got home. It was Dyme's way of making up for deceiving him. She knew it was wrong but the love of money said it was alright.

"OK then!" Dolla cheered as Dyme swallowed for the first time in her life and their life together.

"Eww," she still grimaced when she finally came up for air.

"Eww nothing! That was dope!" he said, hoping to work it into their sxual rotation. Like all couples they had a menu to choose from that would benefit them both.

"Better than Desire?" she teased and cuddled against his chest. The question caught Dolla off guard and the pause made her pop back up. "You gotta think about it!"

"Huh? Naw! You better! The best! The illest!" Dolla cheered. "Shoot you dope for having her do that."

"Yeah, I know," she said even though she didn't and wouldn't have another chick blowing her man. She accepted her little friend was a little slow and didn't mean any harm. "She just better not do it again."

Chapter Twenty-seven

Dolla and Dyme had all their ducks in a row by the time they set up a buy with Lil Pop. Desire came through with a dealer who could get the product off at a profit even though it was just a means to an end. Of course Dyme solicited the proceeds to shop with since it was extra.

Tommy couldn't believe his good luck when Desire came to him with the idea. He had been watching Dolla and Dyme for a way in and the young girl practically handed him the keys. While Dolla and Dyme were plotting on the stud, he was plotting on them.

Lil Pop may have brought strays to her home nightly she set up the meet with Dolla in a nearby hotel. Hotel, not motel with cameras and too much traffic for a jack move. Peppa would sit in a separate room with all the work while Pop sat in another and made the deals. She would text her helper to bring her the work once she checked the money. No money and dope in the same room at the same time. She survived this long by taking precautions like this.

"Get her daddy!" Dyme cheered when they arrived for the buy. She would sit in the car while he went up to make the deal. She had plans for shopping with the stud later in the day.

"I got her mama!" he nodded and hopped out. The lady at the bank would have to miss him today since they were investing last nights earnings with the stud. It was a win/win since Tommy would bring back fifteen grand off the ten they were spending.

Dolla and Peppa pretended not to see each other as he waltzed through the lobby. She shot a quick text up to her boss to let her know he was on the way then went up to the room with the work. It also contained a gun in case things went wrong.

Dolla looked like he belonged as he breezed through in casual linen pants and button down shirt. He cracked a smile at his dapper reflection as he passed by a window. It was a far cry from his every day uniform of Tims and jeans in his homeland of Brooklyn. The love of money had him too and he wanted more by any means.

"Get rich or die trying," he told the handsome man in the glass. The elevator dinged and opened for him to enter. He texted his arrival as he rode up to the tenth floor and got out. Dolla leaned in and pressed his ear to the door for a moment before knocking. He listened for shuffling of feet but heard none.

"Come on!" Lil Pop called in response to the knock on the door.

"Sup cutie," Dolla greeted as he entered the room. His eyes shot all over, up and down before they settled on the blushing stud. She wasn't going for 'cutie' when she pulled her expensive, baggy jeans and Hawks jersey on.

"Sup shawty," she replied and watched his eyes dart around the room once more. "ain't nobody here but me shawty. You can look around."

"Don't mind if I do. Can never be to careful," Dolla said and peeked into the empty bathroom and closet. She lifted up her jersey and showed off her six pack. A black pstl stood out against her yellow skin. A slow twirl gave him a glance of her round ass distorted by the baggy denim.

"I should pat you down this time," Lil Pop half joked. She knew dude was about his business, she just wanted to touch him.

"Have at it," Dolla dared and raised his hands. The stud cracked a crooked smile and came closer. They locked eyes as she dipped low and worked her way up his legs. She flirted near his dick but didn't touch it. She would have found it just as hard as the pstl she found in his waistband.

"Yeah, you clean," she said since she had a gun on her as well. Now that the flirting was out of the way they got down to business. He traded her the bag of cash for a blunt. He began to smoke while she counted out ten grand. "Ten racks, for twenty onions."

"Not bad," Dolla said of the five hundred dollar an ounce price. He was getting seven fifty each from Tommy for each ounce. Dyme wanted to spend the profits but he wanted to flip it again and stack it.

"I gave you the hook up," she said as she texted Peppa to bring his order.

"I'll have to hook you up one day," Dolla shot back. He shot his eyes between her legs so there would be no misunderstanding what he meant.

"We'll see," she said to both of their surprise. Peppa used her key card and came in.

"What?" Peppa frowned. The looks on both of their faces suggested she walked in on something.

"We good," Lil Pop assured her. She passed the work to Dolla and watched him inspect it. He scrunched up like 'it's a'ight' and put it in his bag.

"See you in a few days," Dolla said and stood. Both sets of eyes shot down to his crotch when he did.

"See you tonight since we coming to the club!" the stud corrected. They nodded as he departed.

"You blushing shawty? Let me find out..." Peppa fussed. The last thing she needed was some dude turning her straight and putting her out of a job.

"You tripping shawty. I'm finna fuck his girl, first chance I get!" she assured her. Peppa nodded since she had no reason to doubt her.

*****

"So, what all Desire told you about me?" Dolla inquired as him and Tommy sat down for business in a restaurant near the club. He asked because the girl had told him and Dyme all she knew about the dope boy. From where he lived, to how long he lasted when he fucked her. Everything except him paying her with drugs after they did the deed.

"Nothing much. Just you had some work," he shrugged to conceal the lie. Desire couldn't hold water or tea and bragged how her big brother and sister were getting to the money.

Dolla met him in the eatery to keep this business from the club and he certainly wouldn't bring him to where he and Dyme laid their heads. Not that Tommy didn't know they had an apartment in a downtown high rise since Desire bragged about that too.

"Oh, OK. So she didn't say anything about me being a killer who will kill something about my bread?" Dolla tossed out casually.

"Naw, but I hear you shawty," Tommy laughed at the thinly veiled threat. "I'm good money shawty. With your price I can cut bigger hits and lock down my complex. We gone get money until you switch up."

"A'ight yo. We gone fuck with you then," Dolla sighed. He didn't have much choice since he had no other outlet for the dope. He certainly wouldn't pump anything through his club and had to keep shopping with Lil Pop so he and Dyme could peep her operations to rob her.

Dolla paid for their meals and headed outside to the parking lot. He lifted his hand and Desire pulled up to a stop in her car. She rolled down her window and held out a bag.

"She gone drop off and pick up," Dolla explained without having to explain he planned to keep his hands clean. Get rich or die trying means not going to jail.

"That's what's up," Tommy said and gave him a pound. Little did Dolla know he was plotting the same plot on him as he was plotting on Lil Pop.

*****

"You're up," Dolla said when he came in from meeting Tommy.

"I got em babes!" Dyme said as she came out of the bathroom dressed to at least thrill if not kill.

"Yeah you do!" he exclaimed when he saw her in yet another new outfit. The low cut blouse dipped damn near to her navel showing off almost all of her breast meat. Her legs looked luscious in the tiny skirt she wore for her play date with the stud. She looked so good it distracted him from noticing it was new.

"Yeah she like pussy so much I'ma give her some to look at while I look around her house." Dyme said. She hoped studs liked to showoff as much as dudes when trying to impress a chick out of her panties. They made it hard on themselves but easier for Dolla and Dyme to jack them.

"We gotta peep her stash or stash house. She ain't putting that bread in the bank so she keeping it somewhere!" he reasoned.

It was a reasonable assumption since they watched her sell weight for hours after they copped. Dope boys came and went in and out of the hotel picking up weight and dropping off dough. Dyme wanted to jack a few of them since they were so close to a mall but Dolla kept his eyes on the bigger prize.

Lil Pop made a hundred grand in a few hours so she had to be sitting on a gold mine somewhere. Both Dolla and Dyme were down for almost anything to find out where.

*****

"You can go see a movie or whatever," Lil Pop suggested when she got the text she'd been waiting for. Dyme had just arrived in her subdivision and announced her presence.

"Man don't get caught up in this broad. She don't even rock like that," Peppa reminded.

"Not yet, but when this tongue touch her..." she said. It was the stud equivalent of a dude bragging on his stroke. Peppa let her lick her to several orgasms but was still straight as an arrow have her tell it.

"A'ight," she shrugged and hopped to her feet. Dyme rang the bell just as she reached the door and pulled it open.

"Pop here?" Dyme asked even though she knew she was.

"Pop here?" Peppa mocked and looked her up and down to show her what she thought of her.

"Word," Dyme laughed and breezed by her. She could only hope the sidekick was around whenever she and Dolla came back. She would give her something to mock.

"Sup shawty. Dang, you looking like a bowl of batter after grandma whip up a cake!" Lil Pop complimented.

"And I bet you wanna lick the bowl huh?" Dyme laughed. Peppa sucked her teeth and stepped off. She was so busy huffing and puffing when she pulled out that she didn't register the car that pulled out behind her.

"Lick it clean as a whistle!" the stud declared, ready to prove her point right then and there.

"We'll see. You ready to go shopping?" Dyme asked as she casually scanned the room. She had plenty of etceteras but Dyme knew from experience that doesn't always translate to having money. Some people spend it as soon as they get it and look rich but are almost broke. She should know since she was one of them.

"I really can't get out right now. Hang out for a while. I'll just give you some bread to shop with," Lil Pop said and tried her up like she had tried many straight chicks before.

"I um," Dyme began to decline but a few extra bucks would be nice. Especially with Dolla pinching her off chump change like he had been lately. "I can only stay for an hour or so..."

"Cool. Spark up!" Lil Pop cheered and nodded towards a neatly rolled blunt on the table. Dyme was from the hood and knew better than smoking with strangers if she didn't roll it. That didn't stop her from doing it anyway. The love of money had her in it's grip and it was calling the shots.

"Mhp!" Dyme huffed from the strong weed when she inhaled. Lil Pop watched carefully for her reaction. Dyme kept right on smoking and asked in between pulls, "What, is, this?"

"That's that Loud," she said. It was only half the answer since it was laced with coke and opiates. She quickly lit another blunt of her own before Dyme tried to pass the one she had. She popped a colorful pill before extending one to her guest.

"Nah, I'll save it for later," she said so she wouldn't be rude. Dyme dropped the pill in her purse and kept on hitting the weed. They made casual small talk until the blunts were done and it was time to get down to business. "Show me around?"

"Sho nuff. This the den..." she said as she stood. A crooked smile spread on her pretty face when Dyme wobbled when she stood. "You OK shawty?"

"Yeah, I'm good!" Dyme shot back but felt anything but. She was high as a kite and woozy. Still she pressed on with the tour.

"This my kitchen. A nigga got all the latest gadgets but only thing I cook is crack!" the stud bragged as they passed through a large, stainless steel kitchen.

"You cook up, here?" Dyme asked, hoping to gleam a snippet of her operation.

"Nah, we got a spot for that," was all she got as they hit another room. Then another and a bathroom before they got to the master.

"I..." Dyme swooned and almost fell out. Good thing Lil Pop was near enough to catch her. Bad thing was she was near enough to catch her.

The stud laid Dyme on her bed and stood back to marvel at her legs. The skirt was short enough to see all the way to her promise land. Lil Pop decided to save some for prosperity and snapped a few pics of her pussy .

"Let me get a peek at this thang..." Lil Pop said and pulled the thin strip of panty away and exposed the plumpness beneath.

That led to a sniff, and a lick that led to her pulling the panties completely off and dining on vagina. Dyme was out of it but still felt the pleasure mounting between her legs. She was far away but not too far to bust a nut. The stud greedily sipped her juice box like a thirsty child with a juice box.

Dyme drifted off to sleep off the drgs and orgsm. She felt the same sensation when she awoke hours later. She looked down and saw the stud lapping away at her labia but didn't protest. Instead she spread her legs a little wider so she could get it all. She pulled Lil Pop's face into her crotch and grinded against her lips and tongue. The nut was better than the first and might not be the last.

Chapter Twenty-eight

"What the fuck, yo?" Dolla griped when Dyme waltzed into the club hours after she should have.

"Man..." Dyme said and shook her head to explain all the things she couldn't say. How could she explain to her man than she let the stud lick her bowl and then take her shopping.

"What you find out?" Dolla said and shook his head along with her.

"I know she don't cook up at the house. I ain't see nothing there. She got a stash house somewhere," Dyme reported.

"Yeah, on Roosevelt circle. It's the hood but a few blocks from downtown. A few blocks from the police station," he said since he had followed Peppa. He parked down the block and watched the telltale signs of drg traffic.

Dolla peeked a little more traffic than expected from someone who moved as carefully as Lil Pop moved. It led him to think Peppa may have been making moves behind her back. If so she was on his list too. He expected more info out of Dyme than that. In the end he remembered the old adage, if you want something done right, do it yourself.

"Where you been big sis!" Desire sassed with her hands on her hips. She saw the look on Dyme's face and dialed it back a little. "Are you OK?"

"Yes girl," she said as Dolla pulled off to go run the club. Once he was out of earshot she bragged about her shopping spree. "Girl I copped some bad ass outfits!"

Meanwhile Cynt came over with a trick to treat. Dyme looked around for Dolla and saw he was tied up. She gave a nod and the stripper took him into the private room. Dyme rushed to the office to turn off the recording. This time she didn't have time to stay and watch the action. Too bad because it was plenty of action.

"You want your dick sucked or you tryna fuck?" Cynt asked so she would know how much she had to take off. Head only came with tittes but she had to get naked for some ass.

"I guess a little head wouldn't hurt?" the man asked as if he was trying to convince himself. He nodded in agreement with himself and whipped out the wood.

"Naw, it don't hurt none," she assured him and kneeled in front of him. She was right too and that blow job didn't hurt one bit. In fact it was one of the best the young cop had ever received. They said vice squad came with some perks and they were right.

"There, you, go!" the undercover officer grunted and filled her mouth full of evidence. Of course that part wouldn't go in his report but his case was made. They were selling sx in Club Dimes.

******

"How'd it go?" Dolla asked when he met up with Tommy.

"Like gravy," the dope boy smiled and showed off his new gold teeth. The new product he got fronted was free money so he bought some new fronts. Not to mention he had a stripper laid up in his bed waiting on him to return.

"That is some good gravy," Dolla agreed when the count was right on time. "Let's link up tomorrow and we can do it again."

"Sho nuff," Tommy agreed, then added as an afterthought. "How much can you stand? I can move ten times that much."

"Hmph?" Dolla grunted and peered into his soul. Dolla was a jack boy himself and spoke that language too. "We'll see."

"We will see my nigga," he said to Dolla's back as he walked away. If he could get him up to a key he would chop his whole head off and keep the change.

Meanwhile, Dolla pulled his phone and made a quick call now that he had a reason to. Dyme had linked up with Lil Pop a couple of times that week and had no further info. He needed a reason to get at her or Peppa and now he had one.

"Sup shawty!" Lil Pop greeted with a pussy eating grin on her face. Dyme's juices circled her thick lips like glazed donut.

"I need to bump into you. Asap!" he added. He wanted to put the five thousand profits in the bank but the love of money urged him to flip it all.

"Business or pleasure?" she asked as she watched Dyme get dressed again. She had only dropped by to smoke one and somehow ended up with her legs high in the sky. The shopping money Lil Pop broke her off with justified it her her mind. Besides it wasn't cheating since Pop didn't have a dick and all she did was lick.

"Both," Dolla said and smiled back through the line. He needed a way in so he could peep her movements for himself.

"Fall through," Lil Pop said and hung up. She opened her bedroom door and called for her sidekick. "Say Pep!"

"Sup?" Peppa asked when she finally made it upstairs. She made sure to take her sweet time in protest of Dyme's presence.

"Take her home real quick. Then stop by the spot. I'ma need you to brang some work over," she explained.

"Over where? Over here!" she gasped to show what she thought of it.

"Yeah, over here! Now 'hur-up'!" Pop said in the tone bosses use to subordinates when they forget they are subordinates.

"Check," Peppa nodded in the tone that a Judas will use when ready to cross their leader. Dyme's face went back and forth as she watched the verbal volley. She was happy, high and had a purse full of extra money to shop with. The only thing she loved more than shopping was the money. She loved it almost as much as she did Dolla.

Had Dyme looked up from her phone she would have saw her man pass by as Peppa pulled out of the subdivision. Dolla saw the truck but didn't register the passenger. He knew Dyme was hanging out with Desire and was happy to have her out of the way so he could handle business. He pulled into the driveway and checked himself in the mirror before. He nodded with his spinning waves and hopped out.

"Mmhm," Lil Pop hummed and opened the door as he approached. She was unusually girlie and giddy for some reason. Despite just having sucked his girls soul out of her pussy.

"Sup ma," he greeted with a smile that made the stud remember that she had a vagina herself. It throbbed and got moist with each step he took towards her as a reminder.

Dolla knew he had to press the issue with her if they were going to rob her. He didn't waste a second and moved on her right there in the doorway.

"Hmphh!" Lil Pop grunted when he scooped her into his arms and shoved his tongue into her mouth.

It was a good thing he had a firm grip on her round ass because her knees buckled so hard she almost fell. She went from shock to willing participant in an instant and kissed him back.

Lil Pop had always been a tomboy and that led to girls pushing up on her before she even knew she was a stud. A few dudes got the goodies and ran but girls were more loyal. She developed a grudge against guys and set out to out do them in everything. She played sports better than most and fucked their girlfriends better than most. Plus she could fight and beat up quite a few guys who didn't like her fucking their baby mamas and girlfriends.

A drg plug fell into her lap and she took off in that too. Now she had the work and they had to go through her if they wanted to eat. Now they gladly let her eat their baby mamas and girlfriends.

All that went out the window when Dolla began grinding that thick dick against her. She had the strongest urge to see it. Touch it, and feel it.

"Where is your room?" Dolla asked when he took his tongue out of her mouth. Lil Pop was too fucked up for words and just pointed at the stairs and grunted. She grunted again when he scooped her off her feet and carried her up the stairs.

"Mhgp," she grunted again when he almost passed her room. All she could do was grunt with his tongue on her tonsils. Dolla dipped into the room and deposited her on her bed.

"Take your clothes off," Dolla demanded. He stepped back to watch the show as she complied. Lil Pop transformed into Leticia when she pulled her Hawks jersey over her head. Her big niples poked through the fabric of the sports bra she wore to subdue her softball sized breast.

Dolla felt his dick throbbing and straining in his jeans from the sight. He had no real plan when he arrived but didn't plan for this. He loved his girl and would not cheat on her. Still his erecton somehow made it into the room. It throbbed even more when Lil Pop stepped out of the boxers she wore over her pink panties. The afro below made it look fatter than it really was and made him want to at least see it.

"C,c,can I, I touch it?" the stud pleaded. She didn't wait for an answer before reaching out and taking the dick in her hand. She marveled at it like a new toy. She already had his girl in her mouth today so it was only fair when she leaned in and took him inside.

"Man..." Dolla moaned in sorrow. He knew this was too far and felt bad at how good it felt. He was determined it would go no further than this but still reached down and played in the thick curls surrounding her pussy. The mass of hair was soon soaked in her juice. No man would be able to resist touching it and neither did Dolla. He rubbed his fingers in between her slippery lips, still chiding himself that he was going too far. He vowed not to go any further but made the mistake of pushing a finger inside.

"Shit!" Dolla shouted when he felt how wet, hot and tight she was against his finger. He came instantly from the sensational sensation.

"Mmm," Lil Pop moaned as she pulled him out of her mouth and watched him skeet on her chest and legs. He was still playing in her pussy so she spread her legs.

Dolla could only shake his head at himself when he climbed between her legs. He was still fooling himself when he rubbed his dick head between the froth easing entry into the tight little box.

"Just gonna put the head in," he said mainly to himself.

"OK," the stud agreed just like she did when she lost her cherry some years back. It was just as tight now as it was back then. So tight Dolla just couldn't help squeezing inside.

"Just half," he bargained with himself and took a few short strokes. Just a few before he snatched out and bust another nut on her hard stomach. She leaned up and watched him come on her six pack. Dolla had a dilemma and paused to ponder. He had went too far already so he decided to go on and get his monies worth.

"Sss!" Lil Pop hissed as he worked himself back inside. She gladly sucked his tongue when he offered it. Their tongues did a tango as he stroked her tight box with a salsa rhythm.

"Man you, got, some good, ass pussy!" Dolla said when he came again and filled it with change of a Dolla. He felt so good to the stud she didn't protest when he came inside of her. They cuddled with him still throbbing inside of her and went to sleep.

Lil Pop's phone awoke them both an hour later when it buzzed incessantly on her nightstand. Dolla didn't even budge when she reached over to answer it. Looking down at her pretty face caused him to get pretty hard, pretty quickly.

"Sup shawty?" Pop croaked into her phone. She tried to use her usual stud, husky tone but it was off a little.

"You tell me! I'm over at the Circle waiting 'fo you to tell me what to bring?" Peppa protested.

"Huh? I, um?" Lil Pop replied. She had gotten distracted by the dick throbbing back to life between her legs. She covered the phone and whispered up, "What you was tryna get?"

"This..." Dolla said rubbing his dick against her pussy. It hollered back and got wet and juicy for him. He knew what she meant and added, "Fifteen,"

"Fifteen. Make it sixteen. Give me an hour," she said and hung up. She may have asked for an hour but Dolla didn't last ten minutes inside of her. He added more coins to the change he deposited in her already. They showered together and got dressed. When Peppa arrived they were chilling in the den, smoking a blunt.

"Sup?" Peppa wanted to know when she walked in. The couple worked so hard to appear casual, it came across as anything but. They looked guiltily at each other then away.

"Nothing. You got that?" Lil Pop said sounding close to normal.

"No. It's at the room. I ain't branging nothing here, never!" Peppa said hotly. Dolla just nodded since she proved her worth as a right hand man. Your right hand should check the left when it gets out of line.

"Let me holla at you real quick shawty," Pop snapped and stood. She tossed her phone down and stormed out of the room with Peppa hot on her heels. Lil Pop had a lil limp from the soreness between her legs. They stepped several rooms away into the kitchen but Dolla could still hear the voices. He couldn't make out what was being said but took the opportunity to go into her phone since it didn't have time to time out.

"Where them dollars at?" Dolla mumbled as he went through her phone. He was supposed to be looking for money but ended up perusing pussy in her gallery. In this social media climate, she was sure to have pics of stacks to post to her feed. He found racks at what had to be hundreds of thousands of dollars nestled in between all that pussy. All kinds of pussy too. Young pussy, older pussy, light skin pussy , that good darker the berry sweeter the juice dark skin pussy . The crowd favorite fat girl pussy and some skinny pussy. Some white pussy, Mexican pussy and even one Korean pussy .

"What the..." Dolla said and doubled back to look at one particular pussy he saw. He blinked, rubbed his eyes and blinked some more but it was still Dyme's box all wet and glistening. He wanted to think maybe Dyme sent her the pics to entice her but he recognized the comforter she was laying on. Especially since he just fucked the stud a few times on it.

Dolla was so confused he sat the phone down and stared off into space. He was somewhere near Mars when the two girls returned. Peppa wore a smug smirk that meant she had her way.

"Say shawty, follow her to the room. She got your sixteen over there," Lil Pop announced.

"Bet that," Dolla nodded and stood. He cracked a slight smile as a thanks for the extra ounce she tossed in.

"Sht give me a call tomorrow and we can talk some more," Lil Pop said to even her own surprise. Peppa frowned at the softness in her tone and knew what kind of talk that was.

"Bet," Dolla said and surprised himself as well. He had already went too far but knew he would be back. The ends justified the means and vice versa since they were trying to get rich or die trying.

Chapter Twenty-nine

"You fucked her huh?" Peppa demanded as soon as they reached the hotel where the work was.

"Fucked the daylights out of her!" Dolla laughed. He was curious to see where she was going so he leaned back for the ride.

"You know she done fucked your girl too right?" Pep asked and smirked with mirth.

"Probably. We have an open relationship," he lied so she would keep going. There had to be a reason she was putting her boss on blast. Another reason besides the obvious since she shot a glance down at his crotch. Besides Lil Pop technically couldn't fuck Dyme since she didn't have a dick. He did and fucked the daylights out of the stud.

"Hmph. I do all the work while she get all the credit. If it wasn't for me..." she rambled on. Dolla listened and wondered if he didn't fuck the wrong one. Peppa could lead him to what he was after.

By the time he left he realized there was trouble in Lil Pop's life. According to Peppa, the boss just wanted to stay high and eat pussy . Wolves were nipping at her heels and she was oblivious to the danger. He needed to strike before it all came crumbling down.

Dolla fell back and followed Peppa once they left. She pulled into a 'B' level apartment complex and went inside. He made note that she had the bag of money he gave her when she went inside, but didn't have it when she came back out. He had just found the money stash house. It was time to catch a lick. But first, he had to go face his woman.

Dolla drove slow in an effort to stall the inevitable. He wondered how he should play the situation when he got home. Could he really be mad at Dyme for letting Lil Pop get a little lick. It was a big lick with those big lips but he didn't know that. What he did know was that he got rock hard just thinking about the episode they just

194

shared. He had to change the subject in his head so it would go down before he got home.

"Hey babes!" Dyme cheered when he walked in. He saw the store bags on the sofa and assumed it was why she was so happy. It was partly why but the pill she popped was another part. Dyme found the opiate in the bottom of her purse when she swapped the contents to her new purse. She couldn't wait to go to the club so someone could see it.

"Sup, yo. I got that. I know I said you could keep the change but I went on and flipped the whole thing. The quicker we get this money up, the better," he said and braced for complaints.

"OK, babes," was all Dyme said minus the eye contact. Not that Dolla could tell since he was looking everywhere except in her eyes. They both were just like ole Sam when he used to steal from the register. He died trying and they needed to do better before they followed his footsteps.

*****

"Take this your boy," Dyme said and gave Desire eight of the sixteen ounces. He proved he was good for it the first time but Dolla still didn't put all his eggs in one basket. If he ran off or things went south he could still make up for the loss with the other half.

"Y'all got a good connect! Tommy said the junkies loving it!" Desire repeated. It still hadn't dawned on Dyme that the girl didn't just repeat everything she heard to her, she repeated everything she heard, period. She was an old plastic cup with a hole in it and just couldn't hold water.

"Yeah, ya girl Lil Pop. With her nasty ass!" Dyme laughed. She kept the part about letting the stud eat her out to herself but rambled on and on about Lil Pop's operations. Dolla had filled her in about the other stash spot and she repeated it to Desire.

"Girl that's him now. I'm finna go over there and I'll meet you back at the club," Desire said after reading the text from Tommy.

"Take your time. I'm going to stop by the mall," Dyme said. It made no sense to let the stud suck her soul out for money and not spend the money. Dolla could save all he wanted to but she was going to spend hers. She was still a B.A.B at heart no matter how much money she touched.

Desire drove over to Tommy's apartments to drop off the dope. She had to past her own apartment complex first so she pulled in to make a little deal of her own.

"You brung me a beer?" her grandmother called out as she breezed through the living room.

"When I get off!" she said over her shoulder and closed her bedroom door behind her. She quickly opened each package and took a little coke out of each one. It added up to a nice little package of her own when she was done. She closed them back and rushed back through the living room.

"You gonna brang me a beer?" the old lady asked again in her wake.

"When I get off!" Desire said and closed the door behind her. She mashed the gas to make up for the detour and still arrived earlier than Tommy expected. He was just putting Mzladi in her car with a kiss when she pulled up. Desire wanted to hop out and put up a fuss until she remembered he wasn't her man. He just provided dick and dope but that's not a relationship. The two girls exchanged curt smirks at each other before Mzladi pulled off. They both better hope the other didn't contract anything since he was hitting them both raw like a skinless hot dog. Sheep intestines makes both a little better.

"You got that?" Tommy asked as he led her inside.

"Shole do!" Desire sang happily. She was pleased to be in the loop for her big sister and brother plus Tommy always broke her off for the delivery.

"Hmph?" Tommy huffed when he weighed the work. Desire held her breath and wondered if she had taken too much.

"It's straight ain't it?" she asked and went back to holding her breath.

"Yeah. Barely," he sighed wistfully. The last ones were actually a little over and that's better than being right on. He still slid a little across the table and Desire dropped down to quickly inhale it.

"Sht, while you down there..." Tommy said and fondled her backside. Desire moved a little to help him remove her shorts.

His fingers and coke helped her get nice and slippery for entry. Tommy dropped his baggy, dope boy jeans and pulled out his dope boy dick. Desire winced a little when he pushed inside of her, but kept right on snorting while he started humping.

"Don't come in, me. I gotta go dance," she whined when his stroke grew choppy and his grunts and growls increased.

"Mmhm," he said but didn't comply. His only concern was the impending orgsm building, not whoever had to look at her pussy when she got to the club. She could leak come while sliding down the pole as far as he was concerned.

"Awe man!" she moaned when he pushed in to the hilt and let one fly. She just stayed there and took it so she took another hit.

"Mph, mph, mph!" Tommy said and drug the dick out of her once he was spent. He parted with a little more coke and went to wash his dick in the sink. No time for a shower since he had some dope to sling. Desire had to settle for wiping in his bathroom and padded her panties with tissue to sop up the come on the way back to the club.

"Take this for the dancers," Tommy said when she returned from the bathroom. Desire looked at the gram packages for a second. She knew Dolla and Dyme didn't want any drgs in the club but she was selling it to the other dancers anyway.

Tommy got to work cooking up the coke so he could put it on the street. He broke her off a few grams for her trouble even it was a little lighter this time so he would definitely check it the next time.

*****

"Shawty trying me," Tommy nodded when the next eight ounces was just over seven ounces. The work was short but Dolla still wanted full price.

"What's wrong baby?" Desire asked and rubbed her nose. She knew she took too much out this time but that didn't stop her from doing it.

"Nothing shawty. We good. I'll bring you something for the girls later," he said.

"Um..." Desire paused to see if he was going to part with some coke. He didn't so she simply shrugged since she had skimmed plenty off the top already. Not too mention he didn't fuck her and send her back to work full of come. "OK. See you later."

"Un-huh," he grunted and got back to work cooking coke.

Desire rushed to her car and took a few hits up each nostril before pulling away from the apartment. She was so focused on inhaling the poison she neglected to look up. Had she titled her head she would have seen Tommy watching her snorting his profits. She just pointed the blame where it belonged but it really didn't matter since he still planned to rob Dolla and Dyme anyway.

He was 'Jackin for love too. For the love of money.

*****

Desire was sky high when she reached the club. She knew she would get chewed out for any detours so she headed straight for the office so she could deliver Dolla the money Tommy sent over.

"You got that?" Dolla demanded as soon as she came in. She rushed over and passed the bag across the desk.

Dolla quickly counted it up when he got it. The quicker he did the quicker he could go see Lil Pop. He and Dyme grew more distant by the day as they chased their own desires. Different desires but they stemmed from the same root. The love of money the root of all evil.

Dyme was becoming an instagram model, posting more pics to more likes in her new clothes, shoes and purses. Of course Dolla didn't even know that page existed. Even if twenty thousand followers did.

Dolla was busy counting dollars all day. He multiplied and divided all day in search of that million. Lil Pop was still getting robbed but he planned to flip his daily proceeds every day until he did. In the mean time he had other plans for the stud.

"Yo, I'm gonna run over here and see Pop. Stay here and hold down the fort," Dolla told Dyme. Again he expected some lip since she used to wanna go everywhere he went.

"OK daddy," she said and shrugged. Dolla paused and squinted at her. He almost didn't recognize her with all the makeup and hair. They shared the same space but lately that was about all.

"Sup with that wig yo? You about to rob a bank?" Dolla laughed.

"Boy this is a thousand dollar, Brazilian..." Dyme rattled off in defense of her wig. Dolla nodded and went to handle his business. Dyme stayed behind to handle hers as well.

"Y'all get to it before he get back!" Dyme told Cynt and the other treats who turned tricks in the private rooms. There had been a sudden uptick in business and Dyme could make an extra grand a night.

Meanwhile Dolla made a beeline out to Lil Pop's house. He pulled to skidding stop in her driveway and rushed up the walk. His text was replied by the door opening as he approached. Dolla expected to see the stud dressed in baggy jeans and T-shirt. He didn't mind because she was all girl underneath.

"Hey, word?" Dolla laughed when he saw her posing in black lingerie instead.

"You like?" she giggle like a girl. She was definitely all girl and the ass cheeks hanging from the bottom of her panties proved it.

"Do I!" he exclaimed. Those would be their last words for a while. The next hour was filled with grunts, groans and moans. Dolla had something to prove after the quickies last time. This time he took his time and dug her out properly. Especially since he vowed to himself it would be the last time. He and Dyme may had been drifting apart and it was time to fix it.

"Oooh, I'm finna come!" Lil Pop whined like a kid about to tell on a sibling.

"Come on!" Dolla dared between firm strokes designed for that purpose. Leticia took over for Lil Pop and bust a nut all over his dick. Dolla smiled down proudly at her fuck faces as she squirmed and shivered from the orgsm. He kept right on stroking hoping to make her come again.

"Sht!" he grunted when he realized the end was quickly approaching.

"Come in me!" she pleaded and squeezed her already super tight vagina. Dolla didn't mind hitting her raw since he knew no one else was. That still didn't mean he should come in the chick. He did it anyway and exploded inside of her.

"Yo, I gotta, get back," Dolla moaned. He wouldn't mind going another round but was about his money.

"OK. I had to go get the shit myself since Pep acting funny," Pop said and rolled off the bed. The jiggle of her caramel ass cheeks put

Dolla to the test. He decided he had to hit her at least one more time. Not tonight but it was only right that he gave her some back shots.

"Word," Dolla nodded when he saw she gave him a little extra once again. "Pep is smart yo. Let her handle biz like she been handling it."

"OK, daddy," she giggled. She didn't even count the money when he handed it to her. She was gone off that dick and they both knew it.

Physically the feeling was mutual but that didn't change much. He was going to keep hitting it but she was still getting robbed. He advised her to let Peppa handle business so she wouldn't be there when it went down, since she wouldn't live through it.

Dolla had a hard time getting his tongue back when they shared a parting kiss at the door. He did though and rushed back towards downtown. He made a quick pit stop to drop off the work so it wouldn't be at the club. Dolla was the only one adhering to the rules of the club.

Both Dyme and Desire had side hustles going on and the shit was rushing towards the fan.

Chapter Thirty

Dolla and Dyme awoke wrapped in each others arms. They hadn't been this close in weeks since both had separate lives. As busy as they had been there was no escaping the moment. Both had been with Lil Pop within the last few days but she wasn't there now.

"Mmm," Dyme moaned and basked in his embrace. It felt better than a thousand 'Likes' to lay in his arms.

"Mmm, is right," he and his throbbing erction agreed. They shared their first real kiss in a week. Their lips touched daily but usually while their minds were on other things.

The kiss led to gropes that led licks that led to Dolla sliding inside of her slippery vagina. Getting filled with dick felt better than two thousand likes and Dyme felt guilty about her deception. It wasn't that she didn't love Dolla anymore. Who she was at heart just came to the surface. She wanted to stop but once a B.A.B always one.

The couple came as a couple, showered as a couple and got dressed. They hit the club and made sure it was up and running before slipping up to the office. They made out real heavy in the VIP before slipping away.

"You sure we shouldn't even tell Desire we leaving? So she can keep an eye out?" Dyme wondered as they dressed.

"Desire? That broad can't hold water. We need people to think we in here fucking," he reminded.

"Oh yeah!" Dyme agreed. She was so used to dressing up it felt weird to dress down. This was an armed robbery though and no place for wigs and heels.

Both dressed in all black to blend into the night. Both carried black Macs in case they met any resistance. This should be an easy lick since only Peppa manned the stash house.

Lil Pop was prone to pillow talk after sx and both Dolla and Dyme knew the whole operation. She didn't trust anyone but Peppa so no one else would, or should be inside. The stud mentioned she needed to re-up so she should be flush with cash.

Dolla drove in silence as he contemplated his situation. Dyme had become distant doing just what she was doing now. The social media junkie was posting and liking even as they rode towards their next lick.

Ironically they each blamed the other for the space between them. She was obsessed with fashion and bullshit while he was consumed with making and stacking money. They had nothing in common to talk about anymore so they rarely spoke anymore. Just like they weren't speaking now.

"She gone know it's us,'" Dyme sighed as they pulled into the apartment complex Pop used as a safe house for her money. Dolla heard the unspoken question and replied.

"Yeah she is," which meant Peppa was dying tonight. Both let out another sigh and gave her a moment of silence. Pep was good people but many good people died for the love of money.

"What the..." Dyme fussed when they rounded the last turn towards the apartment.

"fuck!" Dolla added when he saw the brilliantly lit crime scene. He held out hope that it was just the same building and not apartment. His hopes were dashed when they got closer and saw the door wide open and cops in and out. Dolla pulled over and they both got out to join the crowd of onlookers who looked on.

"What happen?" Dyme asked a woman with rollers in her hair. They always have the most information since they're the ones the news crews seem to always pick.

"Someone kicked the door down and robbed her. I think they kilt her," she said. "I ain't think that girl had nuffin going on?"

A hush fell over the crowded crowd when the body bag was carried out to the coroners van. Neither could see inside but they both knew who was in there. Someone had beat them to the lick.

*****

"Hey y'all nasty people!" Desire cheered and cheesed when Dolla and Dyme finally appeared from the office. The big PDA show they put on made everyone assume they were in there doing the do. In reality they shot across town to hit a lick only to see it had already been hit.

"Sup," Dyme moaned as Dolla slinked away to make his rounds around the club.

"What's wrong with bruh?" she asked then saw the look on Dyme's face as well. "What's wrong!"

"Man..." Dyme moaned again and stormed off.

Meanwhile, Tommy walked in and headed straight for the VIP. Desire looked at him oddly since he usually played the tables reserved for regular folk. She rushed up to his side before the other girls could.

"Hey Tommy. What you doing?" she asked and started dancing before he even asked her to.

"Balling!" he proclaimed and waved a waitress over. "Champagne and a bottle of that Henny!"

"OK then!" Desire cheered when he produced a big was of cash. Her ass shook that much harder with all that cash.

It wasn't long after when Lil Pop came in looking like Lil Pop. She wore male clothes on her body and a scowl on her cute face. Both Dolla and Dyme spotted her from opposite sides of the club and made a beeline over to her.

"Sup yo? What's wrong?" Dyme asked since she arrived a split second before him.

"Someone hit my safe house. They kilt my girl Peppa," she moaned. A couple of tears escaped her brown eyes despite the tough facade.

"Word? Come up to the office," Dolla added. He hoped he could get her alone to find out what happened but Dyme was close on their heels. He sat her on the sofa once they were inside asked, "Now what happened?"

"Ion even know. I been calling her for some hours so we could re-up. She ain't never pick up so I went to the apartment and found her skretched out on the 'flo. I checked my money and it was all gone!" Pop said with her head shaking.

"How much!" Both Dolla and Dyme shouted way too eagerly. Pop lifted her head and furrowed her brow at them both.

"A quarter mil. They struck for two hundred and fifty grand!" Lil Pop answered.

"Awe man!" Dyme fussed and stormed out. She made no attempt to hide her feelings on not hitting that lick herself. Pop and Dolla watched her leave and paused for a second before speaking.

"You have any idea who did it?" he asked hopefully. He knew for a fact if they didn't get them now the money would be spent.

"Naw shawty. Err body in the hood know where the stash is but no one knew where I kept my bread. Except me and Peppa," Pop said.

"She must have told someone. How would they know?" he asked.

"Ion know. Why would they do her like that? They did her dirty," Pop moaned again and shed another tear.

"A'ight. Go home. I'ma fall through once we close up," Dolla decided.

"OK," Pop agreed. She wasn't in the mood for loving but needed someone to hold.

Dolla walked her through the club and out to her car. He felt the strangest sensation as he watched her pull out and drive away. Something was wrong with the picture but it just didn't register. The night was too quiet, too still. He should have ran but shrugged it off instead and went back inside.

"That's fucked up B!" Dyme protested when he caught back up with her. She had collected almost thousand dollars from her side hustle while he was out but could taste the quarter mil they almost had.

"Word. I wanna know how someone beat us to it? Pop said no one knew but her and Peppa. I only knew cuz I followed her. You the only one I told and you ain't said nothing to nobody," he pondered and sighed.

"Nope. No one. Un-uh," she said, remembering telling Desire while she was high. She knew Desire was with her all day so she couldn't, wouldn't have done it. The rest of the night was a blur of booties shaking while they mourned the loss of the lick.

******

"How we do?" Dolla asked wistfully when Jamesha and Richard came to the office to turn in their receipts. He tuned out their answers since it fell far short of the two hundred and fifty thousand dollars that got away. He wished he never asked and never knew how much money it was.

"We can still flip it. Help her get her money back up so we can still rob her," Dyme suggested once they were alone again.

"Yeah," he agreed since that was his plan anyway. They quietly closed up shop and headed for the front door. They didn't make it since all the doors suddenly burst open from all sides.

Dolla reacted and reached for the gun he kept in his waist most of his life. It saved his life on more than one occasion in Brooklyn. They weren't in Brooklyn now and not having the gun on him is what saved his life this time.

"Police! Hands in the air! Freeze! Don't move! I'll blow your damn head off!" the cops screamed as they swooped in from every angle.

Dolla and Dyme slowly raised their hands and got arrested.

Chapter Thirty-one

"Yo, what the fuck is going on?" Dolla asked. He and Dyme were handcuffed and sitting on the floor while police ransacked the club.

"Ion know?" Dyme said watching the cops going through everything. She didn't even connect any of the dots that lead straight back to her.

"Clear," Different officers began to announce from different parts of the club. Finally one came out of the office and said the same. He was obviously in charge since people moved when he spoke.

"Separate cars," the vice detective said and looked down at the suspects like they had an odor.

The cops quickly helped Dolla and Dyme to their feet and escorted them out of their club. He was placed in the back of one car and she in another. They looked at each other through the windows until the cars pulled away. He knew she knew enough not to give any statements but also there was no statements to give.

He was mostly legit and nothing was found in the club. His side business with Pop and Tommy was just that on the side. Nothing was sold or moved through the club. Dolla's head nodded at his decision to sue the Atlanta police department.

They arrived at the station and were quickly whisked into separate interrogation rooms. A divide and conquer tactic that fills prisons from coast to coast. The first one to snitch usually gets the best deal.

"Name?" the lead detective asked as he breezed into the room with Dolla. Dolla had the right to remain silent so he did. Especially since they took his wallet and knew good and damn well what his name was. The cop realized he wasn't speaking so he spoke up again. "How does someone with the name, Malik ibn Samir end up owning a strip club?"

Dolla had nothing to say since he definitely couldn't explain that. It was certainly on the opposite side of where he was heading when his parents were alive. Their death left him to the streets and this is what the streets turned him into. The detective still had another suspect to go so he wrapped up by reading out the list of pending charges. Dolla stared off at the wall until he heard why he was here.

"Wait, what? Back up. Prostittion? Sales of a control substance? Bruh, I run a clean joint. I ain't got none of that shit going on!" Dolla protested.

"That's not what I've heard. My confidential informants have been buying sx acts in your private rooms for weeks. They witnessed girls using drugs and even made purchases from them," he reported.

The veteran cop could tell from the look of pure, unfiltered confusion on Dolla's face that he genuinely had no knowledge of what was going on. The best actor couldn't pull off the shock registering on Dolla's face. The cop sat back and watched as Dolla mentally processed Dyme's recent inconsistencies and shopping trips.

"Well, let me go talk to miss Dyme Jackson," the cop sighed and stood. He moved slow so Dolla could stop him if he wanted. He could rat on his girl and help them make a case. That didn't happen though so he left the room and entered one a few doors down.

"A-yo. Why the fuck you got us down here? I know good and damn well y'all ain't found shit in the club!" Dyme pounced as soon as he entered the room. The cop took and seat and did her just like Dolla just did him. He flipped through the reports while she fussed and cussed. He waited for her to run out of steam before he began.

"Name?" he began as always. He only thought she ran out steam because the question set off another tirade that lasted another few minutes. Dyme finally realized she wasn't getting anywhere and calmed down.

"Dyme Jackson, and yes Dyme is my real name. My moms knew I was gonna grow up to be a bad bitch and named me accordingly," she spat.

"Dyme, are you going to drag your man down with you?" was all the detective wanted to know. He seen chicks take charges for their man more times than he could count but never the other way around.

"Down for what? What we going down for? Huh!" she demanded. He began to read out the charges and knocked the wind out of her sails. Just like Dolla she cut in when she heard a foreign charge. She knew about the prostition charges but, "Controlled substance? Ion know nothing about no drugs yo!"

"I said prsotition too," he reminded to point out her slip up. The interview was being filmed and it was a virtual confession. He laughed just like the cop did Kane in Menace To Society. "You know you fucked up, right?"

"Lawyer!" Dyme finally blurted. The magic word ended the interview and caused the cop to stand. He gathered his papers and exited the room without another word since it was being recorded.

*****

"Babe..." Dyme began when she and Dolla were seated together in the magistrate courtroom for a bond.

"Chill," he cut in since there were other people in ear shot. They could talk once they made bond and went home. Dyme didn't like being shushed and pouted until their names were called.

Both came up front and listened to the charges being read to the judge. The man scribbled and added while the cop laid out the infractions. He paused to add it up before he spoke.

"I'm setting bail at one hundred thousand dollars cash or bond. Next," he ordered without even looking up.

"We got that in the bank," Dolla said in relief. That didn't help much since it was the middle of the night. Not to mention they were going to jail, not the bank.

"I'll call Pop," Dyme said taking the words right out of his head. Dolla knew he had the stud sprung and she would gladly put up the ten percent to bail her boo out of jail.

"Bet," he agreed. There was a chance to sneak a kiss before they were separated again but he didn't move on it. Instead, they were taken back to the jail to be processed in.

"Got an hour before we dress you out," the cop said. If they couldn't make bond they would be taken upstairs and put in general population.

Dolla and Dyme sat in segregated cells with other people waiting on bond or a bed. He thought about using his free call to call Lil Pop but knew Dyme got through. He sat back and tried to tune out the loud mouths telling lies about their charges. Dudes claiming to be kingpins but got caught with a dime bag and couldn't make bond.

"Malik i, ib, ibna..." a cop struggled.

"Ibn Samir. Yeah!" Dolla said and raised his hand like it was roll call.

"You made bond. Let's ride," he said and let him out of the cell. Dolla followed the cop to the property window to reclaim what was taken from him. Once he collected his wallet watch and jewelry he was processed out of the jail.

"Sup with Dyme Jackson?" Dolla asked once the process was completed.

"She is upstairs. She ain't make bond," the lady cop shrugged. She popped the lock that separated him from his freedom. Dolla would have to find out what was going on from the other side. He rushed through the door into the waiting room and saw Lil Pop waiting.

"Hey," she greeted them giggled when he looked down at her exposed thighs under the tiny skirt.

"Hey. I gotta see what's up with Dyme. Ion know if she got a hold or..." he was saying until she jumped in and helped him.

"I ain't pay her bond," she explained. There was a terse silence while Dolla processed what just happened. On one hand he had to be grateful but on the other hand she got him completely fucked up if she thought he would sell Dyme out for her.

"A'ight yo. I'll hit the bank in the morning to get your bread back," Dolla said. He didn't need to tell her he would get enough out to bail his girl out too, since she already knew.

"I got something for you to hit tonight," she said and put some sway in her walk. It was enough to convince him to go to her home instead of his own. She passed him a ready rolled blunt when he got in her passenger seat. He lit it and leaned back to enjoy the ride. He was only in custody for a few hours but it was more than enough to know he'd rather be dead than be shackled.

*****

Dolla showed his gratitude when they arrived by kissing down Pop's body. For all the pussy Lil Pop ate she never had hers licked. Her whole body lifted off the bed as if his tongue were an exorcism. She began speaking in tongues when his tongue got to twirling on her love button.

"Man!" Pop protested when a strong orgsm wracked her body. Dolla didn't spare her though. He rushed up and shoved his dick deep down inside of her. He scooped her legs up and placed them on his shoulders.

Pop pleaded for mercy with her eyes but had none coming. Dolla got his footing right and commenced to fuck the daylights out of her. A puddle began to form under her as he splashed in and out of her. Dolla decided to skeet down her throat when the feeling began to build. She came again and contracted around his dick. That made it impossible to pull out so he pushed in and exploded on her cervx. They both struggled for breath for several minutes after the deed.

"What a day," Dolla sighed when he rolled out of Pop and on his back. She rushed to lay her head on his chest and cuddled up.

"I know daddy," she sighed and kissed his chest. He knew she had a rough day too since she lost her money and friend. "I don't even know why Dyme was doing that. I gave her bread err time she came over."

"Yo, she wasn't letting them broads sell pussy or dope up in the club!" Dolla protested in Dyme's defense.

"Ion know nothing about no dope but man, them broads were slinging ass left and right. That Mzladi swallowed so much come in that VIP room she pee seman! And yeah Dyme was down with the lick. She charged them broads two hundred bucks to use the room," she snitched. The room grew quiet while Dolla added that info to the inconsistencies he witnessed.

He knew she was telling the truth but didn't want to talk about it anymore. Instead he gave a head a gentle push to make his request. Pop said 'yes' by kissing down his chest and stomach. His dick was laying on his navel and took it in her mouth. The combination of tongue, cheeks, and lips made him nice and hard once more. Dawn crept on the horizon while she climbed aboard and worked the dick inside of her. The sun rose by the time they finished fucking and fell fast asleep. Dyme would have to wait until later when he woke up and got down to the bank. Lil Pop slept on his chest instead of Dyme.

Chapter Thirty-two

"The fuck?" Dyme demanded when she awoke the next morning. She only went to sleep because she was dog tired from the long day. The thin mattress on the metal slab woke her before the five am breakfast call.

The diva turned her nose up and the cold oatmeal and warm milk. She was hungry enough to take a nibble on what the other inmates were calling a biscuit. It wasn't edible so she gave it to another woman to eat. The crack addict hadn't ate in days and quickly devoured it.

Dyme tried the payphone but neither she or Dolla had collect calls on their cell phones. She stared out the narrow window looking for Dolla to pull up to the jail. An hour passed before she gave up and tried something else. She'd seen several girls use the intercom near the door so she went over and pressed the button.

"What!" the female guard in the booth snapped when Dyme kept pressing the buzzer. She had hoped ignoring her would make her give up but it didn't.

"Yeah um, my name is Dyme, Jackson? I'm not supposed to be in here," she said and felt silly. "I mean, we 'sposed to made bail last night."

"We?" the woman asked curiously. She could tell by Dyme's speech and appearance she wasn't one of their regular addicts or hookers.

"Yes. My friend said she was coming last night to bail me and my man out. His name is Malik Ibn Samir,"

"Spell it?" she said as she began to type. "Sis, he was bailed out last night."

"What? By who?" Dyme asked in confusion. A girl fight in another dorm ended the conversation. The officer called a code that summoned more officers to break up the combatants.

All Dyme could do now was pace, fuss, and pace some more. She tried the phone a few more times but got nowhere with that. A few hours later lunch was served. The fussy diva was too hungry to turn her nose up at lunch. She scarfed down the two bologna sandwiches and child sized juice pack. Then it was more fussing and pacing. Pacing, fussing and watching the clock.

A million scenarios ran through her mind as to why she was still there. Why would Pop bail Dolla out and leave her behind? It crossed her mind that maybe they were fucking but she quickly shook the thought off.

"Nah! Imagine that!" Dyme laughed at the ludicrous thought of Dolla fucking the stud. Even though that was exactly what he was doing at that exact moment.

*****

"Get that pussy!" Lil Pop shouted behind herself. Dolla had her face down, ass up like a whole woman. He was filling up her whole box with good dick that had her rethinking her whole life.

"Oh I got it," he assured her and leaned back to watch the spectacular show her vagina was putting on. Once it coated his thick dick with that good cream he knew the end was near. A few strokes later he seized and pumped her box full once more.

"You should stay here. With me," Lil Pop heard someone say. That same person squeezed their tight vagina even tighter so he couldn't get away. "That quarter million I just lost ain't shit. I got double that put up."

"I love my girl" Dolla sighed even though he realized how much things had changed so quickly.

"Well you gonna have a side chick then cuz I ain't going nowhere!" Pop declared. Dolla chuckled at her determination but didn't say 'no' either. Mention of Dyme made him glance over at the clock.

"fuck!" he fussed when he saw the time. He had an hour to get to the bank to get the money to get her out. "Yo, I need a ride to my car!"

"A'ight shawty," Pop groaned. She really didn't want to be a part of helping Dyme get out since he would be with her. Still, she was sprung and would do almost anything she could to help him.

They could not ignore the sxual secretions on their bodies and had to jump into the shower together. Dolla did ignore the rock hard erction he got watching Pop lather that fine frame. She laughed at it and patted his dick on it's head.

"Poor baby want some more Leticia," she said and gave it a kiss. She knew he had to go and didn't make it any harder. They hopped out and dried off to get dressed to leave.

The ride down to the club was made in silence save the babble on the radio. Dolla felt his heart sink when they reached the club and saw the police tape surrounding his business. A heavy police padlock and chain sealed it from him getting inside.

"They doing way too much!" Pop grumbled hotly. Ironically Dolla patted her hand to comfort her. He leaned over and planted a kiss on her thick lips as he pulled the door handle.

"I'll see, you later," he said to emphasize the fact that he would be back. She giggled and gushed and waited until he got in and started his car. Dolla whipped over to the bank to retrieve ten thousand dollars to pay the bondsman. It was almost two in the afternoon when he reached the counter.

"Good afternoon," the pretty teller told him when he placed the withdrawal slip on the counter.

"I know its after noon," he snapped as if she were chiding him about being late. He needed to be mad at his damn self for spending all morning sxing the sxy stud. Well, former stud because Pop was headed to the mall to buy some more clothing. Dresses, Capri pants, bras, panties and sandals.

"Um? Are you sure this is the right account number?" she asked after trying again and getting the same results.

"Yeah. Dimes LLC," he said and double checked what he wrote. He pushed it back and she entered the numbers once more to appease him.

"Sir, that account has been closed," she informed him. The resulting uproar brought the rental cop running.

"What's the problem sir?" the manager asked when he joined the chaos.

"The problem is she talking 'bout my account is closed! I got a huned racks in that account. I need my bread!" Dolla demanded. He envisioned himself coming back with his gun and taking all the money out of the safe.

"Come over to my office and we'll get to the bottom of this," the manager said and waved the security guard off. Dolla relaxed and followed him over. They took seats on opposite sides of the stately desk and the manager tapped the account number into his computer.

"I bought the club a couple months ago. Been making deposits every day," Dolla explained.

"You used the existing account? You didn't open a new one, or get added to it?" he asked incredibly.

"Um, naw," Dolla croaked as it started to make sense. Ant was so eager to have him keep the account open. Too eager. He even left a few grand in to lure him in. "Who name is on it?"

"I can't give you that information," he said. There was a tense few seconds while Dolla contemplated coming over the desk and beating the info out of him. He felt and and reached for the alarm under his desk.

"A'ight yo," he decided. He knew he could get it out one of the tellers anyway if he had to pay them, feed them or fuck them. Whatever was necessary to find out who had his money.

*****

"What's the emergency, shawty?" Tommy asked when he met Dolla at their usual spot.

"Need to get that bread from you real quick," he said and noticed the brand new Charger on shiny new rims. The new drip dangling from his neck didn't go unnoticed either.

"Fifteen bands," Tommy said as he counted out the money from an even larger roll.

Dolla frowned in confusion, wondering how his worker had more money than he did. He and Dyme had only two thousand dollars in the apartment and nothing in the fridge. Pop's pussy was the only thing he had eaten all day.

"A'ight son. I'll send Desire with some more work later," he said and pulled away with the money.

Dolla dipped across town and pulled to a stop at the jail. The bonding companies were set up across the street so he went in the same one that sighed his bond.

"Yo, I need to post bond for my girl," he announced.

"Didn't we just bond you out?" the worker asked. Dolla confirmed it was, and was charged fifteen percent instead of the normal ten percent. He was back down to those same two grand when he went over to wait in the jail waiting room. His mind drifted between many things while he waited. Getting into jail is a much quicker process than getting out. Dolla eased into a slumber until he heard Dyme raising hll as she came through the door.

"The fuck yo! How you leave me in here all damn day with these damn crack heads! Yo, you know what they feed you in there! Bruh, sup with Pop? How she gone bond you out and leave me? Y'all fucking or something? Huh! And what the police..."

Dolla let her rant and rage without saying a word in reply. He had plenty questions of his own to ask so he let her get her shit off before he did. They were halfway home when Dyme finally looked directly at him and took note of the look on his face. A look she had yet to see since they met. Then again they had only been together less than a year. There was plenty they still didn't know about each other.

"What's wrong babes?" she finally asked softly. Dolla exhaled on filled her in on everything except sx with Pop. They were inside their bedroom by the time he finished.

"Awe man!" Dyme moaned. She ran through another series of questions. Dolla still had some of his own but the doorbell put them on pause.

"That's the food," he said and walked out of the room. Dyme was hungry too but still rushed under the shower to wash the county jail away. She returned wrapped in a towel and found Dolla eating a sandwich. He pushed hers toward her without a word.

A few hours they awoke in the same places they fell asleep. Dyme knew she was in trouble and tried to soften the blow with a blow job. Dolla twisted his lips into a 'yeah right' as she worked his dick out of his pants. They locked eyes while she gave it a few loving licks. His eyes closed when it slipped into her mouth.

Dyme worked her neck and head hoping to get him off. She was too selfish to ignore the throbbing between her legs so she tugged his pants down and mounted him.

Dolla felt guilty about comparing her box to Pop's and shook his head to clear the thought. Despite going all morning with Pop he felt the sensation creeping up his legs. He would usually hold out and wait for her but she wasn't his favorite person right now. Instead he grabbed her hips and slammed himself up and in and out until he exploded.

"Awe man!" Dyme pouted in frustration at not getting off. She rolled off and pouted some more but didn't have any sympathy coming from him.

"Yo, you let them chicks sell pussy in the club? Drugs?" he demanded. Dolla leaned up for eye contact like a human lie detector. "Ion know nothing about no drugs!" she vowed and crossed her heart.

"But the pussy huh?" he asked and pursed his lips. The thought had actually crossed his mind to send her home to Brooklyn and stay down here with Pop.

"Yeah, I did," she admitted softly. "The money yo. The money got me fucked up. You don't know what it's like to grow up with nothing! Sitting on that damn stoop all damn day. Yo bitxhes died on that same stoop! All I keep thinking is I don't wanna die on that stoop. Spend my whole life there and die there!" she whinded broke all the way down.

Dolla twisted his lips again since that had nothing to do with her crossing him behind his back and letting girls trick in the club. Her heart wrenching sobs got to him though so he wrapped her up in his arm. The embrace only made her cry louder and harder.

Dolla felt her though because chicks did die on that same stoop. Murdr, overdose, diabetes and heart attack. Dudes didn't fare much better in those Brooklyn streets and he vowed to never return either. He would get rich or die trying, anywhere but there.

Chapter Thirty-three

"So what we gone do now?" Dyme asked when they next awoke.

Dolla pressed his lips together to keep his first thought from entering the room. She had gotten them in all this mess and now asking him how they were going to get out of it. The rent was due and would eat up fifteen hundred of the two thousand they had left.

"We'll figure out something," he guessed while the wheels turned in his head. He assumed Pop would front him some work so he could keep that money coming in. It was plenty to live on until he could get the club open again.

"We need to find out who name was on that account," she reminded. Partly because they did and partly to remind him that he fucked up too.

"Yeah. Anyway..." he said since he wasn't trying to hear that. "I need to go holla at Pop about some work."

"And I noticed you ain't say for me to come?" Dyme quipped even though she still didn't entertain the thought that they might really be fucking. Why would she when she had been creeping with the stud herself.

"Do you, really want to question me, about that chick?" he asked in a tone that said he knew all about her lsbin tryst in exchange for shopping excursions. Knew all about her getting high off the pills. "Matter fact, you should come. So we can all talk?"

"Naw, I'm good. I need to see Desire. If some chicks was moving something in the club, she would know," Dyme deflected. "But, we still need to rob Lil Pop ass!"

"She ain't got no bread yo. Leave her alone. Just stay away from her. I mean it, don't say nothing to her," he said over his shoulder and headed out. Dyme pondered for a few minutes over his change in plans. She shrugged it off and got dressed to meet up with Desire.

"Hey now!" Dyme cheered when she found a few pills and a few hundred dollars when she changed designer purses. Common sense shouted for her to flush the pills and give the money to Dolla. The devil had other plans and whispered them into her ear. Dyme popped the pills and told Desire to meet her at the mall.

*****

"Girl what happened at the club!" Desire asked when she and Dyme met in the mall food court. She had heard second hand info from a stripper who happened to be turning a last minute trick in the parking lot. But wanted the whole scoop from the source.

"That's what I'm tryna find out. Girl I had to spend a night in jail. A bitch need some food!" Dyme proclaimed. She knew it would better to let the chatty girl chat and see what she knew. She knew Desire knew something when she offered to pay for the meal.

"I got you shawty!" Desire cheered and whipped out a roll of cash. Not a stripper roll consisting on mainly ones. This was mainly twenties, tens and fives.

"Someone had a good night?" Dyme asked and leaned back for the barrage of info she knew would follow.

"My man Tommy broke me off," she said nonchalantly with her belly and box filled with his seeds.

"Oh, he yo man now?" Dyme laughed and listened.

"That boy showed me two hundred and fifty racks the other night! We had sx on it then spent almost half of it the next day. He bought a brand new Charger, put rims on it, bought some drip, some purp, some..." she rattled. Dyme pressed pause and backed up in her mind.

"You said two hundred and fifty thousand?" she said and keyed in on the magic number.

"Mmhm. We counted it a couple times!" she cheered as Dyme put two and two together. She had the girl in the car with her once when it was her turn to keep an eye on Lil Pop's safe house. She remembered talking about the lick with the girl since she got chatty herself when she got high. "Girl he said he robbed somebody..."

"Hmph?" Dyme huffed since that mystery was solved. She couldn't wait to get home and tell Dolla. Then she thought about what he would do to her. It was more her fault for telling Desire than it was Desire's fault for telling Tommy. She knew what had to be done and they had to move quick before Tommy spent the rest of the money.

"What's wrong sis?" Desire asked when she felt the sudden drop in temperature from across the table.

"MmMm," Dyme grunted and filled her mouth with more food. They ate in silence until their plates were clean. "Yo I need you to help me with something?"

"Anything for you sis!" she cheered and jumped to her feet. The shopping trip was abandoned as she followed Dyme out to the parking lot.

"Un-uh. Follow me," she said when Desire reached for her passenger door.

"Um, OK," she said and hopped behind her own wheel. She had to mash the gas to keep up as Dyme whipped out of the parking lot. She followed closely as Dyme drove aimlessly through town until she reached the hood.

Dyme found a building that looked suitable and pulled in. Once Desire pulled in behind her she drove around to the back.

"What is this girl up to?" Desire wondered when Dyme hopped out digging in her purse. Dyme mumbled to herself as she approached still looking through the purse. Desire rolled her window down when she arrived just as she found what she was looking for.

Dyme pulled a pstl and promptly shot Desire right in her smile. That sent her off to the upper room but Dyme pumped a few more slugs her way for good measure. She turned to walk away then turned back and fired one more into her weave.

"That's for sucking my man dick!" she griped and stormed off still fussing. "Since when asking a chick to watch yo man mean give him head! Where they do that!"

*****

"Man you can get whatever you want! I already told you what's up!" Pop replied emphatically to Dolla's request to front him some coke.

"And I told you I can't just bounce on my girl," he sighed. Dyme violated on several levels but his own stubborn loyalty wouldn't allow him to pull the plug. Things had changed enough to accept her as a side chick and Dyme would just have to deal with it. That meant not telling her because he knew good and well how she would deal with it.

"Well, you still my man!" Pop shot back defensively. Dirty dudes had dogged her into being one but Dolla made her feel like a woman. More woman than ever before in her life.

"I am. Now let's get this money!" Dolla cheered. There was no time to make love so they just made out. She gave him what he came for and it was time to go.

"Hmph!" Pop huffed when she looked down at her buzzing phone. "Yo other girl."

"Yo, stay away from Dyme. Me and you gonna do our thing but, don't deal with her anymore. No matter what she say!" Dolla warned.

"I ain't, but shoot she don't want these hands!" Pop proclaimed.

"Nah, she don't," he agreed but only because he knew Dyme didn't do hands. She would put a slug in her melon and be done with it. They made out some more and she gripped his wood through the jeans.

"When you gonna brang this back into my life?" she purred. She wasn't letting it go until he gave her an answer.

"Tomorrow!" he promised and pulled away. Dolla accepted that he now had two girls and he was cool with it. They traded a little more saliva before he pulled away and went to his car.

He got the answer to his unanswered question as to why was Dyme calling Pop when he saw all the missed on his own phone. No sooner did it register then his phone buzzed again from her call.

"Yo," he drawled and started the car.

"Yo? Did you say, yo? Yo, like I ain't just called you a hundred damn times!" Dyme snapped.

"It ain't been no hundred ti..." Dolla was saying as he checked his call log. He indeed had a hundred missed calls in the last few minutes. "Sup?"

"Sup? Bruh, did you 'sup' me?" she spat. He saw how worked up Dyme was and softened his tone.

"Yo, I just got the work from Pop. I'ma meet up with Tommy and..."

"No! Come! Home! Right! Now!" she demanded. She was more than just worked up so he agreed and steered the whip towards home.

Chapter Thirty-four

"Yo, I was..." Dolla explained as he entered but Dyme slammed into him with a hug that knocked the wind out of him. He wrapped his arms around her and walked her over to the sofa.

Dyme rocked and moaned, sobbed and slobbered on his shoulder for a half hour before she even tried to speak. It wasn't quite English though so it took several more minutes before she could get it out.

"I had to. I had to kill her," Dyme moaned.

"Yeah you did. She tried to set you up!" Dolla said. He assumed she was talking about her aunt Lynn and she certainly did have to kill her.

"I did," she agreed. Now he would never find out that she was partly responsible for Tommy getting the info that cost them a quarter million dollars. "I found out who robbed Pop's spot."

"Who?" Dolla growled and stood to go get his guns. Whoever it was wouldn't get to spend another dime of it.

"Tommy! Desire said he said he hit a lick! Said he showed her two hundred and fifty grand!" she told.

"Get her over here! I need to pick her brain," Dolla said. He had no way of knowing that the coroner had to pick her brain up from the front seat of her car.

"Um, I already did. We need to get over to his spot before he spend all the dough!" she urged. She was already dressed and had their bag packed to do the deed.

"Sht he already spent at least half of it!" Dolla said as he added up the new car, rims and jewels he saw Tommy with earlier. They were all the proof he needed.

They marched out to their main car and drove over to the hooptie they kept for missions like this. It was like the good old days as they rode in deadly silence to catch a lick. Even though the money they were going to take back didn't really belong to them in the first place.

"He here," Dolla said when he saw Tommy's old and new cars sitting in front of the apartment. There was a few people out and about but there was no time to wait for the coast to clear totally. For all they knew dude was shopping online from his new computer and spending more of the money.

"I'll go 'round back," Dyme suggested and got out. She went around the building to come in the backside while he sauntered in the front.

Dolla and Dyme met at his front door and leaned in to listen. Neither could hear anything over the bump of the new stereo. That was enough and Dolla used his size twelve key to enter. Splinters flew as the cheap door caved in.

Mzladi was in such a zone sucking his dick on the sofa that it took several more bobs of her weave before it registered. She looked up and squinted at her bosses then frowned at the guns in their hands.

"Really bruh?" Tommy asked and raised his hands. Dolla followed his eyes down to the plastic pstl on the coffee table. He gave a nod and Dyme rushed over to collect it.

"This shit brand new!" she said inspecting the gun. Dolla shook his head at another eight hundred dollars gone from the lick.

"How you finna rob me when I'm getting the work from you?" Tommy wanted to know since he didn't connect the dots to him robbing Pop's safe house.

"Robbing you? You 'sposed to be robbing them!" Mzladi shrieked. She reached for her purse and stood to leave. "You doing the most! I'm finna go!"

"bitch if you don't sit yo ass down!" Dyme demanded. "You gone go a'ight, but not where you think!"

"Yo, I need that money you took from Marietta. That two fifty," Dolla announced. The look of surprise was genuine but he quickly figured where they got the info from.

"Damn Desire! Lil bitch got some fiyah head but that's the only time she ain't talking. Bet she ain't tell you she was pushing work through yo club huh? Bet she ain't tell dat!" he fussed.

"Un-uh! Yo good telling ass telling it all!" Mzladi spat in disgust at his dry snitching.

"I ain't tell them about all that pussy you was slinging in the VIP did I?" he shot back.

"Ya did now!" she snapped. There was no telling how long they would have gone back and forth had Dolla not intervened.

"The bread nigga! Where the bread at!" he barked from behind his gun, looking like a man talking into a bullhorn.

"Bruh, I done spent most of it," Tommy admitted with a sigh. "I ain't never had no money like that and lost my mind!"

Dolla cast a glance over at his woman who experienced the same thing. He should have shot one into the mirror too since he was guilty of the same thing. Dyme took off into the bedroom and looked for what was left. She collected a few bundles of cash, some jewelry and a piece of paper worth seventy grand.

"Here!" Dyme said and shoved the paper in his face. Dolla nodded in approval when he saw what it was.

"Sign it!" he demanded and watched as Tommy signed over the vehicle. He turned to Dyme who was counting the cash.

"Fifty eight," she moaned. Ordinarily fifty grand would have been a pretty sweet lick. But knowing it was two hundred and fifty just days ago threatened to push a tear from her eyes.

"Bruh how the fuck you spent two hundred grand in a few days?" Dolla asked dropping his gun to his side. It was as good a chance as Tommy had coming so he took it.

He was a jack boy himself and knew how these things go. Not a single one of his victims lived to tell when he came through. He made a move but his pants were down from the blow j he was receiving when Dolla and Dyme barged in.

Dolla didn't even raise his gun. Instead he turned and watched Dyme pump one into his forehead. Mzladi began to scream but a bullet sped into her open mouth and shut her up. They quickly collected what was left of what they came for so they could get up out of there.

Dolla had the grim task of retrieving the car keys from his pocket. It came with a bonus of a thousand in cash and some really, really, good weed in his pocket.

They rushed out with their guns out just in case there were any heroes around. There wasn't so they hopped in his car and took off. The tension between the two subsided a little when they made a clean getaway.

"Another sweet lick! Get rich..." Dolla began and paused so Dyme could finish.

"Or die trying!" she added.

*****

"You really think this will help?" Dyme asked when Dolla pulled to the law offices on Howard Stein.

"Chanel said he was the best in town. If we gonna get the club open and get theses charges off we gonna need the best!" he declared.

Dyme had come clean about killing Desire but left out the why. All Dolla cared about was the case died with her. The confidential informants had bought from Desire so they could go dig her up if they wanted to press those charges.

"Well, let's get it," then she sighed and opened her door. The early morning sx had them feeling closer than they had in the months since the shit hit the fan. They actually held hands when they went inside.

"Have a seat," Stein offered and pointed to the burgundy leather chairs facing his desk. His due diligence had all the files laid out in front of him.

"So, how we looking?" Dolla asked once they were seated. They still held hands from across separate chairs.

"Depends. Depends on how much your trying to spend. The drug case is moot but the pandering and solicitation charges are solid. Too many witnesses," he explained candidly.

"What will fifty thousand do?" Dolla said and placed the stacks of cash on his desk.

"That will get her five years. Maybe four and some probation," he replied. "The case and witnesses are all against Miss Jackson."

"Ion wanna do no four years!" Dyme cried, real tears. She looked between the two men to see who could save her.

"It'll cost twice this to keep you out of jail. Fines, probation, community service, but no prison," Stein stated.

"Run it! We'll get it up and get back to you!" Dyme cheered.

Dolla squinted at her since he had no clue how they could come up with another fifty grand. Pop was breaking him off decent enough to pay the bills from helping her with her operations. Plus making her come several times a week, but he wouldn't even try to hit her up for fifty grand.

"I'll need the money in a week. Two weeks tops!" Stein advised. They stood, shook and headed out of the office. Neither spoke until their seatbelts were buckled.

"Where we supposed to get fifty bands from? In a week?" Dolla wanted to know. He turned and cocked his head curiously for a reply.

"You said Pop is rolling. Let's rob her manly ass!" she suggested. Dolla shook his head for several reasons.

First off, Dyme hadn't seen Pop in months. There was absolutely nothing manly about Leticia now. All she wore was sexy skirts and dresses with matching bra and panty sets. Plus she was getting thicker by the day.

"I'm not robbing her," he said so firmly she left it alone. She couldn't help but wonder why but didn't have time to dwell on it. A week wasn't a long time and they needed to do something and quick.

"The Hoe-down! I'll slide up in there and find us a baller to rob!" She cheered and cheesed at her bright idea. Meanwhile Dolla reflected back to his youth as he often did in times of turmoil. (italics)

'Whoever stops asking people for things Allah will make them content. Whoever seeks to be self sufficient Allah will make them self sufficient. And whoever seeks to be patient, Allah will make them patient. None can be given a better gift than patience' (end italics)

The advice from his father was over his head back then but made sense now. Except he was too far gone now.

Four years isn't a very long time for something she did. This was on her but now he had to suffer from it. The pretty girl in the passenger seat was becoming more and more work. Almost too much work in comparison to Leticia.

Dolla and Pop could hang out, laugh, play video games and fuck each others brains out. Dyme was always fussy, moody lately. Now, they had to find another lick and quick.

*****

"Wish me luck," Dyme sighed as they pulled up to the Hoe-down strip club.

"Yeah," Dolla said. He didn't believe in luck and his heart wasn't with it. They got out and went in for her audition to join the elite dancers who danced for the cities major players.

Both of their eyes went wide when they stepped inside the swank establishment. The name Hoe-down was symbolic of the country and western theme instead of just being full of hoes. It was full of hoes but that's another story for another book.

"Can I help you?" a rather large bouncer asked. He sounded professional but poised for the bullshit if need be.

"I'm here to audition to dance," Dyme explained but noticed he was actually talking to Dolla. "This my boyfriend. He came with me."

"There's a no boyfriend policy here. Too many problems," he explained even though he didn't have to.

"I'll be right outside," Dolla puffed up and said. The bouncer cracked a slight smirk. Dolla wanted to pull Dyme out and find another way to get the money.

"I'm OK baby. I'll dance real quick and be right out," she assured him. The bouncer's smirk grew a little more.

"A'ight yo," Dolla relented and retreated. He hopped back in the car and pulled his phone. A swipe and couple taps later and Pop popped up on his screen.

"Sup daddy! You just in time!" she sang happily. Dolla was always amazed how not a trace of masculinity remained in the former stud. His curved dick actually fucked her straight again.

"In time for what?" Dolla smiled at her enthusiastic greeting.

"I was just about to play in this pussy ," she said and pointed her phone between her legs to show what pussy she was talking about.

"Yay!" Dolla laughed and settled back for the show. He adjusted his pants to accommodate the instant erection that popped up. Inside Dyme was dealing with an erection of her own.

"I'm good!" a sultry woman fussed as she stormed out of Newberry's office.

"Oh boy!" Dyme said to herself, knowing some bull sh was behind door number one.

"Next!" the owner said as he stuck his large head out of the door. Dyme was next in line and stood to go inside.

"Hi, I'm Dyme. I'm here to dance!" she greeted firmly as she stepped inside. She looked around the room and realized she was indeed in the big leagues. The office was decorated in expensive furnishings with pictures of the owner with A list celebrities adorned the wall. This was what they were looking for.

"Dancing is just part of what we do here. My customers come for a discrete, clean, sensual experience," he explained. Dyme blinked in confusion so he expounded. "My customers are rich, mostly married men. They spend good money to have a good time."

"And I'm here to dance for them," she shot back. Dyme wasn't that slow and picked up what he was putting down. She clutched her purse and prepared to leave.

"Yeah but men like head. Can you give head? Huh? You probably sucking your broke boyfriend's dick so how about some millionaire dick?" he demanded.

Newberry was used to getting told off and cursed out but didn't mind one bit. His club stayed filled and that filled his bank accounts. There was a line of females down to do what other females didn't or wouldn't do.

Dyme had a week to get this money up and it took four days to get the audition. She sat her purse on the desk and came around to Newberry. She kneeled in front of him and submitted to his desires.

"You, young lady," Newberry grunted as Dyme pleased him. "Have a job!"

Dyme stopped by the ladies rooms after she earned her spot in the club. Most new dancers did after auditioning so they could rinse his seeds from the mouths. That's why Dyme was there but she also had to cry her eyes out, then fixed her face back. It killed her to betray her man again but the way she came up she was used to putting herself above and beyond anyone else.

"You want me to go again?" Pop asked as she recovered from a second nut. Dolla's head began to nod until he saw Dyme exit the club.

"Save it. I'll be over in a couple hours," he said and clicked off. He had taken Peppa's position and helped her move her product. It was good for a couple of grand but not enough or quick enough to pay the lawyer.

"Hey," Dyme sighed as she plopped on the passenger seat. Dolla mistook her melancholy and offered condolences.

"Don't worry. We'll find something," she said and patted her hand.

"I got the job. I'm in," she corrected. She did what had to do and got the job. Now all she had to do was find a baller to rob.

Chapter Thirty-five

"You good?" Dolla asked when he pulled back to the Hoe-down later that same night for her shift.

"Un huh," she said, keeping her head turned. She had been avoiding him all day, hoping he wouldn't try to kiss her. She had brushed, flossed, rinsed and brushed again but still didn't want to kiss him after sucking the next man's dick. Luckily for her he kept his distance. Shd didn't notice he had become more distant by the day.

"A'ight yo. I'm going to shoot out here and holla at Pop," he said. It secretly amused him not to have to lie about where he was going since she would never guess he was doing what he was doing.

"Tell dude I said what's up," Dyme teased and hopped out. Dolla didn't even bother to wait for her to go inside before he pulled off.

Dolla tried to tune out his fathers voice and advice as he drove out to the suburbs. He was fucking up and he knew it. He was stuck on a speeding Merry go round and couldn't figure out how to get off. At least he knew he had to get off, and that was half the battle.

"Hmph?" Dolla huffed at the feeling he felt when he pulled into Pop's driveway. A peace he didn't feel at home. The front door swung open wide as he approached.

"Hey!" Pop cheered like a little girl when her daddy comes home. Come to find out grown women feel the same way when daddy comes home.

"Dm!" Dolla said at the changes in her figure. "You getting thick!"

"You did it!" she giggled and tippy toed up for a kiss. "You gone tell miss thang?"

"Yeah, I guess I'ma have to," Dolla sighed. He knew he would one day have to tell Dyme about this new development.

"Mmhm," she hummed since she didn't believe him. She wouldn't nag though since she used deal with chicks too and couldn't stand a nagging broad. If she couldn't stand a nagging broad she certainly wouldn't be one.

Instead she took him into the dining room and fed him. Once he was full she took him upstairs and fucked him. Once he was satisfied she washed him off and they set out to handle some sales. Meanwhile Dyme was starting her first night in the new club.

*****

"Silly ass costume!" Dyme grumbled as she inspected herself in the cowgirl outfit. She turned to the side and shook her head at her ass cheeks hanging out the back of the leather chaps.

"Not you!" a dancer sang in happy disbelief when she saw Dyme in the dressing room. A lot had to happen for the diva to end up here with her. Especially since she knew what it took just to get in the dressing room of the Hoe-down.

"Sup Amy," Dyme sighed. She almost wished she had been nicer to the girl since she was in the position as her.

"You and Dolla must have broke up?" she demanded as if she had a right to inquire about their relationship.

"Naw. We good as gold!" she shot back and almost got fired on her first day since she was ready to fight.

"Is there a problem here?" the manager asked when she came over.

"No," both sang like sisters answering a parent. The point was made so the woman wandered off to run the club.

"I guess he couldn't mind you sucking Newberry dick since you gone be sucking so much dick in this club," Amy teased. She saw she touched a nerve and backed off a bit. "Don't worry girl it's worth it. It's so much money in this joint! Dudes dropping grands on few dances!"

"Good, cuz I need it!" Dyme admitted. What she wouldn't admit is that she would do anything to stay out of jail. "Where them ballers at!"

"Come on!" Amy said and led her out into the club. Dyme quickly found out she was right when she made a hundred dollars for one song. The rich white men chatted about a business deal and barely paid attention to her.

They were rich but not the type to keep am cache of cash in their house. The real wealthy keep their money in banks and bonds. Not duffle bags and mattresses.

"Yup! There you are!" Dyme sang when she spotted a potential mark. The handsome black man wore brilliant diamonds around his neck and hands. The good shit that flashed blue and white in the strobing lights.

"That's Adam. He from New York. He be spending good but don't be tricking," Amy explained when she saw Dyme staring at the man.

"That's only because he ain't seen the right treat!" Dyme said and sashayed her fine ass over to him. The man alternated his glance between his phone and the large silicone booty bouncing in front of him. The white girl worked it like a black girl but he was only moderately impressed. His mind was on his money and his money was on his phone. The next time he looked up he saw Dyme looking back at him.

"Excuse me!" he said loud enough to be heard over the music and as if his table wasn't occupied with a dancer.

"Hey," Dyme greeted with a soft smile and wave and pretended to keep going. She took another step while thinking, 'wait for it...'

"You're new?" he asked, proving he was a regular. He was and according to Amy he never took the dancers home with him. Dyme came up with the idea to take him home instead. She had to move quick so she and Dolla could rob him and pay the lawyer. He looked even more expensive up close.

"I just started today. I go to school down here," she explained and made sure to stress her up top accent.

"Brooklyn!" he nodded and pursed his lips like he dared her to deny it. All New Yorkers may sound alike to foreigners, but can identify each others distinct dialects indicative of their borough.

"Un-huh. Mr Manhattan!" she grimaced like the borough stunk. It didn't, that's Queens but it broke the ice.

"Come sit we me," he invited and pointed back towards his table.

"Um..." Dyme laughed at the girl dancing for no one at the table. He laughed too and shooed her away with one of the hundreds from the hundreds of hundreds he had in his pocket. Dyme smiled even harder since he was definitely the one.

"I'm Adam," he greeted and raised a hand for the waitress.

"Dyme and yes that's what my mom named me," Dyme replied. She didn't mind sitting and talking since it paid by the song just like dancing. Not to mention talking allowed her to peep who he was and what he was sitting on, that much quicker. So, talk they did.

"Last song!" the DJ announced and the last minute deals began.

"Wow! How long have we been talking!" Adam asked and checked his neglected phone.

"Time flies when you're having fun!" Dyme sang as he broke her off for her time. It sounded genuine because it actually was. She paused for him to invite her home with him but he stood instead.

"Well, it really was nice talking to you," he said.

"Let me buy you breakfast?" Dyme blurted before he could get away.

"Buy me, breakfast!" he repeated like he was shocked. It was a first since chicks usually wanted something out of him.

"You eat don't you?" she asked and giggled at her double entendre.

"Yeah I do once I know it's mine!" he said and peered into her eyes. He thought for a second and nodded his head. "Since this is your first night and all."

"Play my cards right and it could be my last," she purred. "Let me go change!"

"Nah, don't change," Adam said to himself as he watched her nasty walk, walk away. He may have frequented the strip clubs but didn't date the dancers. It being her first night meant he could break his own rule.

"Yo, where you at!" Dyme blurted desperately when Dolla took her call.

"Chill ma. I'm out here," he sighed. It took all he had to climb out of Pop's warm bed and come all the way downtown at two am.

"Fall back yo. I got a baller in my sights. We going to breakfast," she whispered so none of the other girls would hear her.

"A'ight. I'll follow and keep an eye," he said and clicked off. As soon as he did he went back to texting back and forth with Pop.

Dolla frowned when he saw how cozy Dyme looked with dude when they came out of the club. It was pretty hypocritical of him after all the things he and Leticia just did. He felt a little better when he led her to a brand spanking new Bentley. The diamonds on his body threatened to make sunrise come a little early by the way they twinkled in the moon light. Son was obviously caked up and Dolla wanted a slice.

*****

"So what your boyfriend working with?" Dolla grumbled when they awoke the next morning.

He had sat outside the diner where Dyme and Adam chatted over breakfast until the sun had risen. he dropped her off at the apartment and went home. He dropped her off at the apartment and went home. They didn't speak two words when she came in and crawled into bed.

"I could ask you the same thing about pop!" she shot back and snickered.

"Say what you want about her. I brought home two grand for a couple hours work!" he laughed.

"Same amount I brought home,!" she shot back. It had turned into a competition and escaped them both that the $4,000 they made in one day could have easily helped pay the lawyer off.

"Anyway..." he said so she would get on with it.

"Dude is a concert promoter and manager! He works with all the stars!" she said with stars in her eyes. According to her he was collecting major cash from the venues.

"Where he keeping the bread?" Dolla asked with those same stars in his eyes.

"Ion know yet. I ain't been to his crib. Don't even know where he stay yet. I'ma need a couple days," she said.

"All we got is a couple of days," he reminded and stood. sripped to hit the shower but didn't invite her. Nor did she ask to come.

Dolla's phone buzzed when he got under the steamy water. Dyme never worried about other chicks but still checked the phone because she was a chick and that's just what chicks do. She wouldn't have answered it had it been anyone else.

"Sup my dude," Dyme teased when she took her call.

"Dyme?" Pop asked in confusion.

"Who else gone be answering my man phone!" she flaunted.

"I um, we supposed to..." Pop stammered from getting caught off guard. She hadn't spoke to Dyme since their last hook up and couldn't understand why she was being catty.

"Guess yall gonna play some ball or bag some hoes. I'll tell him you called homeboy," Dyme said and hung up.

"Who was that?" Dolla asked when he returned. He dropped the towel and she no longer spoke English.

"Huh?" she she asked while watching the swinging pendulum

"My phone? Who was on it?" he asked and ended the dick display by pulling his boxers on.

"Oh, ya boy Pop," she said casually.

"What you said to her!" Dolla snapped, then cleaned it up. "You know we eating off her right now."

"Chill I ain't hurt your boy feelings," she shot back. They r dressed and departed to go their separate ways. He drove out to see Pop while she took an Uber to meet Adam. It wasn't the end but close to it.

Chapter Thirty-six

"Yo, you all girl for real!" Dolla laughed when Pop met him at her door with a pout.

"Cuz she pssed me off man! I started to tell her!" she fussed until Dolla pressed a soft kiss on her poked out lips. That transformed her pout into a smile and a giggle. The next thing they knew she was riding him backwards.

"Whew!" Dolla exclaimed after they both got their rocks off. They would be late for their meeting but sometimes you have to stop what you're doing and just fk.

"Let's go handle this last biz," Pop said with an aire of finality that Dolla could hear.

"Last?" he asked and watched her wash his wood free of their combined fluids. She almost made him hard again which would have made them even later.

"Yeah, last. I'm done. Finna sell my connect," she sighed. "Gotta focus on us. We going straight. I already told you I got plenty put up."

"I feel you," Dolla sighed just as deeply. He had just broke up with Dyme in his mind. Only loyalty led him to finish helping her pay for the lawyer. He couldn't, wouldn't ask Pop so he would hit that last lick and be done. Plus he was all man and didn't want to come to the table empty handed.

Dolla and Dyme had already drifted apart mentally, all that was left was the physical.

Dyme felt the same way as she and Adam strolled through a museum. He was showing her his side of life while she was still sizing him up for a lick. That's how it started anyway, but by the end of the day she was in like. She decided to make sure he lived through the robbery so they could hang out some more. All she needed to do was get into his house. After the museum they went to an extended dinner.

"I better get going?" Dyme asked when night fell over the outside patio she and Adam were dining on.

"You have to go dance huh?" he asked, almost sounding disappointed. He had been having so much fun he forgot where he got her from.

"Nah, I'm not going back there. One night was too much for me. I mean, I have to figure out a way to get through school but, that's not it," she said and he smiled.

"I know a few people around town. Maybe I can help?" he asked after thinking about it for a moment.

"That would be great! I'm not dancing anymore!" she declared. "When we hanging out again?"

"I have a show tomorrow night so I'll be in afterwards. I hate leaving all that cash in my condo by itself," he revealed.

"So when do I get to see this condo of yours?" Dyme asked coyly.

"Actually, my condo is right around the corner," he admitted and stood. Dyme reluctantly took his hand and walked around the corner.

"Wow!" Dyme heard herself say when they entered his condo. It was decked out in the latest this and the newest that. A huge flat screen TV dominated a whole wall.

"You think this is something. Wait to you see this..." he said and led her out to the balcony.

"Wow!" she repeated at the whole city of Atlanta laid out in front of her. She blinked and panned left and right to take it all in. Adam wrapped his arms around her from behind. Dyme flinched at first then nestled against his body.

Eventually Adam spun her around and pressed his lips against hers. A few cautious pecks later they made out high above the Atlanta skyline. She felt his dick grew stiff and throbbed on her.

"Yoiu want to see my room?" he croaked with a lump of desire stuck in his throat.

"I do but..." Dyme declined but couldn't remember why. Dolla didn't even come to mind at the moment.

"I understand. Don't think I think you're a hoe just because you danced. I never brought one of those girls here," explained.

"Thanks for understanding. Can I get a rain check? Next time?" she asked and gave his wood a squeeze.

"Next time. Why don't you come to the show with me? I'll make you desert when we get back?" Adam asked so next time would be tomorrow.

"I would love too!" Dyme cheered. It was sincere this time since he just invited Dolla and Dyme to rob him. She almost felt guilty since Adam thought he was getting some pussy . When all he was getting was robbed.

*****

"So, how much he gonna be holding?" Dolla asked eagerly. He and Pop had been tossing different business ideas around and he was excited about the prospect. He and Dyme could split the proceeds and go their separate ways. The other fifty grand for the lawyer was coming out of her half

"Phillips arena. Ten acts! It's major!" she said. Both were turned on by the money but turned their backs on each other. Usually they would have went at until the sheets were soaked.

Dolla would save it for Pop and Dyme would give Adam some to ease the pain of losing all that money. Dolla and Dyme fell asleep back to back but woke up face to face. Dyme awoke first from Dolla's buzzing phone. He didn't budge so she eased over and checked to see who was texting.

"Hmph?" Dyme said and twisted her lips. She turned the video chat on and muted the earpiece so Dolla would here.

"Hey, huh?" Pop answered. Dyme didn't speak she just scanned her and Dolla laid up in bed together, then clicked off. "You gone keep playing with me huh? Pay backs a bitch!"

"You wanna eat?" Dyme asked when Dolla stirred awake a few minutes later.

"I could eat," he agreed since it would be a few hours before he linked up with Pop. All she wanted to do was fuck and eat these days. Her vagina was like a new toy and she liked to let Dolla play with it with her.

Dolla and Dyme could have pumped their brakes and went back to where they started from. Back to ride or die and Jackin for love. They didn't and quietly contemplated separate futures with separate people.

"Dude don't have no heat or no security. I'll leave the door open and you can tie us both up?" Dyme suggested.

"Tie up?" he asked and scrunched his face up. They never left witnesses and he didn't plan to start now.

"Yeah, this an easy lick. He ain't bout that life. He ain't gonna come looking for you," she said, nodding so he would agree. "He got insurance and err thing. We good."

"Hmph?" Dolla huffed. This lick should be good for a couple hundred grand no way he was leaving dude alive.

Dolla and Dyme drifted away into their own minds but lusting after the same thing. The love of money had them plotting and planning what they would do when they got it. They ate and made it home without saying a word to each other. They busied themselves in different rooms until it was time for Dolla to leave. He would go spend a few hours with Pop everyday, if they had business or not.

"I'm out yo. Where's my burner?" he asked since they had a lick to catch later.

"In the bag, in the trunk," Dyme replied. "I'll catch an Uber over to the Arena. Three thirty sharp!"

"Make sure that door unlocked. If not, I'll use my key," Dolla said and lifted his foot. That used to get a laugh but not today.

"K," Dyme said and went back to her phone. Dolla took the opportunity to leave before she said anything else. She went to the window and watched the car pull away and sprang into action.

"Adam getting some good Brooklyn pussy tonight and don't even know it!" she giggled and stripped. She was so worked up she had to use the handheld showerhead to relieve herself. She set it to pulsate and aimed it between her legs. The pulsating water gently licked her to an orgsm that made her knees buckle. "Whew!"

Dyme selected a brand new matching bra and panty set. It was perfect to relieve Adam of the trauma of getting robbed. She slipped into a tiny little dress and up into a pair of high heels. The Uber beeped on her phone so packed her pistl in her purse and hit the door.

*****

"Sup yo," Pop teased in a mock New York accent as she let Dolla inside.

"Hey y'all!" he teased right back. His laugh was cut short when he saw what she was wearing behind the door. The flurry slippers were all she had on and he knew what that meant.

"Ooh!" she goggled when he scooped her up and carted her up the stairs. They traded a few a kisses before Dolla put her down and stepped into ensuite bathroom. A wicked smile spread on Pop's face as she sprang into action.

"Two can play at that game," she snickered and grabbed his phone.

Dyme frowned curiously when she saw Dolla making a video call. They hadn't done it in months so she took the call.

"Yo?" she whispered and looked over at Adam to make sure he was busy.

"Sup yo," Pop laughed.

"Pop?" Dyme had to asked when she only vaguely recognized the pretty girl on the screen. She had never seen the Leticia side of LIl Pop. She was cute as a dude but gorgeous as a girl.

"In the flesh," she smiled and scanned her body with Dolla's phone. Dyme was confused when she saw her face, mad when she saw her breast but seeing her stomach just hurt. To add insult to injury Dolla came out of the bathroom just as naked as naked as she was.

"Who you talking to?" he asked and plopped down on her bed.

"No body. Absolutely nobody," she said emphatically since Dyme was less than zero to her. She muted his phone and aimed it at her bed. Now she could could just hope Dyme didn't hang up. She had something she wanted her to see.

Dyme didn't want to see it but couldn't move. She didn't want to watch Pop sit on Dolla's face as he gripped her hips and flicked his tongue. She was frozen in place and couldn't even blink when Pop dipped low and simultaneously took him in her mouth.

A warm tear ran down Dyme's face when Pop lifted her face in ecstasy and came right in front of the lens. It was already bad but watching him lay her out and make sweet, sweet love to her was far, far worse. She knew how this ended but still stayed until the end. Dolla looked directly at his phone and came. He leaned down and made out with her like he loved her.

"You know I love you, right?" Pop asked as they cuddled.

"Love you to ma. Wake me up at two. I got biz to handle," he said and Dyme had heard enough. She couldn't remember the last time he said those words to her.

"Because he don't. He don't love me no more," Dyme moaned and disconnected the call.

*****

"That was so dope!" Dyme gushed when the rap show rapped up just after one am. "This is what you do? For worK?"

"Yup! Pretty cool huh!" Adam said like he couldn't believe his good fortune at his good job. And now a new woman. He leaned forward for a kiss and she met him halfway.

"Can we go to your place? Now?" She asked urgently.

"Yeah, we can. I have to pick up the money from the gate. Wait here," Adam said and rushed off. He walked pretty quickly in general but tonight he jogged since he had some new pussy . Everything is better new cars, homes and clothes but new pussy trumps them all.

He returned in a flash but he wasn't alone. A large man with a large gun on his hip walked along with Adam as he returned with the receipts from the night. He would deposit in the bank first thing in the morning so he could pay his clients for their performances.

"Who is this?" Dyme asked, since he wasn't part of her plans.

"Big George. My guard," Adam said as they moved towards the exit. The large man put a large hand on the large gun and poked his large head out of the back door of the arena.

"Clear," he said and led the way to the car.

"Is he coming with us?" she asked and batted her eyes to remind him of their plans.

"Not in my room, with us," Adam nodded.

"Let me make a quick call. Gotta let my roommate know I'm not coming home," she said. Adam pressed on and hopped into the passenger seat and held the bags on his lap. Dyme wrapped her a her quick call and hopped into the backseat.

It was just before two am when they all reached the condo. Big George sat his big ass in a chair while Adam took the money and Dyme into the bedroom. He slipped into the closet to put the money in his safe for safekeeping until the morning. She watched through the crack in the door and was relieved to see he didn't lock it.

Dyme wasn't wearing much clothing so getting naked was a cinch. Adam came out and went wide eyed with glee at the sight of the naked girl on his bed. He rubbed his hands together like a greedy kid with a plate of cake.

"Time for desert!" Dyme sang and parted her labia to show some pink. Her clitrus popped out of its hood like a Jack in the box. He saw his target and moved in.

"Mmm, my favorite!" he cheered and took a lick. The clean, sweet vagina put a smile on his face as he moved in for his meal. He smacked on his late night snack and removed his own clothes as he dined.

"Ssss!" Dyme moaned to let him know he was on the right path. An intense orgsm was at the end of that road and shook the bed. He lifted up to her face and let her lick her own juices from his chin and tongue.

Adam reached over and retrieved a rubber from the nightstand as she licked his mouth clean. He rolled it on and guided himself inside of her. It was just as tight and hot as he hoped it would be. He started out with light, strokes like a stranger trying to find his way.

They locked lips and kissed feverishly as he humped her. Soon her legs were lifted up in the crook of his arms and he bounced up and down on her cervix like a trampoline. Making love made way to fking and that was just fine by Dyme.

The pace picked up even more just before it came to a sudden end. Adam's whole body seized as if hit by fifty thousand volts. He jerked and spasmed from the orgsm that tested the limits of the latex. Soft kisses replaced the savage tongue swirling from a few minutes ago.

Dyme rubbed his back and squeezed his deflating dick inside of with her vagina muscles. He rolled off but kept her in his arms. They drifted off to sleep just like that. It wasn't long after when Dyme's phone flashed a silent alarm. She didn't need to check it to know what it meant. Dolla was here.

Chapter Thirty-seven

Dolla let out a big sigh when he reached Adam's front door. It was hard enough pulling himself out of Pop's warm bed and hot vagina to come out and catch a lick. Loyalty urged him on so he could set Dyme up and leave her. She would be better off than when he found her so he was cool.

Dolla pressed his ear to the door to see what he could hear. The faint persiflage of a light night talk show could be heard but other than that nothing were stirring not even a mouse.

"Damn Dyme," he whispered when he tried the knob and found nothing doing. He debated whether he should press forward or go back. The love of money whispered and he nodded in agreement. Dolla took a step back and shot glances left and right. His size twelve lifted off the floor and slammed into the door just shy of the handle. The door cracked and creaked but didn't open. He was beyond the point of no return so he gave it two more kicks. It would have been four but the third one did the trick. The door opened and Dolla rushed inside. He came face to face with big George and his big gun.

"Get down!" Adam yelled and pulled Dyme off the bed. He grabbed a gun from under his bed and rushed out into the living room as well

Dyme covered her ears when the apartment erupted in gun fire. It sounded like far more than three men with three guns could possibly shoot. The gun fire stopped as suddenly as it started. A deafening silence followed for a moment.

Footsteps broke the silence just before a figure broke the threshold of the bedroom. Dyme blinked to focus as Dolla came into view. He took two steps inside before he fell dead on the spot. Big George and Adam were both stretched out in the living room but weren't living.

Dyme froze and didn't budge. She couldn't budge from Dolla's dead eyes staring up at her. Soon the room filled with police and CSI techs and she was still stuck.

Eventually she was checked out by paramedics and taken home. The cops advised they would return later to take her statements once she rested. Dyme knew what had to be done and did it. She packed a bag and got into the wind. The Dolla and Dyme saga was over..

*****

Dyme was too numb to even deal with any of the emotions running through her head. The barrage of memories, and regrets along with could've, should've and would'ves threatened to short circuit her brain. She teetered vicariously on the precipice of sanity and insanity.

"Man!" she moaned when the bus rambled by the sign proclaiming New York 100 miles. She copped a sudden attitude with the driver for driving even though she willingly boarded the bus. What choice did she have after police confiscated the cache of weapons from the apartment. She knew they would be linked to several crimes and bodies. Not to mention she couldn't pay the lawyer as wasn't trying to go to jail.

The bus wasn't traveling a hundred miles a minute but still arrived in New York a few minutes later. Dyme was last off the bus because she didn't want to get off the bus. She would have stayed right there in Penn station if she could have. She knew she couldn't so she boarded a train and headed over to the borough of Brooklyn.

If she thought the bus moved fast the train moved even faster. It was a mere blink of the eye and she was back on the block. Chattie and the crew were all happy to see their girl again. Not necessarily because they missed her, more like misery loves company. If they couldn't leave the block they didn't want anyone else to leave.

"Sit right next to me!" Chattie invited and patted the empty spot on the concrete stoop that served as the G.M.G headquarters. The place was vacant since Chattie was having a bad day between her legs.

"Thanks," Dyme sighed and accepted the bunt. She heard the sizzle and tasted the extra in the weed but didn't care. The crew had graduated to smoking woolies and the end was near.

Dyme's new life was sitting on the stoop from sun up to sun down. She slept with whoever for whatever she could get out of it. Most days she stared off into space and tuned out the banal banter. Today was no exception and she missed most of what Chattie and the rest chatted about.

A tinted out car bent the corner and muted the conversation. Dyme sensed something when the girls who never stopped talking, suddenly stopped talking. Chattie stood and slowly eased off with the other girls.

Dyme was from here and knew what was coming. She lifted her head just as the car came to a stop in front of her. The man who jumped out looked so much like his deceased brother there was no need to wonder who he was or why he was there.

"Tell Que I sent you," he said and lifted the gun. She saw what Que saw just before he fired.

The flash didn't even get to fully register before he blasted her from here into the hereafter. And that was the end of Dolla and Dyme. They almost got rich, but died trying.

Epilogue

"Man, that's fucked up!" Lil Pop moaned as she watched her future baby daddy's casket lowered into the ground. Dolla had no other family except the child growing inside of her.

Dyme had gotten in the wind so she claimed the body and arranged the funeral. He had a fancy casket in a shady plot instead of the pine box in a potters field the city would have provided.

Leticia was in the casket along with her man since she vowed to never be with another man. Lil pop was dressed like a dude except for the baby bump that set Dyme off enough to set Dolla up. Dyme used her quick call that fateful night to mock Pop instead of warn Dolla and let him walk into the ambush.

"Malik ibn Samir," Pop read along with the dates of life and death etched into the headstone. She wiped the tears away and manned up since she had a son to raise without a man. The father he would never know was covered with dirt and she turned to leave.